EVA 2040

Volume I

Tyler J Sluys

"Freedom is the open window through which pours the sunlight of the human spirit and human dignity."

-Herbert Hoover

CHAPTER 1

Beep Beep Beep

John Mason awoke and rolled over with a bitter sigh as his hand slammed down onto his retro alarm clock, disabling the noisy and intrusive robotic tone that pierced through his otherwise serene abode. Finding himself in silence, he sat at the edge of the bed with his face in the palms of his hands, spiteful towards that specific alarm style; he chose it because the annoyance motivated him to get out of bed. He otherwise had a difficult time with that. Perhaps because of the excessive amounts of caffeine he would consume in a day. After a minute or two, a familiar voice interrupted his peace.

"Good morning, John!" said Eva.

Instead of answering, John exhibited a lengthy exhale through his nose.

"Would you like me to brew you a cup of coffee, or are you going to be grabbing one on your way to work?"

Again, her statement went unanswered.

"Very well. I can see you are still trying to pull yourself together. If you would like me to make you a hot cup of coffee, please just say the word!"

Eva spoke in a very clear and calm, feminine voice. Her design was of a friendly, customer service-oriented demeanor and many revered her as the greatest technological advancement humanity had developed to date. Since the Conversion, everything was the government, and the government was Eva. She knew everything, saw everything, and controlled everything. Some believe for the better, others say for the worse.

With advancements in surveillance technology, crime became almost impossible to get away with. Society operated primarily on renewable energy sources (although the world was still transitioning away from fossil fuels), poverty was minimal, and the world prioritized the access to and development of Healthcare, education, human equality, environmental health, and technological development more so than it ever had before. Many professed the Conversion as the best thing to happen to humanity as it led to a new utopian world filled with progress, discovery, and prosperity. Others would contend saying the world had become more of a dystopian dictatorship where the lost values of freedom, individualism, and privacy are the very things that make us human and define our existence as people. Some even go further, promoting conspiracy theories that the government had started the events in the mid-2030s that led to the Conversion so that they could design a new world in which they would control all of humanity.

John walked into his bathroom and brushed his teeth. He paused part way through and left the toothbrush dangling out of his mouth, only to be held in place by his lips. He shut his eyes and leaned forward as he placed both hands on the counter to brace his weight. A wave of fatigue washed over him as he fought the urge to yawn, knowing that if he did, his toothbrush would fall out of his mouth. John finished brushing and dressed for work in a semi-formal attire. It was enough to show his professionalism while still being comfortable. He was a police officer prior to the Conversion. Nowadays he worked self-employed as a security consultant. He contracted himself out to various businesses to analyze the vulnerabilities of their company's assets and would then recommend effective and appropriate budget solutions for how they could better protect them. It took him a long time to get the ball rolling for his own business, and there were many complications along the way. Mostly long periods of no clients while he focused on marketing and promotion. The Conversion and introduction of Eva also complicated his business, which forced consultants like himself to adapt to different target areas. After all, why would someone need to focus their budget on crime prevention when it had never been lower? And why would companies need consultants to help protect their data when companies don't even own their own data? Everything was collected, stored, and investigated through Eva. Everything. With frequent AI software updates, John feared that one day Eva would become advanced to where his expertise would no longer be relevant. He questioned if security consultation was a dying industry, but hoped not for the near future. Retirement was near.

John took a quick glance at himself in the bedroom mirror. A tall Caucasian male in his early fifties. His glasses were a little small for him, and its temples gripped his thick dark hair, leaving the greyed edges peripheral to his ears partly concealed. His stance was powerful, grounded, and communicated confidence. A character quality of notable virtue concerning his line of work.

"John, today is *Tuesday April 3rd, 2046*." said Eva. "The weather forecast is cloudy, eight degrees Celsius with a high of fourteen and a slight chance of rain. I would advise that you bring a jacket with you when you leave."

John refused to answer. To do so would be to start his morning with spite and regret. He knew better.

"The time is *7:16 a.m.* I would like to remind you of your appointment today at *8:30 a.m.* with Clarissa Reynolds, who is the Property Development manager with Krucon energy Co. Their address is -----"

"I know where it is."

"Excellent! In order to arrive at an appropriate time, I would recommend that you take the train from -----"

John interrupted Eva again, wielding an elevated tone. "Just leave me to it, Eva."

"Very well, I will leave it to you. If you ever need any assistance, just let me know. I'm here to help!"

John grabbed his jacket and shoulder bag, then exited his apartment. He took his first few steps, leaving the familiar click of his apartment door electronically auto-locking behind him while he continued down the stairs to the lobby and greeted the noise and motion of active city life through his departure of the residential complex. John always valued that first step onto the sidewalk concrete. It made him feel important and alive. A thump in the city's heartbeat. He was his own man and his own boss on his way to make a difference. A battle march that he exhibited with pride. John stopped at the corner of the street and waited for the signal to cross. A woman diverted his attention when she stopped beside him and held her wristlet to her mouth as she spoke. It was the type of boisterous volume where one could not help but eavesdrop.

"Eva, when is the next turn again?"

"In six blocks, turn left, then cross the street and attend the bus stop. Please wait for bus number two-twelve. Once you have boarded, I will update the details for your next stop to your wristlet. If you need any help along the way, please just ask! I am here to assist you! By the way, I have detected your heart rate to be just below your target range. Once you cross the street, I would recommend increasing your walking speed by at least one kilometre per hour to obtain the desired rate."

When the New World Order implemented Eva in 2040, they provided every person a *wristlet*. It was an electronic bracelet that was worn on either arm and synchronized with cellphones, vehicles, and other electronic devices. It displayed a small screen with various touch controls and voice commands, although a primary function of it was to communicate with Eva. The chip inside could be scanned to display the owner's profile. It was a form of personal identification, as well as digital transaction for making purchases, like a debit card. The only other alternative ways of payment in the 2040s were through direct withdrawal in your bank account or by providing a direct transfer of funds that first went through a security clearance check monitored by Eva. Physical cash no longer held monetary value and only existed as relics of the old world. The wristlet contained a microchip that was GPS tracked. Eva always knew where everyone was and what they were doing. Outside of extreme examples, it was otherwise illegal to be in public without a wristlet.

The light turned green, and John and the others crossed the street. One man had his head buried in his phone, too distracted to notice. John could hear Eva behind him inform the man that it was time to cross. As John reached the other side, he looked up and noticed the surveillance camera above the streetlight. The modern world was a place of complete surveillance. *Cold spots* (areas outside of Eva's perception) existed but were uncommon and usually peripheral. When John would notice a street camera, it would usually make him think about his line of work. Today, it served as a reminder that Eva was always watching.

After a few more blocks, John stopped at one of his favorite cafes. It was little things like this that gave him a sense of control and freedom. It may have seemed frivolous, but it was something that didn't require Eva's permission. He approached the counter and ordered his typical. An extra-large hazelnut blonde roast, black, and some napkins. John placed his wristlet against the scanner to make payment, then waited to receive his purchase. Once he received the coffee, he took the napkins and wrapped them around the base of the coffee cup so the heat of the fresh coffee wouldn't burn him. As a younger police officer, he suffered a burn on one of his hands while on duty. The burn has since healed with little scarring, but the incident had left the nerves sensitive to extreme temperatures. A couple of previous incidents of trying to carry scalding hot coffee cups have taught him to develop the habit of wrapping several napkins around it.

John exited the cafe and continued onwards with his work route. After another block, he passed the city's performance theater. An exit door to the side of the building flung open and a young woman with purple hair darted out and slammed into him, knocking his coffee onto the ground.

"SHIT!" he exclaimed.

The young woman shouted back at him, “Watch where you’re going, dickhead!” as she sprinted off into the distance.

John inspected himself for stains. With consideration of the importance of his upcoming meeting, he was relieved to notice that none of the liquid had marked his competent image. He stood still and glanced down at the now empty coffee cup with heavy eyes, almost in grief, while the early morning foot traffic of busy city life navigated their way around him. A large yawn straightened his drooping posture as he thought to himself, “This is going to be a rough day.” After all, John had become dependant upon caffeine. A quick wave of hope washed over him when he remembered that the previous time he visited this client, they had a coffee vending machine in their lobby. John glanced at the clock on his wristlet and figured he had time to stop there before meeting with their company representative. Instilled with optimism, he continued to make his way. Each step displayed a spring of anticipation to arrive at the vendor.

* * *

He arrived at the train station and lined up in the lobby. A sizeable crowd waited in line to scan their wristlet, in which Eva would auto-charge their bank account for the cost of the transit fare. One of Eva’s surveillance drones hovered about twenty feet above the platform, keeping an eye over the mass. In the modern day, it was common to find drones in crowded spaces. Some people felt it helped make them safe, while others believed it was invasive, or even oppressive. They felt it was bad enough that a computer ran the world, but now there were robots watching over them as well. John fell into the category of people with the latter opinion, which was unusual considering his professional background.

As John approached to scan his wristlet, he overheard shouting in the distance. He perked up and focused his attention on the disturbance and observed a man repeatedly swiping his wristlet against the scanner in large and exaggerated animations.

"I'm sorry, but there are insufficient funds in your banking account." Eva said to the man.

"I know! I have to get to work Eva!" he complained. "Put it on a credit and just subtract it from my upcoming paycheck."

"Unfortunately, your credit privileges are currently suspended. As an alternative, I could add it as part of your current time already owed for community service."

The man protracted his lower jaw forward as his eyes widened. He took a lengthy inhale as preparation to shout his following words.

"Are you joking!? It's just a train ticket! I'm not doing MORE community service!"

"Please try to calm yourself. You are performing a public misconduct and if this behavior continues, I'll have to notify the police."

As Eva made her recent statement, the drone hovered over to the man's location.

"OH! You think -----"

The man was interrupted as John rushed over and spoke into his wristlet. "Eva, don't worry about it. I'll pay this man's fare." John looked up in the corner and noticed the surveillance camera had panned over to them as well, mimicking the concern of the drone. John waved at the drone, trying to signal that the situation was under control.

"Thank you for your kindness, John Mason." said Eva. "When you scan your wristlet, I will charge you for two transit fares. Please have a good rest of your day!"

The drone and camera then returned to their original positions.

"Hey, thanks. I appreciate all of this." the man expressed to John.

"Yeah, it's alright man. Just try to get to work." he replied.

"Dude, she's such a bitch!"

John laughed. He found relief whenever he met someone who shared his opinion of Eva. It seemed to be a minority opinion. Either that, or people were hesitant to speak out against her. John scanned his wristlet so that he and the other man could enter the train platform. Upon their entry, the man waved to John in a grateful departure as they walked to separate ends of the platform to wait for the next train's arrival. A few minutes had passed before the next convoy arrived, prompting the crowd of civilians to huddle around the platform's edge. Once the doors had opened, John pushed his way through and advanced to the center of the train, which caused various body parts of his to rub up against the other passengers in ways that in just about any other context would have been inappropriate. The doors closed and the momentum of acceleration caused many passengers to stumble as they sought to regain their footing. It may not have been a comfortable environment, but a cheap and efficient way to get around the city. A method many people relied upon.

* * *

John arrived at the lobby of his destination. In his previous experience, he had to ask the receptionist to meet with his client; however, today he found her waiting for him at the lobby entrance. Their eyes locked almost immediately upon his arrival.

"John Mason, pleasure to have you again!"

"Clarissa, thank you for inviting me back. How has the morning been?"

"I expect a very busy day! But, good busy. Why don't you come with me, and we can get started? If you are ready, of course?"

John stared at the vending machine, then checked the time. It was exactly *8:30 a.m.* He needed coffee, but didn't want to be rude. As a professional, he respected the time of his clients.

"Yeah, I'm ready." he replied. "Let's get to it."

"Right this way."

Clarissa led John into an elevator, and she pressed the button for the 14th floor. As the door to the elevator closed, John filled with immediate regret as the coffee vendor in the lobby became out of sight. He sighed as he thought to himself, "I should have asked Clarissa if I could grab a quick one." The door opened to the 14th floor and Clarissa led John into a conference room. She motioned for him to take a seat in the nearest chair.

"Before we get started, can I offer you anything? Water? Tea? Coffee?" she asked.

John's reply leapt from his mouth with urgent opportunity. "Yeah! Coffee, please! Coffee would be great!"

Clarissa set the machine to brew a small cup. As the liquid poured, a phone rang from the other room.

"Sorry, that call might be something I have to attend." she said. "I'll be back shortly."

She got up and walked out of the room into an adjacent office. John took a moment to take in the details of his surroundings. It was a typical board room. A long oval-shaped table with a conference call speaker in the middle that took up much of the space and was surrounded by black leather wheelie chairs. A grey freshly vacuumed carpet consumed the ground, and the rest of the room was acquainted by various pieces of artwork. One of the walls had been garnished with photographs and short biographical career summaries of all the members of the company's founders, owners, and board of Directors. On the other side of the room, a large, clear glass window substituted the wall.

John stood up and collected the cup of coffee, then walked over to the glass window and stood in awe at the captured overview of the downtown end of Vancouver, British Columbia. Aside from the constant rain, John enjoyed living there. It was an exciting city that had always focused on development. A metropolis with plenty to do and experience that also kept to its Canadian roots. John was proud to be of Canadian heritage but wasn't too confident in what purpose heritage or culture meant anymore, with the world now unified under a single government. He took a moment to remember what living in this city was like before the Conversion. He remembered the mass exodus of the early 2020s when the cost of living was unaffordable for most people, leaving many properties vacant. Back then, people considered Vancouver as a city only for the wealthy. Then the Conversion happened. The housing market, like everything else, became government operated, creating an affordable standard of living. John stood in a reminiscent trance as he considered the world before Eva. He reflected on the freedoms people used to have and wished they could still have; although, amid all unfavourable outcomes, John could at least appreciate the economic outcome the Conversion provided his adored city. A benefit also established in many other areas of the world.

After a few minutes, John perceived his caffeinated beverage to have cooled enough where he could finally consume it. He pressed the edge of the cup to his lips and sipped away, being careful not to burn himself. The wave of desperation he endured all morning vanished. It took away his other senses, and he became lost in the hot, bitter flavour of it.

Clarissa returned to the room and walked part way down the length of the table. She found her seat, then looked up at John, who remained in admiration of the adored landscape.

"Nice view, huh?" she asked him.

"Yes, definitely! I've been here all my life and still don't tire of seeing this city. It changes so often."

"I'm originally from Calgary. I moved here a few years ago when I accepted this position."

"How do you find it here?"

"You know, it's a lot different! People aren't the same. The environment isn't what I'm used to being at sea level, but it's for the best. I used to get migraines back home. In southern Alberta, the weather changes sporadically. Some get headaches because of it. Unfortunately, I am one of those types of people. I don't have that issue living here, with the weather being mild and more consistent. You Vancouverites are so stuck up, though! Calgarians are nicer. I wish I could live with my people, but in your region."

"You're telling me you don't miss the blizzards and temperatures as low as minus forty degrees Celsius?"

Clarissa chuckled and smiled. "Not exactly. I mean, the winter wonderlands are pretty, but I like the rain here."

"Well, I'm glad things are working out for you."

There was a short an awkward pause as they sat unsure of how to progress their small talk.

"So, shall we get started?" she asked him.

"Yes, for sure."

John returned to the table and opened his side bag, revealing a folder filled with documents. He handed them over to Clarissa, then finished his coffee while she examined their contents. Over the next couple of hours, they discussed various security strategy implications for various company protocols, followed by a physical tour of the entire building layout. She impressed John with their overall physical security design, but he pointed out a couple of things of improvement regarding fire safety and emergency evacuation protocols. Clarissa was receptive to John's feedback and took notes on everything he said. It was why she hired him, after all.

* * *

When the tour finished, John said his professional departures and left the property just in time for lunch. He felt his stomach rumble. It was common for him to skip breakfast. Partly because of all the coffee he drank, which is a natural appetite suppressant. However, this morning John didn't have as much coffee as preferred. He stopped by a deli across the street and browsed the menu. After consideration, he approached the counter and ordered a roast beef sandwich with cricket chips on the side, and a large black coffee.

In the modern world, insects were part of regular food consumption. It was a technology made available prior to the Conversion but became a primary food distribution across the world once the Conversion took place. It had something to do with the carbon footprint of operating cricket farms compared to conventional farming methods. An environmentally friendly option that was implemented to tackle climate change. There were also more plant-based alternative foods. People still ate real meat, but it grew in a lab and was developed by 3D printing technology from the DNA of animals rather than from live farming. The current methods for food production differed from when John had grown up, but he didn't care, seeing as how it both looked and tasted the same.

He placed his laptop on the table, eager to resume working on a personal project. He had a potential opportunity to take part in a research program that studied the social and cultural dynamics of various working environments to collect data to discern which types of working environments are best suited to encourage employee satisfaction and work output efficiency. The aim was to establish a link between an employee's level of satisfaction in their role being influential on their productivity. The research program was accepting applications from people who may have relevant expertise in the matter. John expected this research would be a good advertisement for his business while also offering a valuable learning opportunity. He typed away at his application, explaining why he was interested in taking part in this research and his insight into how he believed they should conduct and analyze it.

* * *

A few hours later, he finished and noticed the time approaching mid-afternoon. He analyzed his options. He could head home and beat the rush of everyone coming off normal business hours; but questioned what he would do while at home. Eva was there. Well, Eva was everywhere, but John preferred to be out of the house. That way there were at least real people around him, versus being at home alone where the only other form of company would be in the case Eva piped up about something stupid. John didn't want to take that chance. He forgot to switch her home settings back to *Do Not Disturb.* That way, she would only speak up in the event of an emergency or to answer when spoken to.

He packed up his things and made his way to a pub just down the street from his apartment. Many people had to ask Eva for this type of permission. There were curfews, access control, schedule constraints, and other types of life-style restrictions. John noticed he had more freedom with his actions compared to others he knew. He wondered if it had something to do with being a former police officer. Perhaps his background granted him an extension of Eva's trust? John didn't know, but he took advantage of it.

* * *

John was one hell of a pool player. Not a pro, but the best in his district when he was in the police. He previously took a lot of his fellow officers' betting cash whenever they tried to take him on. John ordered a coffee and cued up the end of the pool stick with chalk. He set up the balls and broke them with the first shot, which already put three of them away. He spent a few more hours at the pub playing pool, taking a break here and there for food and drinks or to socialize with the locals. Eventually, someone caught on to his skills. A small group of cocky younger males. John proved their attempts futile.

After his victory, John departed for home. As he stepped out of the door, he held up his hand to shield his eyes from the glare of the setting sun and completed only a few steps down the alley before being interrupted by a vibration that shot through his leg. An incoming call from an unrecognized number, although that was a common instance with consideration to his self-employment. Regarding the time of evening, he questioned the likelihood the call would relate to work, but answered regardless.

"Hello? John Mason speaking."

"John, hey this is Brian Tallow."

"Sorry, who?"

"Stephanie's Husband."

Stephanie was John's ex-wife, whom he divorced several years ago. John had never met Brian, but knew that Stephanie remarried him.

"Well, what's going on Brian?"

"Hey ugh……"

Some minor grunts came from Brian's end of the call, which revealed to John that Brian had a hard time trying to say whatever was on his mind.

"Well?" asked John.

"Yeah sorry. Hey um, Stephanie is missing."

"Stephanie is what?"

"Yeah, I don't know. She's been gone for two days now. Her phone goes to voicemail. People she works with haven't seen her and even Eva has no idea where she is! Stephanie is gone, John! She's just Gone!"

CHAPTER 2

"John?"

"Yeah, I'm still here."

"I don't know what to do. I've contacted the police and they are investigating, but their database is based off Eva. John, even Eva doesn't know anything! Stephanie went completely dark with no explanation, and it doesn't make sense that Eva wouldn't be able to locate her either."

"Yes, this is strange."

"Well, I figured I should tell you. I imagine it is something you would want to know. Considering your background, I figured you might find something. Do you think you could? I mean, even if Eva doesn't know?"

"I'll try Brian. The thing is the police these days have become too reliant upon technology. Eva does most of their work for them. I'm old school. They trained me during a time before Eva. A time when there was more problem solving. So, maybe I could approach this differently. I'm going to try at least, but I can't promise anything."

"Yeah, ok."

The last words Brian uttered came across in a more confident tone, as if he found a bit of hope.

"Thanks. Please keep me in the loop." said Brian. "This is the best number to reach me at."

"That is good to know. I have a bunch of questions I should ask though. It might help find a lead."

"Sure. Go ahead."

"When did you last see her?"

"Monday morning. I leave for work in the mornings before she gets up. She was still asleep when I left but didn't come home that evening like she usually does. She has been missing all today as well."

"What was her demeanor like when you last saw her?"

"Fine. Nothing out of the normal."

"You mentioned she should have come home on Monday evening. From where? Doing what?"

"She still works at the homeless shelter kitchen, but in a different role than when you guys were together. She still cooks, but now she is in a leadership position and works in the evenings. After serving dinner, they clear out the homeless and she loads up all the dishes and stuff to be run through the overnight wash cycle, as well as setting up a few things for the next day's breakfast crew. She then locks the place up and is the last one to leave."

"Ok, and when does she leave?"

"It varies, but usually about 9 p.m."

"And what time does she usually arrive home?"

"Like, 9:20 or 9:30."

"What is her exact route home? Does she make any stops along the way?"

"I don't think so. And I don't know. I have never ridden with her on her route."

"But she does drive?"

"Yes."

"Does she still have that black SUV?"

"Yeah actually."

"Can you tell me the plate number?"

"Ugh.......... I should know this. Sorry, I don't know it."

"Ok. In that case, is there anything unique about her vehicle that would stand out? Stickers? Damage? Anything like that?"

"No. There used to be a crack in the front windshield, but she recently got it replaced."

"And her vehicle is missing as well? Or still parked at the shelter?"

"It's unaccounted for."

"And we know for sure that she was at work that evening? Locked up and everything?"

"Yes. I've called her work, and they confirmed it. There's recorded footage on the surveillance system of her locking up and then leaving; although the camera view on the exterior does not cover where she had parked. So, she is officially missing from that point onwards."

There was a long pause. John heard only the sound of the cool evening breeze through the line.

"Anything else?" asked Brian.

"Yeah, one more thing. I know this is private and might sound invasive, but I promise it's relevant and I need to know."

"Okaaay....?"

"How have things been going between the two of you? You know, with your marriage? Has she been distant or closed off at all?"

"No! Not that I know of, at least. Things are going smooth. We just celebrated our anniversary a few weeks ago. Why do you need to know about that?"

"You never know. I'm not saying this happened, but sometimes people might be unhappy. There could be infidelity. Someone else involved. You never know. I'm just trying to cover all angles."

"Oh, I don't think that's what happened. No. Nothing like that."

"I need you to send me the most recent photo of her. I'm going to need that."

"Not a problem. I'll do that right away."

"Thanks. I think that's everything I need. Thanks for the call. I will let you know if something comes up."

"Okay."

"Bye."

John hung up the phone and placed it back in his pocket. He stood still for a moment and stared at a random spot on the ground to process what he just learned, then ran his fingers through his hair before he continued home.

* * *

The night was troubled with the restless tossing and turning of unsettled thoughts and distant memories. John reflected on their marriage, divorce, and how they first met. It was back when he was a police officer. He had to respond to a call that had happened downtown. There was a violent situation that happened at the homeless shelter Stephanie worked at. One of the homeless bumped into the back of another while they were sitting down to eat a meal. The person became irate, then stood up and threw their soup at the other, which led to a fist-fight. That was when John first saw her. She was beautiful. Tall and slender, with rosy cheeks and bleach-blonde hair tied back into a ponytail. John always had a soft spot for blondes and Stephanie always preferred those of the tall, dark, and handsome type. A couple days later when John had a day off, he went by and asked her out. She didn't recognize him out of his uniform, but he jogged her memory. Before long, they dated. John was never shy around women and didn't fear getting shot down. You'll never score unless you take a shot on the net. That's how he saw things.

* * *

The next morning, Eva offered to brew John his morning coffee, to which he declined. He wanted coffee as usual, but preferred to make it himself. The coffee brewed while he made his breakfast. Eggs on toast with an orange. Once he sat down with all of it at his kitchen table, he realised how tired he was because of the little sleep he got the prior night. He was going to rely on caffeine today, but that was nothing new. John relied on caffeine every day.

He turned his home settings for Eva to *Do Not Disturb,* then sat for a long while strategizing on how he was going to begin the investigation. He knew that finding Stephanie was going to be a challenging task. Luckily, he had his day mostly free. Originally, his plan was to do some business networking on various social media platforms, but finding Stephanie was an obvious priority. The only thing on the day's agenda that wasn't flexible was his upcoming deposit. A *deposit* was an appointment that Eva routinely scheduled for people. Everyone had to do it, and you had better have a good excuse to reschedule. It involved going to a clinic where they would take blood samples. The reason provided was to do routine health checkups to keep track records of various biomarkers to ensure the quality of the person's health. The other reason stated was to look for pathogens early on to prevent a potential pandemic before it became a problem. Eva advertised it as a safety protocol following the Covid-19 pandemic that started back in 2019. The coronavirus pandemic changed certain aspects of the future world, but many people didn't believe these explanations. Why would it be so strictly enforced if there were no additional or alternative purposes? Why couldn't people have autonomy over their own health decisions, like when to go to a doctor and what tests they should do? That's how it was in the old world before the Conversion. And if it really was about pathogens, why was there a lack and disregard for other safety procedures that are typical of a pandemic response?

By the time John finished his breakfast, he knew of where to begin the investigation. He cleaned up his dishes, then exited his apartment, leaving the familiar noise of his apartment door auto-locking behind him.

* * *

John visited the nearest police department. A plan unlikely to succeed, but worth the try. He opened the entrance door and approached the front desk, where a uniformed female police officer greeted him. He glanced at her name tag, which read: *Miller*.

"Hello."

"Hi, I was hoping you could help me with some information." said John. "I'm a private detective looking for someone."

"Um……"

She froze for a moment, unsure of how to respond. Her youthful appearance gave John the impression she was likely new to the police force and had not encountered a situation like this before.

"I suppose that would depend on the specifics." she replied. "Why are you trying to find this person?"

"Missing. The husband hired me to investigate."

"Have they filed a report with us?"

"Yes, he did. I was hoping we could share information and work together. I was wondering if there is any information you have already collected that may be useful?"

"Police records are confidential. I don't think we can be openly discussing something like that to civilians. Seeing as how we are already aware; I assure you we are working on it."

"Yeah, I figured. Thing is, I'm an ex-member. I'm familiar with how these can go. Missing persons can sometimes be a lower priority. I know you guys have other things keeping you busy, and police resources can be spread thin among multiple matters. Therefore, they hired me. This way, I can assure the client that there is someone working around the clock with their sole focus on their particular concern. I just want to bring her home to her husband as quickly as possible. I'm sure you can appreciate that."

"Could I just scan your chip quick?"

John figured she was only asking so she could identify who was poking their nose in police business. It probably had no significance in getting the information he was looking for. It wouldn't have been back when John was in the police, but he knew he was grasping at straws. John scanned his wristlet on the reader attached to the counter. The computer monitor was facing the other way so that only those behind the counter could view it, but John figured Miller was probably browsing through his ID profile. A quick moment passed, then Miller glanced back up at him.

"Okay, Mr. Mason. Like I said, there really isn't much I can do for you; however, if you were to find something of significance, you are more than welcome to drop by and fill us in. Anything you provide to us could always be useful towards the investigation."

"Can I please speak with the on-duty Sergeant?"

Miller exhibited a strong and lengthy exhale before she replied, "Sure," and departed from John's field of view as she walked into a back office. She returned after a moment and asked that John take a quick seat and the Sergeant would be out shortly. John found a chair and waited. It wasn't long before another woman in a police uniform walked out into view. She had three stripes on the shoulder patch of her uniform, which John recognized as the ranking of Sergeant. She looked over at Miller, who then pointed to John sitting in the chair. The Sergeant then approached the counter and motioned to John, who stood up and made his way back over.

"Hello Sir. My name is Sergeant Garnier. You requested to speak with me?"

"Yes, I'm a private detective working on a missing person's case. My client filed a report with your department yesterday, but also wanted additional resources invested into finding his wife. I was hoping we could work together and share some information. I was curious about -----"

"Yes sir, one of the other officers has informed me of your inquiry. I apologize, but there are policies in place that prevent us from sharing confidential law enforcement records with civilians. As a former member, I imagine this is something you could understand."

"I understand. Is there at least some sort of lead you could provide? To point me in the right direction?"

"Well, any leads we may have would already be under investigation. I assure you that the Vancouver police department has taken a special interest in this case, due to its rather unusual nature. We are doing the best we can. That's all I can say."

John thanked the Sergeant then turned to exit the building. His shoulders sunk and his head hung low as disappointment overtook him. He figured things would go down like that, but it was at least worth the attempt. John's expectations had come true. He was going to have to do things the hard way.

He made his way over to the convenience store across the street and purchased a coffee for himself, along with some sandwiches and cigarette packs, which he then carried out in a large white bag made of *reebo*. Since the Conversion, the production of plastic materials had been banned, and the replacement was the development of a new flexible paper-like material that could easily be factory manufactured for cheap and at a low carbon footprint. Plus, no trees had to be cut down in its making. The new substance was called *reebo* and was water resistant, tear resistant, biodegradable, and recyclable. It wasn't plastic or paper, but something kind of in between.

John had bought these items with an intended purpose. Since his original plan failed, John knew he would have to resort to the auxiliary.

* * *

He took the goods over to the proximity of where Stephanie worked, having known that place would crawl with the homeless. Even with minimal poverty levels in the current world, there were still those who were homeless. Not because of lack of employment opportunities or affordable housing markets, but there would always be those who refuse to assimilate or couldn't because of things like addiction and mental illness. It was hard to find narcotics in the present day, but even things like alcohol could be restricted if someone was exhibiting addiction behaviors. Eva would lock the person out from being able to purchase those substances or go to certain places where they could encounter them. Allegedly, it was for their greater good. Even so, there were still people living with substance addictions. As the saying goes, where there is a will, there is a way.

John knew the homeless were the eyes and ears of the street. If something shady happened to Stephanie on Monday evening, the homeless of the surrounding area was John's best chance at locating witnesses. He surveyed the area and discovered an alley that led to a large run-down building. There were two street camera mounts. One at each end of the alley, but the cameras themselves were missing from the mounts as if the locals didn't take lightly to being spied on. Shopping carts and tents lined up through the entire depth of the alley, along with the dense population of their holders and inhabitants. Upon his entry, the eerie flock of piercing gazes greeted John. They felt territorial, almost threatening, but John persisted in the confidence he could handle himself. He only took several steps before a dishevelled older woman intercepted him. Her smile revealed the absence of several teeth.

"I haven't seen you walk through here before." the woman said.

"I'm just here as a friend," replied John, "and I've brought gifts in exchange for information. Any chance you guys could help me try to find someone?"

Upon finishing his sentence, he pulled some sandwiches out of the bag to show what he brought. John then turned his head over to his left to meet a voice yelling over at him.

"Best to go in that building there and speak to Jasper. If anyone can help you, it's him."

The remark came from a middle-aged homeless man who sat beside a tent made of boxes and blankets.

John replied, "Ok. Thanks." then tossed a pack of cigarettes over at the man as a token of gratitude. He then headed over to the beat-up building just further down the alley.

John proceeded inward and let out a shiver as he took in the grisly details of the foreign environment. Graffiti overtook the stripped floor and barren walls. The absence of internal lighting left the rooms dim. The only luminous source was the streaks of sunlight that poured through the broken windows. As he advanced deeper, he observed the nude wrists among the inhabitants. Not one person wore their wristlet. As he passed by the first room, he observed a skinny man covered in tattoos and dressed in nothing but shorts. He had a rubber tie around one arm and was injecting himself with a needle filled with some sort of unknown substance. A young woman lay beside him and rested against his shoulder. She eased her body gently in a graceful wave, as if to some slow rhythm that only she could hear. John assumed a high from the drugs had taken her away, but did not grant it much attention. He was there for a purpose and didn't want to stay any longer than needed. A couple more rooms passed, and John ended up in what appeared to be a common area. There, a large man with messy dreadlocks and dark skin intercepted him. His voice was deep and raspy.

"What's a cop doing in my home outside of uniform?"

"I'm not a cop. Just here looking for information." John explained. "I've brought gifts for you all and was told to speak to Jasper. You must be him?"

Jasper nodded, then motioned towards one of the other people in the room, who then took the bag from John and distributed the sandwiches and cigarettes among the others.

"Before we can talk, you must leave your wristlet and cellphone at the door." said Jasper. "We don't allow that shit in here. She's always listening. We will return them to you when you leave. You've got my word on that."

Someone from the room approached John's left arm where the wristlet was worn and held out their hand. John paused briefly, considering his next actions.

"Well?" asked Jasper.

John took his wristlet off and handed it over.

"Before I give you my phone, I have to show you a photograph." said John.

John brought up the picture of Stephanie that Brian had sent him, then held it out for Jasper and his people to see. They took the photo in Stanley Park at the edge of the water that separated it from North and West Vancouver. The Lion's Gate Bridge was distant in the background. She stood by herself, smiling. An example that after all these years, she kept her beauty. John made sure everyone got a good look, then handed over his phone to the person who took his wristlet. They then withdrew themselves from John's view and left the building, granting John the opportunity to explain his situation.

"She went missing on Monday. She works in the kitchen just down the road. Her last known details were locking everything up around *9 p.m.* that evening, then didn't come home. Been missing ever since. I was hoping somebody here knew her, and knew what happened."

Jasper answered, "Yeah, we know her. Sweet lady. Always treats us well, but doesn't put up with any bullshit either."

"Sounds like her." John replied.

Another man from inside the room spoke up and said, "Hey, I might know something."

Everyone else in the room turned to look at him. He stood up from his sitting position against the wall, then took a step forward and cleared his throat before he continued.

"I was scrappin' for copper that night, and I saw a kidnapping in the parking lot just around the corner from that kitchen. I would have done something, but I was alone and there were a bunch of them."

"How many?"

"Five? Six? Something like that. It was dark. I couldn't say for sure it was her, but it would be a damn coincidence if it weren't. We haven't seen her at the shelter since, to be honest."

"What happened?"

"They nabbed her and threw her in a van before taking off down Hastings street."

"East or West?"

"West. Then I lost sight."

John's heart sunk. It felt like he swallowed a brick.

"Anything else?" John asked the man.

"Yeah, once they threw her in the van, one of them got into a vehicle that was parked in that lot and took off following them."

"What kind of vehicle was it!?"

"Some kind of larger vehicle. Black, or some other dark color."

"An SUV!?"

"I think so. Yeah, actually. It was an SUV."

"Fuck!"

A thick awkwardness swept in between each of them as they stood silent, unsure of what to say next. Finally, Jasper broke the reticence.

"Must have been one of those government kidnappings."

"Ugh, what?" asked John.

Jasper clarified, "The government. They've been taking people off the streets. It's been going on for a long time now."

Several other people in the room nodded.

"What the hell are you talking about!?"

John sensed motion in his peripheral view and drew his attention to his side, where a woman approached him.

"We don't know why. Maybe because they don't obey Eva?" the woman explained. "Everyone has a different theory, but everyone knows kidnappings will get you jailed up. Noone can get away with that type of crime anymore. It was either someone with some real balls or the government. Probably the government. I wish there was more we could do for you."

"Well, what the hell am I supposed to do about that!?"

John's concerns failed to meet insight as he received only shrugs and diverted eyes. The same awkwardness resumed its founding until Jasper recognized the situation to be without progress.

"Anything else?" Jasper asked John.

"I don't think so. I'll come back if I need more information. With more supplies, of course."

Jasper nodded. John turned to walk away but stopped after a few steps when a curious thought overtook him. He always wondered about the effectiveness of the new prison systems. Since the Conversion, criminals were subjected to a variety of behavioral programs that intended to rehabilitate the offenders into productive members of society. The goal was to tackle the root cause of their behaviors and teach them self-confidence, real world applicable skills, and give them the tools to be successful once integrated back into the world. The facilities were highly hospitable and treated the inmates with respect. It operated by the principle that if you treat a person like an animal, then it will promote feral and barbarous behaviour, but if you treat them with respect and dignity, then you will receive similar congenialities.

Conventional penitentiary systems were reserved for those who could not rehabilitate. Repeat offenders, or those deemed a danger to society. For these reasons, prisons of the traditional sense were excessively brutal.

John looked back at Jasper. "Hey, about these new rehabilitation programs. Do they really work?"

"Kind of. They certainly help some of those who are just lost and trying to fit in somewhere. There is less re-offending; Although, for others who don't care that much, there's less fear of going to prison. It's nice there. Nicer than the streets and shelters. Why do you ask?"

"Just curious. I used to be a cop."

Jasper's eyes grew wide as he pointed at John. Not with anger, but delighted amusement.

"HAH! I knew it! You all got the same look. It's in your walk, your stance, your tone of voice. HA-HA!"

A feeling of embarrassment and self-consciousness washed over John. Something he had long gone without experience.

"Yeah? Anyway, I better be going. Thanks for the information."

Jasper waved as John turned away and walked out of the building. The same person who took his things waited for him at the exit and returned them to John upon his departure. John put his phone in his pocket and his wristlet back on, then walked down the alley back onto the street. He stood for a moment and thought, "Is the government really kidnapping people? Why? And why Stephanie?" John heard rumors of a similar sort, but figured it was just some unsubstantiated crazy talk that conspiracy theorists spread. He didn't know what to do next and wondered how he was going to track down the government undetected by Eva. It seemed impossible. John only made it back half-way through the length of the alley before a voice from his wristlet interrupted his thoughts.

"Hello John! Are you doing okay?" asked Eva.

"Why?"

"Several minutes had passed where I couldn't detect your pulse. I was contemplating sending emergency services over to your location to check up on your well-being."

"Just a glitch. Don't worry about it."

"That's my job, silly! I'm just looking out for you. I'm glad everything is alright. While we're talking, I just want to remind you of your upcoming deposit at *6:45 p.m.* this evening."

John forgot about it. He had been so distracted by the details around Stephanie's disappearance. This was one of the few times ever that he was glad Eva started talking to him. He checked the time. It was only *11:13 a.m.* He had lots of time to figure something out, but he needed to come up with a lead today. Tomorrow, he had work appointments. Not to mention his concern that if he spent too many days wandering around areas of the city outside of where he frequents, Eva might ask questions or impose restrictions. He had to be careful.

John walked in a random direction. He wasn't a person who could sit still for long periods of time, especially when thinking about something. Was it natural? Or perhaps due to all the caffeine? It wasn't long before he came across a commotion at an intersection just a couple of blocks ahead. It looked like a protest of some sort. Something that was uncommon in the modern day. For a moment, John remembered the pre-Conversion world when citizens had the right to conduct a peaceful protest. Nowadays it was banned.

John picked up the pace to get a clearer look. Police had the area secured. A few drones flew over the area and John could see that the street cameras within the block were all turned to focus on the protest. There were people with picket signs that said various unfavorable things about Eva and the New World Order. The people in the crowd were all chanting the same thing in perfect unison as if they had rehearsed prior.

"EVIL EVA! EVIL EVA! EVIL EVA!"

Amid the chanting, there was a man with a megaphone who gave a speech. He spoke with passion, as if on a critical mission. Like a prophet, set to deliver a revelation. The crowd enthusiastically concurred between his statements.

"They have stripped us from our freedoms and privacies!"

"Yeah!"

"We are people, not dogs! We will live no longer with a short leash around our necks!"

"Yeah!"

"They have robbed us of the very things that make us human!"

"Yeah!"

"They have hacked our lives!"

"Yeah!"

"They -----"

One of those last words struck John like a bolt of lightning. *Hacked.* He couldn't even hear the speech or the crowd anymore. Not over his jarring epiphany. He figured the best source of information on how to track down the government would be from a government resource itself. It was at this moment John knew what he needed to accomplish. He needed to hack the system. He was going to hack Eva.

Chapter 3

Of course, John himself would not hack Eva. He wasn't tech savvy enough, but he knew that was needed to be done. How else was he going to learn about Stephanie's whereabouts? John had to find someone who had the skills to do what seemed to be an impossible job while also having the willingness to operate on the shady side of the law.

It didn't take him long to think of a contact. When he was an officer, he had worked on a case with a juvenile criminal, who faced mischief charges regarding computer hacking. They offered to expel the charges in exchange that he lent his hacking skills in cooperation to bring a larger priority criminal to justice. They found the case complicated as it involved a legal gray area, which regarded getting critical information about the suspect through the hacking of personal data. With consideration of the specific circumstances, a Judge ruled it in their favour as being non-invasive of a citizen's legal right to privacy. The kid's skills were beyond notable recognition. A total computer whiz. John believed it was a shame he didn't use his talents for a more honourable cause. When John previously worked the case, there was an issue with his work email in which it temporarily did not receive incoming traffic. He remembered he had sent the case file to his personal email address, so he could view it while the IT department resolved the issue. John wondered if he still had that file buried deep within his personal email traffic. He had to check. He searched through his email history over the next couple of hours until he finally found it. “Crap! Won’t open!” John thought to himself. His cell phone failed to recognize the file type. It was too old for his current software. He browsed the internet and searched for previous software versions with hope he could access the file. After several attempts, John found one that worked. He reviewed the file’s contents, then read the suspect’s name out loud. “Wesley Atterton.” A teenager then, but John knew that now he would be in his mid or late twenties. The mug shot was old, but it was the only means of identification in the file. He figured the address was probably outdated, but it would at least serve as an investigative starting point. John didn’t even have a plan yet about what he would say to him. Would Wesley even be interested in helping John? How would he convince him? After all, hacking Eva would have serious criminal consequences. That was a bridge to cross later. Until then, John's focus was to find him.

* * *

John perused the case file several times over as he traveled to the clinic for his deposit appointment. He arrived and scanned his wristlet at the counter to check in, then found an available seat to abide the service. He took a moment to ingest the environment. It was a typical medical clinic waiting room. He observed the cry of a young child from a room down the hall. A suggestion of disfavour towards needles. A television advertised a weight loss program on the wall across from him and a second television was on the wall above his head. He couldn’t see the program, but identified it as a local news broadcast through the narration. The reporter spoke with a concise and professional demeanor as they relayed the details of the story to the audience.

“A violent incident left a young woman in critical condition as she struggles to recover in Surrey Memorial hospital. What began as a fun night out with her friends turned into a nightmare. Last night, someone attacked her in a dark alley during her route home. Kelly stated she was trying to take a shortcut to the nearest train station but had to cut through a dark alley in order to get there. It was here that a man grabbed her and told her to give him her phone and purse. She tried to scream and break free, but the man overpowered her and pushed her, causing her to fall and hit her head. A few good samaritans found her moments later who described her as lying unconscious with no one else around. Kelly awoke in the ambulance to find that her purse and other belongings had been stolen. Joining us now is the leading investigator on the case."

"Surveillance footage in the area captured the incident, and by working with Eva, we could uncover the offender's digital footprints. Earlier this morning, we arrested the offender and brought them to justice, where they will face sentencing. I'd like to take the time to remind everyone to please use their best judgement when they leave their homes. Try to travel with a group and preferably in open occupied spaces with lots of other people around. I'd like to remind everyone about the Buddy Up application available for free. Eva will use it to connect you with other people in your area that are traveling a similar route as you, and then recommend the safest path to take together to get there. That way you never have to travel alone through dangerous places. I'd also like to take the time to give a reminder to any potential criminals listening to this broadcast. Due to the surveillance technology and sophistication of Eva in the modern world, unsolved crime is at an all-time low. If anyone out there is thinking of hurting someone, or performing any illegal acts, I would like to encourage you to reconsider. It is very easy for us to find people these days. If you commit a crime, you will be caught and there will be consequences."

John swallowed heavily. After all, this applied to him. He was conspiring to commit a major crime. John took a moment to reconsider his intentions. If he were to be caught, his career would be over. There would certainly be no return to his line of work as a convicted felon. His reputation would be destroyed. His concerns caused him to consider giving up and leaving Stephanie's circumstances to the police; however, if it truly was the government behind her disappearance, then there's nothing the police could do. Eva would shield Stephanie from them. No. The only way Stephanie could be rescued was if John found her. He was her only hope, and he would not give up on her.

"John Mason?" asked the medical receptionist.

John looked up.

"Room 4 please."

"Thanks."

John made his way into room 4 down the hallway. He sat in the chair and waited alone only a moment before the nurse walked in.

"Please confirm your name and date of birth." asked the nurse.

"John Mason, March 2nd, 1994."

The nurse took out an alcohol swab and swabbed John's arms. Then prepared the Needle.

"Make a fist. Quick pinch."

The nurse inserted the needle and the transparency of the vial soon diminished as bright red blood consumed its volume.

"Hey what's all this about, anyway?" John asked her.

"Well, we do routine check-ups on people. It gives you your results so you can see your biomarkers on your health app. Plus, if anything is ever off, it helps us catch things earlier."

"Like what?"

"Anything health related that could affect you or someone else. We wouldn't want another Coronavirus going around or something like that. We just want to always be on top of things."

John didn't believe her. When the nurse finished, she put some cotton over the needle insertion point with some medical tape and asked John to keep applying pressure. She then took a sticker label with his personal information printed on it and placed it over the vial of John's blood sample. The vial was placed with a piece of paper in a reebo bag, which then went in a small hatch in the wall to be collected and filed.

Along the route home, John googled the address listed in Wesley Atterton's file. It was a 3rd floor condo in a larger apartment complex. Security was tight, and John certainly didn't have a good reason for Eva to grant him access. Even just asking her could generate suspicion. John knew that if he was going to get into that building, he would have to resort to more creative measures.

* * *

Once John got home and finished his dinner, he finally had a plan for how he would try to get in. His father was a retired handyman and still had his work suit and tools. John figured he could ask to borrow the uniform. The plan was to watch the foot traffic of the building entrance and when someone would come either in or out of the front door, John would try to get in posed as a maintenance worker. He figured it was likely people wouldn't ask questions that way. John called his father, but his mother answered.

"John!"

"Oh, hi mom. Is dad around?"

"He's somewhere around, fiddling with something. He's always working on something."

She yelled through the house at his father. "Bernard! Hey Bernard! John is on the phone for you!"

John heard the distant yells of his father echo back. "What!?"

"It's our son!"

"Housson? I don't know a Housson. It's probably one of them telephone scammers. Just hang up already!"

"It's John, you old fool! He wants to talk!"

Over the next minute, John could only hear various muffled background noises that he couldn't identify. His father then answered the phone, out of breath, and struggled to muster up his words between wheezes.

"John!"

"Dad, hey. Question for you. Do you still have your old work uniform lying around?"

"Yeah, I think so. In the garage."

"Could I please borrow it?"

"Well, it would probably fit you. What do you need it for?"

John did not enjoy lying to his parents, but he knew they were both loudmouths. They regularly communicated pretty much everything to Eva. They gossiped with her as if she were a guest in their home. She knew about everything going on in their lives. John couldn't tell either of them about Stephanie or his true intentions.

"I could use it for a job I have coming up. Someone hired me to infiltrate their business. It's a test on their physical security controls. My plan is to sneak in disguised as a worker. I think it'll work."

"Oh? Yeah ah…… ok. When do you want to come by and get it?"

John could hear his mother in the background getting excited at the thought of him coming over.

"Oh, I'll make us a roast tomorrow! With a salad and some of those lemon potatoes he likes. He never ate them as a kid, but remember when he started growing up, he began to enjoy them? Bernard, do you remember that?"

"It sounds like I'm coming over for dinner tomorrow." said John.

"Okay, we will see you then."

"Bye dad."

* * *

When the morning arrived, John awoke in his usual state, an inattentive slop of weariness. John dragged himself through his usual morning routine, then left to meet his client.

A company hired him to help them set up a plan for an auxiliary location with the capability to host their primary operations in the event of a critical incident. This would include things such as natural disasters in which their company temporarily could not operate out of its usual location. John gave them the usual advice, but also suggested they consider a potential partnership with some other like-minded companies that would unify their resources into an operating facility that would not depend upon any single company's resources. A legal unification, in which each company tips in their share of resources into a larger pool used as needed by any of the shareholders in the event of a critical incident. The concept would spread business risk across multiple enterprises, mitigating the severity of impact any of them would face should a critical incident occur. John knew that something along those lines would have to be approved by Eva. There were always government guidelines to follow for these sorts of things, but if they were careful about who they partnered with, John couldn't imagine a probable deterrent for his proposed action plan.

* * *

In the evening, John arrived at his parents' house. As soon as he knocked, he could hear the relentless bark of Bigslie (his parent's dog) on the other side of the door. It was one of those small, yappie creatures, far too overconfident for its size. Eventually, the door opened, and his mother dragged him inside. She was always so happy whenever he was over for a visit.

"Come on in! I'll put on some tea." she said.

John stood in the middle of the living room fending off the snarling of Bigslie at his heels. Just then, his father walked into the room.

"Oh, Bigslie is angry."

John chuckled and replied sarcastically, “Oh? How did you figure that?”

“I got this new upgrade for my hearing aid. It tells me what the dog is saying.”

“It does what!?”

“Well, you know those scientists. They’ve been learning more about animal communication. With dogs, there are nuances in the way they bark or whimper. They say it’s a simple form of communication.”

“And your hearing aid is a canine translator now?”

“Yup! Well, it can only tell me certain emotions or mannerisms that it detects in the animal. Like fear, jealousy, pain. That sort of thing.”

“Or rage, clearly.”

“Yeah! I downloaded the software upgrade wirelessly at a reasonable purchase. It’s pretty neat!”

“I figured a person wouldn’t need a dog translator to know that Bigslie doesn’t like me very much. He doesn’t seem to like anyone aside from you and mom.”

John’s mother yelled from the other room. “Bernard, put that mutt out in the yard!”

John’s father tried to scoop up the dog, but he hopped out and returned to snarling and barking at John’s heels, almost with a vengeance. The second attempt proved successful, and he carried the dog outside and closed the sliding glass door, keeping the frenzy at bay. John’s mother then placed a small cup of tea on the dining table and told John to have a seat and try it. John blew on it for a bit to cool it down, then sipped it.

“Woah, that’s good tea! What is this?” John asked.

“Well, it’s called Golden Eyebrow!” she replied. “It’s from the Wuyi mountain or something like that. It’s a rare tea that’s hard to get, but you know how I’m always looking for new teas, right? Well, I was at the store doing some shopping.

I had to buy a new set of oven mitts because your father burned a hole in one of them the other day and I saw an ad in my social media thing for this beautiful new set that's woven from these rare fibres. Oh, they feel so smooth! It reminds me of when you were just a boy. Your hair then was so thin and smooth! Like silk fibres! Hey Bernard! Do you remember John's hair when he was little?"

John tried to get his mother's story back on track. "So, you were browsing for some tea…."

"Yes! After I bought the oven mitts, I stopped by that tea store I like that's over there. I spoke to the lady and told her I like to try new teas and she showed me all about this Golden Eyebrow that's hard to find. It was expensive! Do you think it was probably being overcharged there? I think it was overpriced. She told me about that tea and about how it comes from China, but her son had actually just been to China. He was there on some kind of business trip, but he also plays table tennis a lot and the Chinese are really good at table tennis. So, while he was there, he did some tournaments to get better. He played in some, and do you know what she told me happened, John? She said that -----"

It was about this point when John's attention span had run out. He looked over at his father, who didn't pay attention either. Instead, his father stood peering out the window with a gawking stare on his face. His eyes squinted.

"That damned neighbour! Never mowing their front lawn. Just lazy!" he muttered.

"Bernard, you've played table tennis before, right?" John's mother asked.

"What?"

"Table Tennis!"

"Table Tennis!? I'm talking about the neighbour for crying out loud!"

"What's going on with the neighbour?"

"Never mowing their front lawn!"

"Why do you care about that!?"

"Because Margarie! It makes the street look run down. It lowers the property value for all of us trying to live around here!"

"Just mind your own business Bernard."

John's father muttered inaudibly under his breath. His eyes never relented their gaze. John's mother then sat down next to him at the table and grabbed his hand.

"So, when will you start dating again?" she asked him.

"Mom! I don't know!"

John's mother than leaned forward and pinched his cheeks with both hands.

"You were always so handsome! Every day you spend not dating is a waste of your good looks! John, they're going to go away one day, so make sure you use them! Find yourself another Stephanie! I always liked her, you know."

Just then, John remembered why he was there. He got up from the table and went over to talk to his father, who had not moved from his curious viewpoint.

"Dad, about that maintenance uniform?"

"Oh right. I think it should be in the garage. Let's go down and look. I could also use your help with something."

The two of them walked towards the garage when John's mother reminded them dinner would be ready soon and not to take too long. Once in the garage, his father went over to a workbench and took a long time to bend down and drag out a tire a few feet so he could get at it with some more open space. His father had a back issue, likely from a lifetime of working with tools. He moved his head around in all directions from a kneeling position to look for something on the floor, then the top of the workbench. His eyes then locked onto an object on a shelf further down in the room."

"Hand me that spoke, will you?" he asked John.

"Hand you what?"

"Haven't I taught you anything!?"

"Dad, I promise I have never heard of this before."

John's father took his time to get back up to his feet, then sauntered over to the shelf and grabbed a circular metal object, which he held up for John to see.

"The spoke wrench!" he exclaimed.

"Oh."

"Hold this in place for me."

John stabilized the tire while his father cranked away at it. It didn't take long before he finished. John then dragged the tire back into its spot below the workbench so his father wouldn't have to stress his back. When John stood back up, he noticed his father returning the spoke wrench on the shelf, who then turned to look back at him.

"Let's get that uniform." he said. "Why do you need it again?"

"A client hired me to infiltrate their building. It's a test of their security protocols."

John's father issued a blank stare as he tried to make sense of John's statement. "Infiltrate?"

"Yeah. They want to make sure unauthorized people can't easily get into areas that they shouldn't be in."

"I thought you installed security cameras!"

"Where did you get that idea!?"

"You said you worked with security equipment. You told me about that job some years ago, where you had set up the security cameras for some energy company."

John's eyes glanced up and over to the ceiling corner to trace along with the various thoughts that bounced around in his memory. He tried his best to recognize how his father got that impression. Eventually, John had the notion.

"Dad, I'm a security consultant. I think you are referring to one job I had where I analyzed a company's surveillance and access control layout. Sometimes I make suggestions on camera placements and overall surveillance design strategy, but it usually involves the development of newer facilities than pre-existing ones. I do advisory services, not installments."

"Security consultant? Oh. Alright then."

John could tell his father didn't have a full grasp on the explanation that he gave him. He then followed his dad over to another area of the garage, where he pulled out an old beat-up duffle bag. As he unzipped it, the opening revealed a dark blue colored jumpsuit inside.

"That's it!" exclaimed John's father. "Oh, I fixed a lot of stuff in this thing. Brings back memories."

John zipped the bag up and carried it into the house, followed by his father. He had also taken a tool belt with him to enhance the image of the disguise. John set the bag by the front door before he joined his father on the couch while his mother worked away at the stove tops. The honey baked ham filled the house with a sweet aroma, which enticed their stomachs into a thick hunger.

"John, would you like some more tea?" John's mother asked.

"No. Coffee would be nice, though."

"Coffee!? It's nearly in the evening! You'll never get to sleep tonight if you have that now!"

"It'll be fine, mom."

"No. I'll make you a decaf then."

"Just give the boy what he wants, Marg!" pleaded John's father.

John's mother didn't acknowledge her husband and set a pot of decaf coffee for brewing. John's father sought Eva's attention.

"Hey Eva!"

"Hello Bernard!"

John sighed and thought to himself, "Ah shit."

John's father continued, "What's that song? You know. *Bum Bum CHA! Bum Bum CHA*! Play that song for me!"

"I'm sorry. Could you please be more specific?" Eva requested.

"You know, that one with the gay singer that died a long time ago. *Bum Bum CHA! Bum Bum CHA!* He had that mustache!"

"Are you by any chance referring to Freddy Mercury?" Eva asked.

"Freddy Boy! Yes Freddy! He was in that band."

"Freddy Mercury, born September 5th, 1946, was a British singer and songwriter who achieved worldwide fame as the lead vocalist for the rock band Queen."

"Queen! Right. Couldn't remember. Hey, play that song by them!"

"Which song by Queen would you like to hear, Bernard?"

"The one that goes like, *Bum Bum CHA! Bum Bum CHA*!"

"Dad, it's we will rock you." said John.

"That one!"

"Sure thing Bernard!"

We will rock you by *Queen* played out of the living room wall speakers.

"Isn't she great John?"

John replied in a sarcastic tone, "Sure."

"Alright you two, dinner is ready!" said John's mother.

The three of them lined up in the kitchen with their plate and grabbed what they needed before sitting down together at the dinner table.

"Are the potatoes just like how you remember them?" His mother asked him.

"Yes mom, they're great."

"What about the Ham? Too sweet? I was worried about using too much Honey?"

"No. It's good."

"Really? Are you sure? Because the recipe said to use only two cups. I've found that this honey isn't as sweet as the other brand I usually get. So, I used two and a half cups. I just wanted to -----"

John's father interrupted her, muffled by a mouthful of food. "He said it's fine!"

"So, your father met with a surgeon about his back!" said John's mother.

"Oh?" John replied.

"They are thinking about replacing some of his spine with synthetic vertebrae. You know, because he has such awful back pain. They think it'll take most, if not all, of the pain away. Plus, he'll be super limber again!"

"Dad, that's great news!"

"Bout time! Too many damn things to fix around here!" John's father asserted.

"No! You'll have to rest!" replied John's mother. "Doctor said no fixing anything for at least a few months after the surgery. It probably won't happen for a little while still."

"That's still good news." said John.

"It's a new technology, better than the previous type of synthetic vertebrae." said John's mother.

"How so?" asked John.

"It's stronger and more flexible." she explained. "Plus, they can sense the patient's pain levels and they will release those endorphins into your body. Your father should have a more comfortable recovery that way."

"That's impressive." John remarked. "I didn't know they developed that sort of thing."

"They are certainly coming out with some interesting technologies to help people." John's mother stated. "My friend Stacy got her eye fixed. They took those stem cells, and she had to do a series of injections into her eye over a period. Eventually, her eye became perfect 20/20 vision! And just the other day I saw a man that was jogging down the street with one of those robotic legs. They look strong! I wonder if they are better than the real ones."

“Well, think about it, Marg,” said John’s father, “I bet if I were made of steel, well, I know I’d be stronger. That’s for sure! Heck, I could become one of those new bionic athletes! Like the ones on television!”

“I’d bet that would be enough to get you out of retirement, Dad. You seem bored these days.”

John’s father enthusiastically continued his line of thought. “Or maybe I’d just be a runner. How about a swimmer? Yeah, I could do that. I bet with a leg or two made of steel I could swim from here all the way to Nanaimo!”

“You’d sink to the bottom of the ocean!” John’s mother declared.

John laughed hysterically. His father looked offended at first until a grin plastered across his face once he recognized the humour. “Well, maybe you’re right about that one.” he admitted.

The three of them finished their dinner, immersed in the small talk of current events and fond family memories. His mother kept bugging John about being single. Eva had to remind John’s mother that the oven was still on, and at her request, Eva auto-turned it off. John’s father made a few more classic rock requests along the course of the visit, getting half of the song titles wrong. Once they finished, John said goodbye and headed home with the duffle bag that contained the uniform and tool belt.

* * *

The next day, John had a lunch presentation at a business gathering. It was designed for various company representatives to network together and discuss ideas. There were a few key speakers invited to give presentations about various topics and how they apply to the business environment. John gave a thirty-minute presentation titled: *The Critical Importance of Security and Safety Mindset within the C-Suite.* He rocked it. A few audience members had detailed follow-up questions about some technicalities in his presentation. John was prepared and answered them to a high professional detail which exceeded their levels of satisfaction.

* * *

Once he finished, he returned home to change into his father's uniform, then made the journey over to the apartment complex listed in Wesley Atterton's file. John stared out of the train window as the stations passed him by. He noticed some new buildings being put up and recognized the structural material as a new type of brick that absorbed and stored sunlight internally as a power source for the building. These new structures still had connections to external power sources, but the fact that they were partially self-powered lowered the demand for extraneous resources. They also had small water turbines built into the tanks and pipelines of the building so that as water ran through them, it generated a current that supplied additional power. John thought to himself, "Captain Planet would be proud!" He remembered how he grew up watching that cartoon. A childhood favorite of his. Since the Conversion, the modern day contained a prevalent green focus. Eva held certain restrictions on some people and businesses. It was due to an environmental health code that sought to limit the consequences of superfluous human consumption for the greater good of the planet.

* * *

John finally arrived at the apartment building and stood outside in his father's uniform with the tool belt around his waist. He pulled out his phone and pretended to be busy speaking to someone as he waited for an opportunity for entry. Approximately twenty minutes had gone by before someone pulled up into the parking lot. John waited for them to exit their vehicle and approach the building door. They scanned their wristlet and held the door open for John as he came walking in behind them. He was in!

A building resident noticed John and asked him, "You must be here to fix the heating on the main floor finally!"

"Oh, yes!" John replied. "Sorry it's taken so long. There was a bit of a mix-up, but we're finally getting around to it."

"Bout time. Thanks for coming. Have a good one."

"You too."

The disguise worked! John put his phone away and went up to the third floor once the man was out of view. He questioned where he was going to change. No one was around, so he figured he would just quickly do it inside the stairwell. He put his clothes that he wore underneath over the top of the uniform. What would he do with the tool belt? Well, it was mid-afternoon. Most people would be at work. He didn't plan to be longer than necessary and questioned if he should just leave it in the stairwell and come back for it once he finished. John realised he didn't have a better idea and placed it in the corner, then exited the stairwell into the hallway and approached apartment *#305*. He took a big inhale and held his breath as he knocked on the door. Nothing. John waited a bit, then knocked again. Still nothing. He wondered if one of the neighbouring residents knew something. John tried several doors in the hallway, but only one of them answered. The interview proved futile, as the person was not familiar enough with the residents in apartment #305. There was one last door at the end of the hall. As John approached it, he took in another big breath before he knocked. No answer. That was John's last chance. He would have to come back later and try again if no one would answer. He went to knock one last time, but stopped his fist just about an inch from the door when he heard the lock unlatch from the other side. A short older woman answered the door and looked up at him.

"Yes?" she asked.

John cleared his throat. "Hello Ma'am, I'm sorry to bother you. I am looking for someone around here, but they didn't answer their door. In fact, I'm not even sure that they still live in this building. I was hoping a neighbour could answer some questions to help me locate them."

"Oh? Well, I'll try. Who is it?"

"I'm looking for a man in his mid-twenties. His name is Wesley Atterton. He lives in apartment *#305* just over there, or at least he used to. Do you know him?"

"Well, why are you trying to find him?"

John hoped this woman would not be nosy. In his experience, some people were content to help, while others were highly suspicious and didn't take too kindly to strangers poking around. This was John's only potential lead, so he hoped for the better before he offered his reply.

"I'm a private detective hired to find him. He had a relative pass away and there's an inheritance for him. The problem is, I'm worried the address I have listed here might be outdated."

"Oh, I thought they handled that stuff through Eva these days. She usually knows where people are and has their banking information, doesn't she?"

John's heart skipped a beat. He made a mistake. His mind raced to come up with a suitable answer.

"It is! It's just, um, these sorts of things require a witness to be present when signing. That's where I come into the equation."

"Oh, I see. Well, why wouldn't Eva know where you could meet him? I thought addresses and other personal information were always up to date with her."

"FUCK!" John thought to himself. He screwed up again. He scrambled for another quick answer.

"Eva is a very complex system, but she's not without flaws. We are having a server issue with some of her files. In the meantime, we must resort to older sources of information until we can return certain aspects of her memory bank to a restored function."

The woman thought about it for a few seconds. In his mind, John projected the same thought over and over "Please believe me. Please believe me. Please believe me."

"Well alright. I'll try to help anyway that I can."

John let out a wave of relief, but did his best to mask it. He thought about showing the old photo to the woman to ask if she recognizes him, but then he remembered the photo was a mug shot which could certainly blow his cover.

"Thank you. I appreciate your help. I'm looking for a Caucasian male around his mid-twenties. Short, brown hair and big ears. He's quite skinny. About 5 feet 8 inches in height. Freckles, and a bit of an overbite. Does that sound familiar?"

The woman pointed down at apartment #305 and replied, "Oh yes, he used to live just over there. He hasn't been there in a while, though. I remember that troublemaker. Always cursing and arguing with his mother. You could hear it coming from down the hall. Rambunctious child!"

"How long ago?"

"A year, maybe?"

"Do you know where they went?"

"No. I avoided them."

"Okay. Do you know anything about them at all? People they knew or places they visited?"

"No. I'm sorry, I don't."

There was a long pause.

"I suppose you'll just have to wait until they fix the server and get Eva to help you."

John nodded. It was a lie, but he tried to make it seem genuine regardless of feeling like he was lost in a void of hopelessness. He had no lead. It was possible he could come back another time and try some neighbours who weren't home, but that was a big stretch. John thanked the woman for her time, then as he turned to walk away, she spoke up again. "There was one thing. It's probably nothing."

A sense of hope shook him. "What is it?"

"Well, when I saw him come and go, he usually had some bag with him and a hat. There was a weird sword and shield symbol on both. I remember that because the hat and bag always matched."

"This symbol could be important. What exactly did it look like?"

The old woman's eyes glazed off into the corner while she brandished a scrunched-up wince on her face. "It was a sword and shield knocking together. They were white, and the background was black. There was some sort of writing around it that was also in white, but I don't remember what it said."

"The writing was part of the logo?"

"Yes, I think so."

"Okay. That might help. I'll try to see what that is. Otherwise, I'll just wait for Eva to be up and running again. Thank you for your help, and goodbye!"

John made his way back down the hallway, collected the tool belt from the stairwell, then exited the building and sat at a bench at the end of the street. He browsed the internet on his phone in search of anything that matched the logo described to him. It took some time, but John found something that stood out. There was a popular Virtual Reality video game called *En Guarde*. The logo for the game was a white sword and shield with a black background. The letters *En Guarde* were written over it. John discovered there was a large gaming club just on the outskirts of downtown that regularly held tournaments for the game. He searched their website and eventually found an advertisement for an upcoming event that read:

Tune in this Saturday April 7th at 10:00 a.m. as Galactic Emperor defends his reigning title in the Arena! It's going to be a death battle! Tickets on sale NOW!

To John's fortune, below the headline was a photograph of Wesley Atterton! John couldn't believe his luck. Wesley was Galactic Emperor. Not only did he figure out a lead to find him off a seemingly unreliable tip, but he knew exactly when and where Wesley was going to be tomorrow!

CHAPTER 4

John could hardly believe that he found Wesley. He figured that if he was going to tail Wesley away from the gaming tournament tomorrow, he should become more familiar with the surrounding area. He made his way over there to scope the place out, purchasing a spectator ticket along the way so that he could attend the next day's event.

He surveyed the perimeter upon arrival. It was a large building with a few different entry and exit points. He figured there would be a large crowd during the event, making it easy to lose his target; especially with the consideration that John had never previously worked as an undercover. He knew the surrounding neighbourhood well already, but to become familiar with all potential departure scenarios, John also surveyed the alleys between the streets, paying special attention to the cloistered spots. After all, he knew he would only need to follow Wesley long enough to confront him in a safe and secluded area. When John felt he had acquainted himself enough with the surrounding areas, he went home and called Brian.

"Good to hear from you, John." said Brian. "I've been waiting. I hope you have good news?"

"Well, sort of. Sorry I haven't given you an update yet. I have a lead. It could go bad, but I'm trying to do everything I can. It has taken effort to come this far already. I just wanted you to know I'm still working on it."

"Ok. Thanks for calling. I appreciate that."

"Have you heard anything back from the police?"

Brian replied with a lower toned and drawn-out pitch in his voice. "No."

"Yeah. Ok."

There was a long pause as each of them scrambled to think of anything additional to say of relevance until John spoke up again. "I'm doing everything I can. I care about her too, you know."

"Yeah, I know. Thanks."

"We'll be in touch. See ya."

"Bye."

* * *

When John arrived at the gaming tournament address the following day, he stopped shy of his approach to the main entrance and took a few deep breaths to ease the knot in his stomach. After a brief pep talk with himself, he entered and scoped out the building interior. The area was dimly lit, with a variety of colored flashing lights. Purple carpet covered most of the ground and the walls were painted in a large array of different colors. John could see a variety of gaming stations over to his left that included a mix of newer games and some classics. Over to the right was the bar and dining area. John noticed a sign in front of him from where he walked in that read: *En Guarde Tournament 2nd level.*

John noticed a staircase ahead that led upwards. He walked over and got in line, waiting to be permitted into the upper level. He was relieved to notice that the line of people was short, which granted him the confidence he could keep his target. When John queued to the front of the line, Security scanned his wristlet, proving his receipt for ticket purchase and granted him entry.

The second level contained four small cages in the center with signs above them labelling them as *Arena 1-4*. The flooring in them appeared to be of a smooth and hard rubber. Similar to what is used in an indoor rollerblading rink. The same purple carpet stretched across the rest of the room, which appeared to be the spectating area. Barricades of chain-linked fencing separated the arenas from each other, identifying their own play space. Large screens perched at the top of each arena and another rested on one of the back walls of the room. There were two potential exit points in the room. The staircase by which John entered and an emergency exit door. John remembered from his perimeter patrol the previous day that there was a fire escape on the side of the building that led to one of the back alleys.

He recognized it must be where that door led to. As the time passed, John noticed he previously misjudged the number of people that would be at the event based on the population of the line that he stood in, failing to consider how early he had arrived. The place filled and before long; the area smelled of body odour and the temperature increased to a warm amplitude. A slight humidity also overtook the room's atmosphere, due to the large number of people being condensed into a confined area. One of Eva's drones flew in and surveyed the crowd, but there was too much going on in the room for John to identify where it had come from. He sweat as his heart rate increased, knowing it might be difficult to keep track of his target through the crowd once he exited the playing arena; however, if Wesley really was some sort of celebrity among these people, John hoped he could still track his movements by reading the energy and body language of the crowd.

Suddenly, the lights came on and a loud intro theme played, followed by an advertisement for the game. An announcer dressed in one of the game's logo t-shirts then stepped into arena #1 accompanied with a microphone and engaged the audience.

"Lllaaaadies and gentlemen! Welcome to the 2046, Vancouver local tournament, Foooorrr En Guarde!"

The announcer threw his arms up in the air as he finished his sentence. Everything he said corresponded with an energetic display of bodily animation, which seemed to play a role in the buildup of hype within the crowd. The room brimmed with cheers and roaring applause. John could hear someone a few feet away from him yell at the top of his lungs. "Yeeeesssss! Emperor is gonna kick some ass! He's gonna kill you all!"

The announcer continued, "Alright En Guardians, we have an exciting show for you tonight! A show filled with violence, weapons, gore, and one of the most dominant En Guarde champions the game has ever seen! Galactic Emperor!"

The room erupted in applause. The announcer gave the audience time to express their mania, then held his hand up. When the energy of the room partially subsided, he made additional announcements regarding the company's sponsors, prize offering for the players, a prize draw for the spectators to take place later in the day, and events being hosted at the arcade unrelated to the current tournament. It wasn't information that was important to John, so he did not pay it much attention. Instead, he watched and waited for his target to arrive. John observed that the players would likely approach the arenas from somewhere in the sidelines. When the announcer left the arena, the large black screen at the back of the room turned on and served as a leaderboard for placings of the tournament players and a display for information for the day's upcoming matches. By viewing it, John determined the event was a sixteen-player tournament reserved only for those who were of a professional level ranking. Wesley Atterton's gamer tag was listed as a player in the event. The matches were one on one, best two out of three games with a load out select available after the first game of each round. The leaderboard displayed that there would also be some exhibitions taking place as well that were not part of the tournament. Some being one on one, two verses two team battles, or a four-player free for all. A different voice from the original announcer came on through an intercom speaker. The words bellowed throughout the room.

"Announcing first games of Round 1 pairings. NoobSlay3r2020 to arena 1 vs Mysterii to arena 2. Dragonmage to arena 3 vs DawnBlade to arena 4."

The screen on the wall then displayed the players' gamer tags over the arena numbers. The announced players made their way into the corresponded arenas and took a few quick minutes to equip themselves with the virtual reality set. It was a headset with a controller in each hand, while the shoulders, elbows, hips, knees, and feet also had sensors on them. The screens above the arenas now turned on and read: *Match Pending,* while the staff members and players set the game up.

The first game soon fired off. The screens above each arena now showed the game through the first-person perspective of the player within the virtual world. It was a fighting game where the players took each other on in a battleground setting, like gladiators but with advanced weaponry. There were a variety of weapons and power-ups that could be picked up to get an advantage on the other player. A fence made of laser beams marked the boundaries of the arena, and was hostile to the characters, making them take damage if they contacted it.

The player in arena 3 lost almost immediately. The game brought them to a menu where they customized aspects of their character. John figured this must have been the load out selection he learned about from the leaderboard. John wasn't a gamer. He dabbled a bit here and there when he was younger and had owned a gaming console, but that was the extent of his gaming experience. During that time in his life, John was more interested in playing hockey and chasing girls. En Guarde impressed him, though. A thought entered his mind that he might return sometime to try it out. Provided he could experience it in a non-competitive setting.

John snapped out of his thoughts, realising he could not allow himself to become too distracted. A task that was becoming ever more difficult with all the lights, sounds, and rowdiness of the mob of obstreperous gaming enthusiasts that surrounded him. John looked around again for his target. He couldn't see anything except what appeared to be some sort of disruption further down within the crowd. John noticed a bunch of people were facing the other way from the gaming event, as if they had drawn their focus to someone. He pushed his way through the crowd, but by the time he got close, things had already dissipated.

Round 1 finished. The players unequipped themselves, then departed from their arena. The leaderboard screen was updated to show the current player standings, then the previous voice from the intercom announced the next sequence of round 1 match ups.

"Announcing the next match ups for the first round. J@mesposeidon to arena 1 vs Galactic Emperor to arena 2. J3ster To arena 3 vs KageYama to arena 4."

John waited in deep anticipation. The crowd in front of arena 2 swayed until someone had emerged to the front. Several people slapped him on the back and fist bumped him as he made his way into the arena. It was Wesley! He looked pretty much just as John remembered him. He wore the En Guarde t-shirt and corresponding hat; all the while brandishing a very confident, almost mischievous smirk on his face as he got himself immersed within the complex setup of the virtual reality equipment. The energy that came off from the crowd was electrifying. A crackle of a boisterous storm of frenzied inequity. He was clearly the crowd's favorite.

Once he set himself up, he motioned to them in acknowledgement and gratitude, like how a king would beckon their people. The round started. Galactic Emperor made a dash to the center of the battleground where a shield had spawned while his opponent went for a weapon drop that was located closer to the outskirts. Once he got the shield, Galactic Emperor then pursued after his opponent, while maintaining the inside footing of the fighting grounds. His opponent was on the back foot, but played with an aggressive style, and swung his flaming axe at Galactic Emperor in desperation to strike a clean blow. John could hear confusion and criticism of Wesley's play strategy come from the surrounding crowd.

"What the hell is Emperor thinking?" a spectator asked.

“I have no idea!” replied another spectator. “He doesn’t even have a weapon!”

Galactic Emperor strategically timed each parry of his shield with a surgical accuracy and robust fortitude that staggered his opponent’s character off balance, minimizing the distance between them and the lasers bordering the edge of the battleground. Eventually J@mesposeidon took damage by being repeatedly knocked into the laser fencing. Upon recognition of what was happening, J@mesposeidon used a dash ability to get himself out from being cornered, but by this time, the health of his character had already been halfway depleted. J@mesposeidon finally landed a blow on Galactic Emperor, which took some of his health away. He went in for another strike, but Wesley did a jumping flip within his arena, which caused his character to do a mirrored movement in the virtual game, evading the attack. With the path now clear, he sprinted towards a distant weapon drop. Many spectators cheered, impressed and in admiration of his athletic ability, while others were left astonished in disbelief, as if they have never witnessed a player perform a maneuver so adroit. Galactic Emperor picked up a sword and took J@mesposeidon head on. The two exchanged blows until Galactic Emperor parried an attack that stunned his opponent, then used his shield to knock the axe out of his opponent’s hand before finishing with a spinning 360-degree backhanded sword strike that cleanly decapitated him. His lifeless body then dropped to the floor, squirting blood out of where his head used to be.

The two players then went into the load out menu and made customizations for the next game, which started off differently than the first. The map of the battlefield was different and contained two levels connected by ramps the characters could travel up and down. J@mesposeidon took the high ground and went for a long two-handed spear while Galactic Emperor stayed on the main level and collected a jet pack. It wasn’t long before the two met on the main floor of the battlefield. By using his jetpack, Galactic Emperor underwent a series of evasive maneuvers to dodge the spear thrusts of his opponent. Another weapon drop spawned on the 2nd level of the map and Galactic Emperor made a boost with his jetpack to get ahead of his opponent, but J@mesposeidon used his dash ability to close the distance between them, then struck Galactic Emperor with his spear. Galactic Emperor used the last of his jetpack fuel to make a jump from the main floor up to the 2nd level where the most recent weapon spawn had dropped, but J@mesposeidon threw his spear at him which caused him to lose momentum and he crashed into the ground. J@mesposeidon then sprinted up the nearest ramp to the 2nd level and collected the blast cannon. He displayed awareness that Galactic Emperor was almost dead and wielded no weapon. When the next weapon drop hit the map, J@mesposeidon made his way to a vantage point from the 2nd level that overlooked the drop point where the flaming axe had spawned. He waited in that location, fully aware that Galactic Emperor desperately needed a weapon and expected his arrival. When Galactic Emperor came into view, J@mesposeidon fired the blast cannon several times at him as he grabbed the axe. Galactic Emperor used his invulnerable ability, which granted him temporary immunity from taking damage and the energy blasts had no effect. The two of them rendezvoused in the center of the battlefield on the main level where their battle of wits persisted. J@mesposeidon was out of ammo and resorted to using the blast cannon as a blunt weapon. With no ammunition, it was inferior to the fire axe that Galactic Emperor had just picked up, but it was all he had. Not to mention the fact that he was leading in health inspired the confidence that he would be victorious. The two chopped away at each other with Galactic Emperor taking away most of the health of his opponent, before he succumbed to a beat down of the blunt end of the empty firearm his opponent wielded.

The two players returned to the load out screen and made their appropriate customizations for the final game of the round. They were tied 1-1. The third game took off more aggressively than the previous two. A hasted melee of tenacity and determination with Galactic Emperor taking a slight lead. It was close, but his reaction times were just slightly ahead of the other player. J@mesposeidon could recognize that he was losing and would have to resort to a different approach if he were going to win. He retreated, hoping to play more evasively until he could accumulate a weapon or power up that may give him an advantage. Wesley seemed to have better control over his character than his opponent and eventually closed the distance, stabbing him in the back. Desperate to shake him loose, J@mesposeidon jumped off the edge of the 2nd level down to the main, but Galactic Emperor used his freeze ability on him. By the time J@mesposeidon reached the ground, he found himself imprisoned within deep, thick ice, which temporarily barred him of all movements. Galactic Emperor approached his helpless opponent and used the power glove to rip off his enemy's armor. With his bare chest exposed, the visual aspects of the game then went into an X-ray mode where the organs of his opponent's character became visible and brightly highlighted. John could not identify the meaning, until he heard someone beside him in the crowd comment, "It's a lethality! He's gonna perform a lethality!" Galactic Emperor raised his sword arm in an inspiring fashion, then drove his blade through the exposed area of armor, penetrating the heart of his adversary, who then collapsed lifeless onto the ground. The fans went wild in commendation of their champion's triumph.

The match then came to a closure, and Wesley advanced to the following segment of the tournament. Over the course of the next few hours, he won the rest of the rounds until an intermission took place just before the finals. It was Galactic Emperor vs Stonewall for the championship. There were some team game exhibitions that took place during the main event's intermission, but most of the crowd was not interested in them. It had now been a few hours since the start of the tournament and John needed to use the washroom. He knew he had time to spare since the championship match wouldn't start for a while. John did his business, but as he re-entered the spectating area, he bumped shoulders with another younger man by accident and caused him to drop his hotdog onto the floor. The man turned around to confront John.

"Yo, what's your problem!?"

"Sorry." replied John. "It was an accident."

"Accident my ass! There's no way you didn't see me! Are you trying to start something here?"

As he finished his last sentence, he shoved John forcefully in the chest that started a flashback from his time in the police academy. They were practicing a self-defence technique in a martial arts dojo that involved a takedown into an arm bar that was utilised off this exact type of shove.

"Mason! You're finally getting it!" said the combat instructor. "Just swivel your hips a bit more on the descension and you'll get this down perfectly! Come on Cadet, one more try."

John's training partner squared up to him, then forcefully extended his arm to shove him off balance. John grabbed his partner's wrist and twisted him off balance, then moved to an adjacent position on his partner while maintaining control of his arm. He then lowered his center of gravity and stepped backwards and sideways in the motion of the letter *C,* which caused his partner to swing down into a prone position. He then locked up the arm, putting hyper extended pressure on the elbow joint until his training partner tapped his free hand on the ground, signaling that he couldn't take anymore of the pain.

The vision died and John's focus returned to the present moment. He noticed the younger man staring at him, eagerly awaiting his response.

The young man persisted, "Well? Are you?"

John took a minute to contemplate how he was going to handle the situation, then took a deep breath and gave his response in a poised demeanor.

"No sir, I'm not. I'm just here to see the event like everyone else. I really am sorry about your food, and if you'd let me, I'd like to pay for it, please."

The man's posture relaxed as the tension in his face released, suggesting the dissipation of emotion and return of rationality.

"I guess. It was twenty credits."

The man and John both opened the funds transfer app of their wristlets, then held them close enough together for the wireless connections in the devices to recognize each other. John sent twenty credits to the other man's digital ID, then figured he would break the awkwardness by attempting to establish some sort of common ground.

"About that last match, Galactic Emperor really put on a performance, didn't he?"

The man's attitude towards John changed from hostility into an affable and accepting sentiment. Almost as if they were friends.

"Dude, I can't believe how he was farming those drops! His opponent never stood a chance at getting any good spawns in that first game. If you ask me, I'd say his character movement was quite suspicious. I don't think I've ever seen someone else corner cut like that. It was gust! Also, I think his build in the second game had too much burst. He probably didn't need it and don't even get me started on those offensive stack builds."

John exhibited his best effort to pretend like he understood what the other guy meant, displaying an artificial tone of confidence and a forced smile of sincerity.

"Definitely. I've had similar thoughts about that. I think Emperor is going to take the win here today in the finals. Regardless, it should be a good one. Enjoy the last round."

"I will! You too."

John walked away and repositioned into a spot where he felt he could best observe his target in the upcoming round. Several minutes later, the previous announcer returned to arena #1 with the same microphone.

"Alright folks! The time has finally arrived to start the final round of the Vancouver En Guarde Championship!"

The crowd responded with astounding excitement.

"But first, it's time to announce the winner of this event's prize draw! Today's winner will get one month of unlimited free gaming redeemable at any of our locations! And without further ado, today's winning ticket number is……….774688! Would ticket number 774688 please report to the front desk on the main level to collect your prize! Again, that's ticket number 774688. Please report to the front desk on the main level to collect your prize!"

John could see someone from the crowd nearly bushwhacking his way through the thick of people, clearing a route over to the staircase that connected both floors of the building. John figured that must have been the lucky prize draw winner.

The announcer continued, "Ok folks. Can you guess what time it is?"

Cheering

"I said…. does anyone know what time it is!?"

Cheering

"It's time for the moment we have ALL BEEN WAITING FOR! Two of the best En Guard players in the region facing off one on one, in a best of three games DEATH BATTLE!"

Cheering

"Introducing first, the challenger. Playing in arena #1. The one, the only, STONEWALL!"

The crowd had a mix of some people cheering while others were booing.

"And finally! Last, but not least. Playing in arena #2. Introducing the reigning and defending champion. One of the best players En Guarde has ever seen! The elegant, the extravagant, the magnificent, the one and only……… GALACTIC EMPEROR!"

The crowd went ballistic as Wesley made his way past them into arena #2. He took his time getting set up within the virtual reality equipment, showing off along the way in an appeal to his fans. Some of the event staff motioned to both players as if checking in on their status with both players returning a thumbs up communicating they were ready to begin. The first game went to the challenger, and the second game went to the champion. As the players made their customizations for the final game, the air in the room grew thick with the anticipation of eager fans. They knew this was it. The moment that would crown a new regional champion.

The third and final game of the tournament began with both players heading to the nearest weapon drop before they clashed together in the center of the battlefield. They seemed evenly matched, with many strikes being paired with blocks and parries. The round went on for several minutes, with little progress being made on either end, almost as if the champion and the challenger were both too skilled for each other. Before long, both players seemed nearly overwhelmed with conspicuous weariness, but refused to relent as they pursued their offensive with an immense tenacity and will for victory. Eventually, both characters were almost dead, leaving the impression that another hit on either of them would define the new champion. The vaporizer then dropped on the 2nd level of the battlefield. Stonewall beat Galactic Emperor to it and threw away the weapons he was already holding in order to pick it up. He turned to face Galactic Emperor who was sprinting towards him and fired off a few rounds that all failed to make impact. Understanding that there was only one shot remaining in the vaporizer, Stonewall took a steady aim. The entire room went completely silent in anticipation of what would happen next before an audience member vociferously expressed an observation that broke the silence. "Oh shit! He's got the theft lasso!" A glowing rope appeared in the hands of Galactic Emperor, then extended towards Stonewall and snagged the weapon out of his hands. Now with the vaporizer in his own possession, Galactic Emperor took careful aim and fired off the last remaining round. The energy blast hit Stonewall square in the chest, who then exploded into bright dust. The audience erupted into a cheerful applause in celebration of their champion's victory. After voyaging through a series of worthy opponents, Galactic Emperor won yet another En Guarde tournament.

When the energy of the crowd finally died, the event staff proceeded with the closing announcements. The announcer returned to arena #1 and officiated Galactic Emperor as champion once again, then thanked everyone in the audience for supporting the event. The closing ceremony took place, which involved the top four players receiving their prizing. John's patience was tested as Wesley remained afterwards to do an autographing and photography session with fans. When the last had been accommodated, Wesley grabbed his things and said his farewells to some of the event staff members before he departed out of the building, accompanied by a small group.

John did his best to stay back far enough to not draw suspicion, but not too far that he would lose his target. Wesley and the group walked down to the edge of the street. They stood around talking for a few minutes before they shook hands and made separate departures. Wesley went through a back alley that came out to a busy street. As Wesley approached the crosswalk, the light signaling to cross had just switched off, and he ran to beat the flow of traffic. John knew it was a major intersection, and if he didn't make the cross, he could fall behind and lose his target. John sprinted, desperate to make it across. As he stepped onto the crosswalk, traffic started up at the green light. A vehicle nearly struck him as it slammed on its brakes. The piercing shriek of the car's horn echoed through the city intersection and drew a magnitude of public attention to him as he finished crossing. John's hair stood on end. He noticed the gazes of others around him and wondered if Wesley had noticed. That's all that mattered to him. John took several more steps and peered through a temporary break in the foot traffic where he recognized Wesley ahead, uninterrupted by the commotion that occurred at the intersection. John's relief was brought to an abrupt halt when Eva suddenly spoke up on his wristlet.

"Hello John! I couldn't help but notice you crossed a little too late back there! The cross signal had already ended and I'm afraid you stepped into oncoming traffic. I am glad to report there are no injuries, but I'm afraid you will have to be reprimanded for public endangerment. Seeing as how this is your first offense, you'll be pleased to hear the repercussions as being only a first tier fine. When you next log on to your banking account, you'll notice a deduction in the amount of $412 credits. If you have questions about the fine, or the offense committed in subject, please ask me and I'll be happy to fill you in on whatever information you need!"

John thought to himself, "Aww for fuck sakes!" while he jogged to keep up with his target. John followed Wesley to a train station and got in line several spots behind Wesley. Eventually, they both made it through the lobby and waited on the platform for the upcoming convoy. When it arrived, Wesley waited for the egress of people to exit, then he and a small crowd of other people stepped aboard. John entered through the other end of the train and braced himself with the wall as it sped up in departure. He watched as two other people on the train approached Wesley. One of them pointed at their phone and asked him something. The conversation was not audible to John, but it seemed as if they recognized Wesley. They took photographs with Wesley before he stood up from his seat and made his way to the door as the train approached the upcoming station.

The train came to a halt. The crowd exited, and John followed Wesley down the set of stairs that led to the street. They traveled across several major streets until eventually passing through a residential area that led to a park. John worried it would become difficult to follow Wesley as the houses, shrubs, and fences introduced a cluttered view. Wesley took a sharp turn and disappeared down a bike path that could not be observed from John's current position. The foliage obstructed any hope of an outside view. He hurried to the spot he last saw Wesley, then entered blindly to pursue the long trek of the bike path. As John stepped in, he fell prone onto the ground, completely unaware of what he had tripped over. He rolled over in confusion, trying to make sense of what had happened, then saw it. John froze with his hands held innocently in the air as he stared into the barrel of a handgun pointed directly at his head.

CHAPTER 5

This was the end. He failed Stephanie and now she would never be rescued. These were the thoughts that raced through John's mind before he was captivated by the voice disclosed behind the firearm that said, "The honesty by which you answer will determine the mercy of your death." John saw more clearly now. The person behind the handgun was Wesley. Somehow, he identified John was following him. John figured Wesley must have hidden around the corner of the bike trail entrance and tripped him as he entered through.

"I know you heard me. Tell me who you are."

"John Mason. I'm a former police officer. We expunged your criminal charges to get you to assist us with that case several years ago."

"Yeah, I think I remember you. So, you're working undercover now, huh? What do you want with me?"

"I'm not in the police anymore. I followed you away from the tournament because I needed to speak to you privately, and it was the only way I could find you."

"About?"

"I need your help with finding someone. She was kidnapped. This isn't for certain, and might sound crazy, but Eva may have had something to do with it. I need someone skilled in computer software. I don't think I can find her on my own."

"Who is this person you're looking for?"

"My ex-wife. She went missing earlier this week. Witnesses say she was abducted in her workplace parking lot. They threw her in the back of a van, then one offender drove off with her vehicle."

John waited for a reply but received only silence.

"Please, I have no leads!" John begged. "I don't know what else to do! You're the only one I know with the possibility of any skill set that might find something for me."

"You think I can just hack Eva? Is that it?"

"I don't know what else to do."

"Roll onto your stomach and put your hands behind your back!"

John complied and Wesley patted him down, but found nothing.

"Alright Mr. Mason, this is what we are going to do. I'm gonna find out for sure whether you're telling me the truth. You're going to stay in this position until some friends of mine arrive. If you try to fight, run, scream, or touch your wristlet, consider yourself lead-brained!"

"Who is coming?"

"Like I said, we are going to find out exactly who you are and what you want. If you have been telling me the truth, then I promise you there is nothing to worry about."

It must have been at least a half hour that John stayed in that position. The damp soil stained his clothing and his lungs filled with an earthly musk with each anxious breath. He must have taken over a thousand of them before he heard many pairs of thumping footsteps approach within a close distance. John could hear a muffled conversation between Wesley and whoever had arrived, but he couldn't make out the words. The footsteps then approached both sides of John and then his vision went dark as his head was tightly wrapped in a cloth bag. They handcuffed John and yanked him up to his feet. He felt the barrel end of a handgun dig into his back as he was told to walk to the entrance of the bike path. He found himself barely able to stand, let alone walk. His legs were deeply asleep from being wound up like a pretzel for so long. An overwhelming painful sensation of pins of needles flooded his entire lower body, which consumed his full attention and challenged his best efforts to bear. They stripped John of his wristlet and cellphone and threw him in the back of a van where a burly man kept watch over him. John couldn't see the man, but he felt a large shift in the van's weight move onto its back tires as he climbed in the back. They shut the door behind them and the rumble of a fired-up engine vibrated through the vehicle's metal hull, almost tickling John as they drove away.

John tried to count the number of turns and stops, committing them to memory as best as he could; although his efforts turned fruitless, as he eventually forgot the lengthy sequence. John was lost. He didn't know where he was or where he was being taken. Eventually, he felt a forward shift in gravity as the van traveled on a descent. A clanging sound of metal echoed through the area, like a heavy parking garage door had just opened and closed behind them. The van didn't wobble as much as before, suggesting they had reached smooth pavement. John wondered if they were underground. The van made several more turns, then came to a complete stop. John could hear the slam of the driver and passenger doors as they opened and shut before the door opened to the vehicle's back component where John had lay captive. He felt two pairs of hands grab him and pull him onto his feet, where a reunion took place between him and the familiar feeling of a handgun dug into his back as he was told to walk forward. John was still blind but figured all he needed to do was continue to walk in the direction he was being led. Aside from the sense of immense panic within him, he also felt relief, knowing that momentarily he would be face to face with whoever was behind all of this.

They took John into a secluded room and forced him into a chair equipped with several bodily restraints that left him immobile. He worried that he would have to endure a brutal interrogation, maybe even torture. He knew he wasn't lying, but his thoughts about the methods these people may resort towards to discern that concerned him.

John remained captive in pure darkness until the door finally opened and he could hear several pairs of feet enter the room. They yanked back the cloth that consumed his vision. He winced as the rough fabric dragged across his face until the blinding light of the room pierced into him, shielding John from identifying anything more than a blurry figure that stood before him. A buzzing sound emerged from directly behind John's ears as a pair of electric hair clippers ran through his head. Small piles of hair fell onto the floor one by one until John was completely bald. The person behind him then took a warm gel and lathered his bare scalp with it, which engulfed the room with a potent chemical smell that stabbed the senses. A strange device was then placed on his head. It was like a metal helmet covered with sensors and wires, which took several minutes to set up. John felt beads of sweat form along his forehead. He had never previously encountered anything like this device and didn't know what to expect next. A luminescent glow emitted off the various sensors, showing the device became operational.

By this time, John's eyes had adjusted to the bright light in the room, and he could identify the visuals for his new environment. Florescent lights suspended from the ceiling engulfed the room in an artificial luminescence. Bland white tiles made up the walls and ground. A wide trail of rusty brown stains led from the base of the chair that bound John along a slight decline towards a small drainpipe in the center of the room's flooring. John could sense there were many people in the room, but there was only one in his view. The figure became clear. An older man of slight precedence to John, with white hair and thick glasses. He looked over at someone behind John in anticipation, as if waiting for a cue. An unidentified voice behind John replied, "Good to go Sir!" The older man then turned back to face John.

"This device on your head accurately monitors your brain activity and will tell us whether you are lying." said the old man. "We are going to ask you a series of questions and you are going to answer them truthfully. Anything short of the truth and we will discern your deception. I assure you I am not the most patient of those among men. Do you understand?"

"Yes."

Nearing the end of his time in the police, John had heard about the development of a new mind reading lie detector technology. The developers had not completed the project as they were working on perfecting the last remaining bugs. There had been talk about replacing current lie-detectors with the new technology, as it was recognized to be vastly more accurate and didn't depend as much on the interpretation of an interrogator. It was a technology expected to be used as court reliable evidence in criminal cases, believed by many to become a revolution in the integrity and continuity of court evidence procedures for proving any potential guilt among offenders; however, nearing the end of its development, some test subjects had proven to develop negative side effects. Due to ethical concerns, the project was terminated.

The older man then asked John a series of interrogating questions. He looked up at one of the other people in the room behind John as if receiving assurance between each provided answer.

"What is your name?"

"John Mason"

"What interest do you have in us?"

"I don't even know you! I was following someone by the name of Wesley Atterton to seek his help in finding someone."

"Who are you looking for?"

"Stephanie Houghton. October 9th, 1995. Well, she goes by Stephanie Tallow these days."

"What is your relation to this person?"

"She is my ex-wife. Her husband contacted me to find her. She has gone missing."

"Why not leave this matter to the police?"

"I'm not sure they can help. She was taken, and possibly by the government. I don't have reasons to believe anyone else could have done it."

The old man paused briefly, then continued with the line of questioning.

"How has this investigation of yours led to someone named Wesley Atterton?"

"He is the only person I know with extraordinary computer skills. I've seen him hack into databases before. If I am correct about Eva being behind my ex-wife's disappearance, then I would need someone who could grant me any leads from the inside."

"Under what circumstances have you previously been associated with this Wesley Atterton?"

"I am a former officer for the Vancouver police department. Before the Conversion, we made a deal to expunge Atterton's criminal charges provided he lend assistance in the arrest of a criminal case. For a younger person, he was a real tech protégé. He's the only person I know that might be both able and willing to give me a clue about where to go next."

"Do you have any associates working with you?"

"No."

"How did you find this Wesley Atterton?"

"I still had access to the old case file involving Mr. Atterton. Yesterday, I went to the old address listed in that file where a neighbouring resident gave me a clue. That clue led me to discover that Mr. Atterton frequented a gaming club where, earlier today, he took part in a virtual reality tournament. I followed him away from it when he got the upper hand on me and called you guys. Now here we are."

The older man stared at John for a moment. His glare pierced through him, as if not intended to analyze John's words, but his soul. He then motioned to some others in the room behind John, who powered down and removed the device on his head. Everyone but a large man left the room, who remained to watch over John. When the door closed behind them, John faintly heard the older man argue with someone else in the adjacent room.

"Fucking Moron! What did I tell you about going to those gaming events!? You are drawing attention when I ordered you to lie low! What if he was a cop or a government agent? You could have led them right to us! Do you understand how bad this could have gone, you careless fuck!?"

"Hey look, maybe we can use him. I'm supposed to be a ghost, remember? If he tracked me, maybe he can help find Drax. The guy has some skills and a motive we could use for leverage. He's desperate!"

"Don't try to justify your actions! You are becoming sloppy! From now on I'm putting a leash on you! I want to know everything that you do! I don't care if it's as harmless as buttering toast or slipping into your sister's panties! You don't even get to take a shit unless I tell you to, understand!?"

The man who watched over John realised their voices were coming in audibly through the walls and went into the other room to inform them. The voices then became imperceptible, and the man returned to the room to monitor John. They both lingered mute for what felt an eternity of awkward silence with the only flare of hope being that John briefly heard someone from the other room vouch for his relevance. They would know John told them the truth after all, not to mention he no longer had ties with any authorities. His affiliation with law enforcement was prior to the Conversion. The world was much different back then. They wouldn't find that to be a threat, would they? John's anxious speculations came to a halt when the door re-opened and the others returned to confront him.

"What are you willing to do for her?" the older man asked.

John ruminated about it, then replied with a tone of palpable sincerity. "Anything. I'll do whatever it takes."

"Even at your own expense?"

"I think I've proven that by coming this far."

The older man nodded in approval. He motioned to someone behind John, who took a damp towel and wiped the potent chemical gel from his scalp. Once clean, they released John from his captivity. He sat there in the chair unbound, listening carefully as the older man spoke to him again.

"You can call me Farell. I oversee these operations. I have a proposition for you, but I'll grant you the courtesy of answering your questions first."

"Let's begin with the obvious one. Who are you?"

"We are The Patriots. You've probably heard of us."

Those words struck John. *The Patriots*. They were a terrorist organization, or at least that's how the media portrayed them. They were the primary opposition formed shortly after the Conversion, whose united purpose was to destroy Eva and restore freedom and natural order to humanity. Their members and associates were branded public enemy #1. Subject to brutal torture, preceding execution. Or at least that's what the rumours were.

"What are you going to do with me?" John asked.

"Nothing bad if you behave. We might be able to help you."

"How so?"

"Got a job for you. In return, there's a good chance we could help you get Stephanie back, but you will need to pull through for us first."

"What do you need me for?"

"Our leader, Drax, was captured. He's being held, but we don't know where. We've run out of leads. You've proven capable of tracking people down, and perhaps we could use someone that can think outside the box."

"So, if I find where he is, you'll help me get Stephanie back? How do you know where she is?"

Farell nodded, then took a deep inhale before he continued. "We will explain that shortly, but yes. That is the deal and I assure you that we found her. Consider this an exchange. We would work closely together. We will monitor you, but give you the help you need. If you bring us the payoff we're looking for, we will get your woman back to you."

John took a moment to contemplate what he might get himself into.

"You understand the direct corollary of your involvement, don't you?" asked Farell. "You'll be an enemy to the government. An enemy to Eva."

"I understand."

"And your decision?"

"I won't abandon her. I owe her."

"Very well. Stand. Follow Lev and see Wesley."

Everyone left the room except the burly man who watched over John.

"I'm guessing you're Lev?" John asked him.

The man did not respond. He pointed to the door, providing the inference to leave. Lev led John through a large common space in the adjacent room, like a lounge that contained a full kitchen and a small bar counter that housed several brands of alcohol behind its display. A large metal desk cluttered with computer monitors and various complex circuitry occupied the back corner, manned by Wesley, who sat in a leather computer chair at the cockpit of its convoluted arrangement. As they approached, Wesley motioned to a spare adjacent seat. John sat down and waited in anticipation for whatever would come next.

"YOOO! Ha-ha, how's this for a turn of events, eh?"

John did not reply. He stared at Wesley and waited for anything of relevance to happen.

Wesley continued, "Yeah alright, so here's the thing. If you're going to work with us, you'll have to poke around as needed without Eva getting in the way. I've modified your wristlet. She can't track you anymore."

"Um, how does that work, exactly?"

"Right, so it's really complicated. Um…."

Wesley rested his chin between his thumb and index finger, taking a moment to consider how he was going to approach his explanation.

"They programmed Eva to recognize patterns and to look for certain triggers, or abnormalities that would prompt her into an investigation. She monitors everyone and everything, but it is only when specific things occur that provoke her to take a response. This could be to monitor for keywords in conversation, analyzing daily behaviors, spending habits, places being visited, things like that. When something happens that Eva would recognize as an irregularity or some sort of prohibited action, she will then conduct a course of action relevant to how they programmed her to respond. It is important to understand that Eva only handles the minor and medium complexity investigations with more complicated manners allocated to a government official who will then analyze the next course of action based on the circumstance and data that Eva has collected. The main point to take away here is that Eva is essentially passively monitoring each person, rather than actively. Unless something draws her attention. Are you following so far?"

"I think so."

"Cool. So, all we have to do, rather what I have to do, is make the edits of your average day into her system to trick her into believing you are still living life as you normally would. Meanwhile, with your updated wristlet, you can roam freely underneath her capability of detection. Well, semi-freely. Don't be careless about it. That way, her programming will detect nothing abnormal to provoke her into investigating you. The government doesn't end up on your ass that way."

"What about the GPS in the chip?"

"Not a problem. Your wristlet is now cloaked from her GPS detection. I'll have to work with you in coming up with various examples of what a typical day of yours would look like, then I can input that information into my computer which will auto-generate a GPS paper trail in real time each day as if you were living life normally. That way, you can operate as needed without generating suspicion."

"You really can hack her after all!"

"Well, aspects of her, and not always. Different security measures defend different areas of her data, which change periodically. It's like solving a highly complex riddle, only to eventually be locked out again with a new puzzle to decipher. Not to mention she receives regular software updates, becoming more complex with each subsequent upgrade. Therefore, we always work with urgency. The longer our fight continues, Eva only becomes more powerful."

"How am I supposed to make calls or purchases?"

"I've also cloaked your cellphone. You can make purchases as needed, but ONLY as needed. You will not be accessing your personal banking account, but a small, separate one of ours that I have created for you. Consider it an allowance, just for the everyday little things. The purchases will be untraceable. When I work with you on establishing what an average day of yours looks like, we will go through your banking statements so that similar data will be replicated into your daily profile that is uploaded to Eva's system."

John nodded, then looked around the room. He spotted remnants of various supplies and food boxes that have been left around. The room contained furnishings of a surprising quality that surpassed John's expectations for what an underground base would contain. Typical household appliances were scattered throughout the establishment, offering a sense of hospitality.

"How have you guys been getting by all this time?" asked John.

"We ugh, accumulate banking information from various people around the world and transfer tiny amounts of their funds ever so slightly into a series of bank accounts which transfer those funds into other freshly created bank accounts, in which the original accounts are destroyed. Then rinse and repeat. Forever. Think of it like an infinite game of hot potato where each person is swapped out by someone new once they've passed along the tuber."

John's eyes narrowed at Wesley while he continued with his following statement, "Ah, I see. So, you guys scam innocent people then."

"A word of advice. Drop the Moral Police attitude if you want to fit in around here. We do what we do because it's the only form of untraceable income for us. Besides, it's going towards a better cause."

"What about all of my GPS and wristlet data prior to when you guys brought me here?"

"Already taken care of. Eva currently thinks you're at Queen's Park. I began tampering with your wristlet immediately once we put you in the van, so there's no GPS trail that could lead anyone back here. Regarding your investigation so far, Eva hasn't been spooked. So, either you didn't do or say anything that she would have flagged, or she couldn't identify it. The speakers in the wristlets work best indoors and even then, they can't shut out all background noise. You know what it's like trying to talk to someone on the phone while they are outdoors, right? There are things like wind or noisy city-life that can drown conversation and make it difficult to determine exactly what's being said. And that's considering that the phone is right up to your face. She does still incriminate people if they are careless. Not thinking about where they are, what they are doing, or what they are saying. Things like that. She can pick up on various cues."

"What about all of her drones and public cameras?"

"PASSIVELY, monitoring! If something spooked her into investigating you, she, or an actual person in the government, would review the data and would certainly determine an inconsistency with your log of daily activities versus your physical absence in the surveillance footage of those areas. It would prove that you were never at those locations; Therefore, you are going to AVOID flagging Eva's suspicion, so that type of data is never reviewed. Got it?"

John nodded. "Okay. I understand."

"This is the sole principle of why we haven't been caught yet. So, I can't stress the importance of being mindful of your actions. Be careful about where you go and what you do, and don't raise any suspicion!"

"Like become a renowned gaming champion?"

Wesley's jaw clenched and his eyes narrowed in reply to John's witty remark as if what was said had challenged him, but then he quickly turned and looked away. An awkwardness swept in between them, soon to be halted when Wesley remembered about the information he still required in order to build John's daily profile imitations. Over the course of the next hour, John answered a lengthy series of personal and daringly private questions about his lifestyle which Wesley then inputted into the computer program. The level of detail incorporated into its design impressed him. Not only did it include everyday mundane tasks, but John would even periodically receive funds into his personal banking account under the guise of various company names and clients that he would typically receive payment from. When they finished, the system oriented a routine detailed to John's lifestyle, which was then employed into immediate operation.

"There. It is now in effect." said Wesley.

"What about my actual upcoming appointments?"

"I'm afraid you will have to cancel those. We can't take the risk that you might cross contaminate what you're actually doing with the illusion this program is creating for you. If you interact with somebody who somehow gives Eva the impression you are involved in something separate from the information she is receiving by your end, she might notice the contradiction in her data and that would become a problem. A big problem."

"Yeah alright. I get it. So, what now?"

"Well, we are finished here. Farell wanted to speak with you again. Go have a seat over on the couch and I'll let him know we're ready."

John went over and did as Wesley instructed. It didn't take long before Farell and several other people entered the lounge room, claiming their seating arrangements. Farell grabbed a chair and set up directly in front of John's view, as if to address him in a candid and personal matter.

"Meet the gang." said Farell. "You already know Lev and Wesley. This is Rio and Kade. There are more of us, but they are occupied with tasks."

Farell pointed to each person as he identified their names. Rio was a middle-aged woman with a strong, toned structure. She exhibited a powerful, unwelcoming body language which communicated her uptight demeanor. She stood with her arms crossed and jaw clenched as she slowly chewed a piece of bubble-gum. Her eyes were wide and fixated on John, like an attack hound waiting to strike. Lev was a man of impressive size who took up the entire half of the couch he occupied. His chest hair became exposed, overlapping the collar of his shirt when he found his seating. He didn't seem to speak much and his movements seemed slow and calibrated, which mismatched his otherwise intimidating stature. Kade was slender, dark-skinned, and dressed in a sleeveless basketball jersey. He brandished a warm, satisfied smile as if he were glad to have recognized a new member in the team.

"Seems like a small crew." John commented.

"We are a worldwide organization, but yes. I'm afraid we have recently suffered large losses of numbers. Let's get to it John. We would like your help to find Drax. He is our regional leader who was captured just earlier this week. We are normally very careful about who we bring into our establishment, but as they say, desperate times call for desperate measures. I am aware of your background and levels of expertise. I anticipate they will provide use for our cause."

"Here's hoping. I need you to tell me how you know Stephanie is alive, where she is, and your capability to return her."

Farell looked over and extended his hand out to Wesley, prompting him to speak.

"So, I've gained access to an area of Eva's data, which seems to be documented case files for the people the government has abducted." said Wesley. "They refer to them as test subjects and it appears as if they are becoming subjected to various forms of...... experiments."

John swallowed heavily. "What kind of experiments?"

"Genetic," he replied, "but I can't determine the specifics. The reports are littered with science jargon."

"And you know where she is being held?" asked John.

"Yes. Well, no, but I think we can schedule her release." replied Wesley. "See, while sifting through all the scientific mumbo-jumbo in the reports, I've noticed a commonality. They often refer to something called *Serum 3V-12,* and it seems to be that the test subjects who respond adequately to it eventually become safely released back into the public. I don't know why."

"And what happens to those who respond inadequately to Serum 3V-12?" asked John.

"Their files are discontinued." replied Wesley. "We can only speculate what that means."

John leaned forward and raised his voice. "Tell me what Stephanie's file says about 3V-12!"

"Hey take it easy!" shouted Wesley. "I've read the most recent updates and there is no mentioning of Serum 3V-12 anywhere. They still have her. Relax."

John took a moment to calm the tension in his body. He took a big breath, then continued.

"So, I help you find this Drax of yours and then what? How are we going to get Stephanie?"

"Theoretically, I make an edit in her case file stating the desired outcomes of the Serum 3V-12 testing, then file recommendation for her public release." explained Wesley. "I could easily forge the signatures and everything. Should be a piece of cake!"

"THEORETICALLY!?" objected John.

"Well, it's not like I've actually done it before!" replied Wesley. "Look, every case file with that in common gets discharged shortly afterwards, but if you have a better idea, then we are all ears!"

John sat silent and unable to think of a response.

"John, you should know about what happened." said Farell. "Drax was out on an errand with some of our members. We were doing a supply drop off to what was supposed to be other Patriots from another region. Our members were attacked, and either killed or captured in the firefight. We can't say for sure, but we think we may have had a mole. This is no longer a concern, as whoever it may have been did not survive the encounter. Drax was taken and we're sure he's been interrogated. He's the toughest son of a bitch I've ever come to know, and he would die a brutal death before giving the rest of us up. Regardless, we still cannot be certain about the level of information they may have extracted from him."

"You're sure that your remaining members are ironclad?" asked John.

"Passed the helmet test and everything." Farell assured.

"But you all still have your hair." John pointed out.

"That's just for the first use." explained Farell. "The gel helps the sensors get a stronger identification of the user, basically charting a map of their unique neurology. It's relevant so the machine can discover how the person's unique thought patterns operate; however, regarding any follow up uses, the machine would calculate its results based on the person's signature neural identity it already discovered in the initial trial."

John nodded in acknowledgement. The room was quiet for a moment before Wesley poked fun at Lev.

"Except in Lev's case, there weren't any thoughts to detect. So, we had to pass him as safe under the assumption he isn't smart enough to think of a lie, ha-ha-ha."

Kade laughed while Lev sneered at Wesley.

"So, where should we start from here?" asked John.

"Not sure just yet." replied Farell, "But I have a meeting with one of our contacts later this evening. I anticipate it will lead to a clue. John, for now, take a load off and familiarize yourself with the place. In the morning, I will brief everyone on the plan. While you are with us, Rio will be your direct report. Go to her if you need something."

Farell then stood up and left the room while the others remained. Kade then turned and looked at John. "Ayy, you thirsty or something?" he asked him.

The mere mentioning of water invoked a heavy wave of dehydration that swooped over John. He hadn't eaten or drank anything since leaving his home that morning.

"Yeah, now that you mention it," replied John, "I could really use something."

Kade went over to the fridge and pulled out a cold bottle of water, then took some protein bars from a box in the corner of the kitchen counter and tossed them over to John. The sensation of cool water streaming down the back of his throat sparked him to relax. He had been in a state of fight or flight all day and this was his first opportunity for any sort of intermission between all the stress and anxiety.

"Hey guys, we never got to finish our discussion from earlier." said Wesley. "I still think a silverback gorilla could take on a grizzly bear in a fight."

Kade scoffed and replied, "Naw, man! You ever seen the size of them grizzlies!? I told you, they are twice the size!"

"Okay, but a gorilla has opposable thumbs, right? And a larger arm span which pretty much makes all the difference. And they gotta be stronger than a bear. They could easily tear a human's limb right off! Imagine just being able to grab and hold back a bear from being able to do anything to you and then you can just bite or rip it apart whenever you want to. And I think Silverbacks are bigger than you think they are."

"Grizzlies are bigger, stronger, and faster."

"Bruh, I promise you they are closer in size than you think."

Wesley and Kade raced to take out their cellphones and began researching, shaking their heads in disbelief at the other person's stance on the topic.

"Ha! A Silverback gorilla's bite force is 1300 PSI, while a Grizzly's is only 1250 PSI!"

"That's not a significant difference! Look, a grizzly weighs about six hundred pounds while a silverback is around four hundred. That's not even close! Grizzlies are also more aggressive AND have four-inch-long claws! They have a top running speed of thirty-five miles per hour in comparison to only fifteen miles per hour of the Silverback gorilla! Checkmate!"

"Well, but that's just flat numbers. Take into account the intelligence of a gorilla vs just a bear. They are closely related to us, after all."

"Bears are straight up smart. They have to scavenge the forests and shit. And figure out how to find food and survive!"

"And a gorilla doesn't? Look, a gorilla lives a lot longer than a bear, right? So, if we are comparing the two in their prime adult stage, then a gorilla has been around a lot longer than a bear has. Plus, bears hibernate part of every year, so they're just sitting in a cave sleeping much of the time. A gorilla spends its whole-ass life trying to survive, and totally beats a bear when it comes down to matters of experience. Are you going to rule that factor out entirely?"

Kade threw his hands up in the air. "I'll lose my mind with this guy!"

"Rio, you agree with me, right?" asked Wesley.

Rio responded with only a facepalm. Wesley sought reassurance from John.

"John?"

John shrugged. Wesley let out a sigh of regret in advance at having to consult Lev.

"Lev? What do you think?"

Lev responded revealing a thick Russian accent. "I think little boy talk too much."

Kade laughed while Wesley appeared embarrassed. He attempted to deflect his embarrassment by pursuing the debate topic with Kade. They clashed with each other in a fiery exchange of counterpoints until Lev and Rio lost interest and left the room. John waited for an appropriate pause in the discussion between Kade and Wesley, cautioning not to interrupt one of them. When the opportunity struck, John spoke up.

"Someone care to show me around this place?"

"Aww my bad." Kade admitted. "Let's peep it!"

Kade motioned for John to follow. The room connected to a long concrete hallway. Old, dingy LED lighting dimly pronounced its visibility. Various rooms were connected among the extension of the corridor, most of which were open and not barricaded by any sort of door. Kade's voice bounced off the concrete halls as he called out the various areas to John before stopping at one last area as the tour came to it's end.

"This is the quarters. That one there is Rio. You should know that if she's gonna be your supervisor. These here are unoccupied. Just take an empty one. Showers are just over there. Try to use the water sparingly. Everyone does their own laundry. Toilets are behind there. Wesley fucked up, so Farell put him on bathroom duty for the next while."

"Got it. Appreciate the tour." said John.

"It's all good. See you in the morning."

John spent the rest of the evening lying in bed. His head became a whirlwind of confusion as he debated with himself the moral stance involved in working with The Patriots. He disliked Eva and the new social system but could still recognize the benefits that it introduced to the world.

* * *

After a few hours, the cognitive dissonance within John nearly drove him mad. Needing to distract himself from his own mind, he got up to explore his new subterranean home. When he approached the lounge room, he noticed that the television was on. A man whom he hadn't met yet sat in a lazy boy and waved at him as he came into view.

"Name's Milton." he said. "You've gotta be John? The new guy!"

"Something like that."

"Yeah, I had trouble sleeping my first few nights. Well, I still do sometimes."

John sat on the couch and observed the television program. It was some sort of documentary about how the latest global environmental policies over the last several years have positively influenced the return and flourish of wildlife in various areas of the world. "Well, that's just great." John thought to himself. He hoped to take his mind off these sorts of things.

"How long have you been around here?" John asked.

"I joined the patriots just a few months ago. I'm a newbie as well."

"Can I ask why?"

"I guess I just needed something to fight for. I've been a fighter my whole life, but now, I'm long out of my prime. My coaches just about forced me to retire, saying it was for my own good. Otherwise, I'll just end up getting myself hurt. Turns out I'm not cut for the normal life. Tried doing the daily nine to five for a while, but it's just not for me. Being a warrior is in my blood. I've gotta fight for something, and I never really believed in this whole post-Conversion world. So, coming on board with The Patriots was a natural transition for me."

A couple minutes went by, then John mustered up the courage to ask about something that had been itching on his mind. "Hey, I gotta ask about your cause. Just to ease my mind. The only things any of us on the outside ever hear about you come from the media. Would be nice to learn about the people I'm affiliating with straight from the horse's mouth."

"I can respect that. We believe in freedom. We believe in the very fundamental spirit that makes us human. Look, we're not meant to be living this way, under a normalised slavery regime serving a computerized overlord. Our mission is simple. We exist to fight the system. We want to destroy Eva and return the state of humanity as it was before the Conversion."

"I'm not vouching for it, but in my observations, many people seem satisfied with the system. I've had many people tell me Eva makes their lives easier, and it has led to an explosive array of developments for the world."

"There are bits of truth in that, but at what cost? Think of the various industrial revolutions we've brought to ourselves throughout history. All of which were accomplished without Eva. We can work through our problems on our own. Think of all the social and technological progress we've established in just the last handful of generations! I'm talking about the decrease of things such as racism and gender inequality, and the advancements in fields like medical science, physics, energy, I could go on and on! People can develop progress on our own, it just takes time. In fact, I would argue that freedom of life, choice, and expression are only advantageous to these purposes."

"How so?"

"With the freedom to do, say, or think how you like, people can establish a wider variety of perspective in which they can share with the rest of the world. Some will be good, some will be bad, but the good will persist and be drafted into opportunities that lead us towards innovation. It's just natural selection. The things which are beneficial to our species will endure and diversify while that which are detrimental to us will eventually fade away; however, consider the opposite. Control and censorship prohibit the spread of ideology. It creates tunnel vision, and bars our species from the windows of opportunity that would otherwise develop."

John nodded and replied, "I see where you are coming from."

"With your background, do you believe that truth has anything to fear from investigation?"

John took a moment to consider before he replied, "No, I don't"

"That's right. You can't have truth without investigation, you can't have investigation without honesty, and you can't have honesty without freedom; therefore, there is no truth in the absence of freedom. Some say that all truths begin as blasphemies, but how do we find our way to those truths, lest we dare to challenge and explore our beliefs and ideas?

"Alright, you've made your point."

"Not to mention the absurd and unjust amount of power it places into the hands of those who are in charge. To quote the famous John Acton, power corrupts, and absolute power corrupts absolutely. Man, the nerve of the elites to think that they, and ONLY they, could know what's best for us, what makes us happy, or how we should best live our lives. It's just evil. Pure EVIL!"

Milton recognised his emotional state and took a few deep breaths before he continued. "Sorry."

"Don't worry about it. I asked, didn't I?"

"Yeah, I suppose. Thanks for letting me rant. I'm going to bed. See you at the morning debrief."

"Goodnight."

John found himself alone, distracted by his own thoughts, while the flashing images on the television illuminated the room. He would have changed the channel to something else had he even recognized the type of program that still played. Milton's statements left John immobilized with heavy contemplation. He sat there in a trance and glared through an empty void, completely oblivious to his surroundings until eventually he found himself captured by fatigue and succumbed to a rooted slumber.

CHAPTER 6

John awoke to the violent thump of someone kicking the couch that he rested on. His eyes focused on a mix of familiar faces; among another not yet introduced to him.

"Farell will be here soon." said Milton. "John, you wanna go track down Lev and Wesley? Tell them the briefing is about to begin."

"On it."

John departed the room with a spring in his step. Something that rarely existed as a part of his morning but considering the abrupt nature of how he awoke and the fact that he was given a task, he made along without dragging his feet. John thought to himself, "Okay, I don't know my way around here that well. Where would be a good place to start?" He went to the quarters in anticipation that Lev, or Wesley, may have slept in.

John found the quarters vacant, then glanced his eyes over at the corner. He remembered the tour of the previous evening, where Kade had explained the bathrooms were in that direction. John explored the area, but upon a closer inspection, he noticed two opposing directions. He went left. Dead end. John backtracked and went right, which led to several unmarked doors. Having not known of where they led, John pushed the nearest one. It opened about a foot into the room, then came to an immediate halt, followed by the surprised shouts of a person within. "Hey? hey STOP! Someone is in here! Don't you know how to knock for CHRIST'S

SAKE!?" John only partially saw into the room, but it was enough that he could tell Wesley had been masturbating. He closed the door, then took several steps back and shook his head in disappointment. Once recomposed, he tried the other doors with a knock and verbal announcement prior to entry. The other bathrooms were empty. John thought to himself, "Okay, where to now? If I were Lev, where would I be?" Several seconds later, he had the idea.

John departed from the living quarters back into the main hallway. Once he neared the end, he heard the deep penetrating sound of clanking metal that rattled through the area. It grew louder with each step as he neared the source. It led him to the gym, where he observed Lev lying down on a bench press station. The clanking metal echoed the vicinity as the enormous weights rose and fell with the momentum of each forceful repetition the behemoth performed.

"Pyat'nadtsat! Shest'nadtsat! Sem'nadtsat!"

John waited for Lev to finish his set and thought to himself, "Glad he's on our side!" The series of metal clanks came to a halt as Lev racked the barbell back on the supports, creating a final BOOM, more worthy of impression than the previous. He then sat up out of breath while thick beads of sweat trickled down his face.

"I was told to come get you." said John. "Farell will give the briefing shortly."

Lev nodded, then walked over to the corner of the room where a heap of clothes rested on the ground. He picked up a shirt and dressed himself, concealing the sweat drenched sleeveless already worn. The two of them left the area and rendezvoused with the others back in the lounge room. They found their seating arrangements, and the tension among them was thick in anticipation of the boss to give word.

"Now that everyone is here, we can begin." said Farell. "Last evening, I spoke with our contact from within the Vancouver police department. He gave us information on a probable lead. There is a prisoner transport scheduled to take place this evening. Well, technically early tomorrow morning. The official purpose on paper is to transport the prisoner to a medical facility for additional sample tests following concerning results of their latest deposit; although our contact is expecting the situation to be a capture."

"By capture, you mean kidnapped for experiments?" John asked.

"That's right. Look, it is going to be dangerous, but the mission is to tail the convoy and see where they bring the prisoner. It could reveal the location of one of their facilities. John, as a security expert, we need your analysis on an infiltration plan. Provided that things even get that far."

"Understood." replied John.

"I don't like the sound of this." Kade expressed.

"Neither do I, but it is all we have." replied Farell. "I have decided who to dispatch on this mission. Rio, Kade, Lev and John. You guys will take part. I have tasks for the rest of you."

The person John did not yet know spoke up in objection. "Uh, Sir! Why not take the van? It can host an entire squad of us."

Farell took a big breath before he gave his reply.

"The headlights on that thing are too bright! We are trying to tail, not ambush. "Besides, standard protocol for prisoner transfers usually involves only two or three lightly armed officers. Still, the four of you involved will be equipped, of course. Take one of the other vehicles and operate with caution."

Farell allocated other duties to the rest of the crew members, who then got up one by one and departed the lounge to tackle their fresh assignments. They left quickly and with fervor, which gave John a powerful impression that The Patriots were a group of disciplined, zealous martyrs, deeply proud and devoted to their cause. Most people may have found this type of environment intimidating, but it reminded John of his time in the police force. He found inspiration in that, even though he was unsure if he fully embraced the Patriot ideology.

Farell assigned the last remaining Patriot their task, leaving him and John alone. He stared at the ground for a moment while his mind searched for the words appropriate for the matter of attention.

"John, you'll have to forgive the rather candid and surly nature of what I'm about to address, but I assure you of the necessity. It is something I must bring up with all newer members."

"What's on your mind?"

"I trust your motive; however, if the thought ever crosses your mind, you should know that treason is dealt with in the outmost authoritative gravity of consequence. Those parents of yours on Mathers Avenue………"

Farell connoted his statement with the hand gesture of firing a gun. John's lips separated as his eyes widened. An expression which Farell received as confirmation that John had understood his sinister warning.

Farell continued, "Head to the armory. Stoiya is expecting you."

When John arrived at the Armory, a woman greeted him at the entrance. Her appearance conquered his attention. One pigtail dyed purple and the other green with each lip in matching lipstick color to her hair. She wore a camouflage rib cut top and tight short shorts that firmly hugged the curve of her hips. The diamond in her belly button piercing sparkled as light reflected from it with each sway of her movements. She extended her hand outwards to greet him, revealing a tattoo of a large caliber bullet on her wrist. They shook hands, then she motioned for John to follow her inside. The room was split into two components. The first had various weaponry tightly organized over the walls, counters, and shelves. A shooting range made up the second half of the room, with several targets displayed among varying distances. John followed Stoiya as she skipped to one wall and handed him a firearm model he recognized immediately.

"I'm sure you have experience with this one, yes?" she asked him. "It's the standard sidearm for the Vancouver Police Department."

"Sure do! Been a while, though."

"Well cutie, it's time to clear the cobwebs! Follow me over to the range here for a bit of SHAZAAAM!"

Stoiya skipped to the range. John followed and took a standard firing position at the counter. At Stoiya's request, he showed her that he knew the basics, such as loading the clip and chamber, and turning the safety on and off.

"NOOICE! Alright Johnny boy, I'll go over here and start up the targets. Show me what you got!"

A bunch of targets then popped up across various areas of the shooting range. John did his best, but it had been several years since he fired a gun. He only hit four out of the twelve targets, all of which made an impact among the outer rim. He looked over at Stoiya, who cringed back at him.

"I can do better." assured John.

Stoiya walked behind him and grabbed his butt, prompting his posture forward. He flinched, surprised and uncomfortable.

"Hips forward just a tad! Should help you out a bit." she said. "Relax your breathing and don't rush your shots. There's not too much a girl can do with an early shooter!"

John loaded a fresh clip into the gun as Stoiya went over to the controls to restart the targets. John took advantage of the moment and closed his eyes, remembering his training from the academy. He existed in a state of tranquility before a loud ding started the next round of targets.

POP! POP! POP!

John fired off the handgun with confidence and clarity. The anxiety from the previous attempt left him and he felt reassured, knowing he performed better the second time around. John took a glance down range to confirm his accuracy. He hit ten out of the twelve targets. One of which being a direct bullseye.

"Okay, fine! "There's room for improvement, but I suppose you ain't half bad after all." Stoiya admitted.

She then handed John the holster for his firearm model and some spare clips. John sheathed the weapon.

"By the way," she continued, "don't worry about fingerprints. It's coated in eltrasium."

"Eltrasium!? I thought that stuff was just a myth!"

"Sweetheart, I bet there are tons of stuff we got you thought was just a myth!"

Stoiya complimented her statement with a smile and a playful wink.

"Huh, no shit." replied John.

"Oh, and don't even think about coming in here and playing with my toys! Hands off! You keep that one for now, and maaaaybe I'll let you graduate one day."

"I wouldn't dream of it, but why are you giving me one in the first place? The whole self-defence thing is perfectly reasonable, but I just want the expectations for myself to be clear. I'm not going to kill anyone."

"Well, nobody PLANS on killing, but shit happens hot stuff! Better to have one and not need it than need it and not have it!"

Stoiya's latest comments churned John's stomach. If he needed to defend himself, he would, but he was not a killer. He considered how far would he go to protect his fellow Patriots, but failed to provide himself a confident answer.

John spun around again, viewing the array of weaponry displayed in the room.

"Where do you guys even get all this stuff?" he asked her.

"We have good friends. A lot of militaries. Many people in various armies around the world have been good to our cause. It's hard to find people more patriotic than soldiers. They are used to fighting for freedom, after all."

"Yeah, I guess that makes sense."

“Your team is waiting for you back in the lounge. Put those glutes to work!”

“Alright, I’ll head back there. Thanks for the piece.”

Stoiya replied with an enthusiastic gesture of finger guns. When John returned to the lounge, he observed Rio attending the bar counter while Kade and Lev sat among the stools. Wesley typed fanatically at his computer, but stopped and looked up when he noticed John had entered the room.

“So, you met Stoiya?” he asked him. “She’s something. I don’t get the whole colorful hair while wearing camo thing. It’s like, Yo, you wanna be seen or not!?”

John chuckled, then noticed Rio motion for him at the bar counter. She followed up with him once he found his seat.

“What’ll you have?”

“Coffee please.”

She glared at him. John looked over and noticed the hard alcohol in the other glasses. Lev and Kade looked at him, anticipating his order. John understood that they held off on their beverages until everyone had been served.

“Alright, whiskey.” he conceded.

Rio poured two glasses. She gave one to John and kept the other for herself, then set the bottle down on the counter. Rio, Lev, and Kade raised their glasses in the air together. John recognised it as the beginning of a toast and followed suit.

“To the mission, and the cause!” said Rio.

The four of them clanked their glasses together, then took a drink. Each shot down in a single guzzle. Rio raised the bottle at them, offering more. John and Kade declined. She put the whiskey away and grabbed some vodka. The lid popped, and she poured herself and Lev another round. A smile cracked across Lev’s face, granting John the impression that it was a favourite of his. Wesley interrupted their attention when he again piped up from the other side of the room.

“If you are going to waste alcohol on that thing, I suppose I’m glad it’s none of the good stuff. That brand is just cheap, fermented potato water!”

Lev shifted his weight as if to stand up from his stool and confront Wesley, only to be met by Rio, who grabbed him by the sleeve and yanked him back to his previous position.

Lev expressed his frustration. "If boy wasn't too good with computers -----"

"I know, big guy!" interrupted Rio, "Just let it go."

Lev muttered something in Russian. A heavy grin persisted over Wesley's face as he returned to work on his monitors.

"In all seriousness," John began, "how does a guy make a coffee around here?"

Rio pointed to the kitchen behind John. He turned around and noticed the coffee machine on the counter.

"You'll find the grinds in the cupboard just above it." said Kade.

"Okay, thanks."

John made coffee and spent the rest of the day getting to know the various crew members. A futile attempt to distract himself from the upcoming mission.

* * *

Time dragged on, but eventually midnight arrived, and the team crewed up for the mission. They drove out to the vantage point, then parked and waited for the upcoming convoy. Kade was the designated driver. Lev sat in the front passenger seat. Rio was in the back seat behind Kade and John was behind Lev. Kade lit a cigarette, took a puff, then glanced up into the sky as small bits of rain drizzled onto the windshield.

"Sheeiit. Looks like a storm' bout to come." Kade commented.

Lev agreed with a grunt. Kade then turned over his right shoulder to look back at John and held up his pack of cigarettes.

"Want one?"

"Nah, I can't. I quit that stuff a long time ago. Toughest thing I ever had to let go of. Well, almost the toughest."

John turned his head to stare out the window in reminiscent thought. A brief moment went by before he returned to his senses and continued his statement. "It's funny. The moment I quit was when I started drinking all this coffee. I guess I just traded one substance for another."

Kade nodded and puffed away with the cigarette. A couple minutes went by until an armored van passed them.

"Ayy John, you recognize that?" asked Kade.

"Yup! That's definitely a transfer unit." he replied. "There's no other route away from the prison, so they'll be leaving through here."

"Yeah. We got em. By the way, don't worry about what you say in here." said Kade. "This vehicle's Eva proof, courtesy of Wesley."

"I figured as much, but thanks." said John.

Kade continued, "I know the guy seems a fool, but he's really come through for us. Many times."

"He like, how you say? You know, like wrench in gears!" said Lev.

John and Kade laughed at Lev's remark, but the humour quickly died over the serious anticipation of the risk they were about to take. The rhythm of rain drops splattering across the windshield increased, along with John's heart rate. He clasped his hands together to prevent them from shaking and closed his eyes to divert his full attention to breathing. Approximately twenty minutes passed, then the convoy returned and drove past them.

"Alright guys, uh, and lady!" said Kade. "It's showtime!"

Kade conducted a gentle pursuit. They pursued through several roads, then bright crackles of lightning asserted their presence across the night sky, followed by deep booms of thunder. The rain increased to a flooding downpour and distorted the team's visibility despite the windshield wipers being on the maximum setting. The convoy turned left, then another left, and another left, and a fourth that returned them to the previous intersection they initially cornered.

"I don't like that." expressed Kade.

"Could be counter-surveillance." John added. "Hang back more."

Kade pulled the vehicle back to create a larger distance between them and their target. The convoy progressed through the next intersection, but the light went red before Kade could follow. He brought the vehicle to a complete stop. The team noticed the convoy's turn signal blinking several intersections ahead.

"Wait for them to take their turn out of view," said John, "then make a rip through the red light and catch up."

Kade did as instructed, then Eva interrupted the team mere seconds after they went through the intersection.

"Hello Reginald! I have detected a traffic violation at the previous intersection. I'm afraid that the light was still red when you passed through, and you'll have to be reprimanded for public endangerment. Seeing as how this is your first offense, you'll be pleased to hear the repercussions as being only a first tier fine. When you next log on to your banking account, you'll notice a deduction in the amount of $467 credits. If you have questions about the fine, or the offense committed in subject, please ask and I'll be happy to fill you in on whatever information you need!"

"Reginald?" John asked.

"Don't worry about it." replied Kade.

Kade brought them to where they last spotted the convoy and mimicked the same turn. When they repositioned on the new road, the four of them were shocked to find a long, empty street. The transport unit was nowhere in sight.

"Fuck! Where did they go!?" asked Kade.

"Just get ahead a bit more." replied John. "We can't be far behind."

Kade accelerated with great prospect. The street took a curve, then revealed the transport unit once Kade guided their vehicle around the direction of the bend.

"Got em." said Kade. Eva's voice then came through the vehicle's monitor again.

"Hello Reginald! I have detected another traffic violation at the previous intersection. I'm afraid that your vehicle was traveling well above the permitted speed limit, and you'll have to be reprimanded for public endangerment. Seeing as how this is your second offense within the same day, you'll find the repercussions as a second tier fine. When you next log on to your banking account, you'll notice a deduction in the amount of $1080 credits. If you have questions about the fine, or the offense committed in subject, please ask and I'll be happy to fill you in on whatever information you need!"

A few seconds after Kade straightened the vehicle out from the recent turn, the convoy van ahead of them picked up speed.

"Fuck!" Kade exclaimed.

"You idiot!" shouted Rio.

Kade cautioned the others. "Everyone hold on! This is gonna get intense!"

The accelerator was floored, and both vehicles sped through the area. The convoy truck took a winding turn ahead.

SCREEEEEEECH

The sound of screeching tires penetrated the block as they made a loose turn, desperate to keep up with their target. The vehicle's tires barely held traction on the road, but leveled out.

"Hey! Be careful!" said Rio with a shaky voice.

Eva's voice came through the monitor once again. "Hello Reginald! I have detected another traffic violation at the previous intersection. I'm afraid that your vehicle is still traveling above the permitted speed limit, and you'll have to be arrested for dangerous driving. I have dispatched the police to your location. Please pull the vehicle over and turn yourself into the custody of your local law enforcement."

"Fuck off Eva!" yelled Kade.

"Oh, this is bad." Lev expressed.

"Great! Just Great!" shouted Rio.

"Hold on guys!" said Kade as he held his breath. "We're not done yet!"

The tires screeched again as Kade guided the vehicle through another sharp turn, desperate not to lose the target, but almost lost control. Eva's voice came through the vehicle's monitor again.

"Reginald! I'm afraid I'll have to request again that you pull over your vehicle. If you fail to comply, I'll have to cut power to your vehicle's engine and your actions will be considered as resisting arrest."

"Pull over you idiot!" demanded Rio. "We have to get out of here!"

"Don't worry guys!" replied Kade. "She can't power us down!"

"Kade! This is a bad idea!" expressed John.

"Reginald! I'll have to -----"

SMASH

Lev drove his fist through the dashboard speaker, bringing Eva's statement to an end.

"Oh shit!" Kade gasped. "I think we're hydroplaning!"

"Shit!" exclaimed Rio.

"We got this!" shouted Kade. "Hold OOONNN!"

They hit a concrete road construction barrier, which knocked them into the air. A sequence of loud slams and bangs occurred as they landed upside down on the street. Several seconds went by. The only sounds being grunts and groans until Rio pulled herself together and checked on the others.

"Welfare check! Everyone sound off!"

"Yo!" replied Kade.

"Good." replied Lev

"John?" asked Rio.

There was no reply.

"JOHN!?"

"Yeah! I'm good!" he finally replied.

"Everyone, get out now!" she demanded.

The team struggled to drag themselves out of the wreckage, brandishing only minor cuts and scrapes. When they brought themselves to their feet, they could hear police sirens approach from the distance.

"We have to get out of here!" Rio expressed between her frantic breaths. "Follow me. I know where to go!"

Rio led the team through many back alleys and narrow streets until they came down a winding bike path which proceeded to a secluded area underneath a bridge. The team stopped for a moment to catch their breath, completely exhausted. After a moment of rest, Rio spoke up to confront Kade, panting between her words.

"I can't believe what you just did! Why did you do that!?"

"What!? We couldn't lose them! We don't have any other leads!"

"What was your plan exactly!? Did you think they would lead us back to their base knowing we were following them!? We should have pulled off and come up with another strategy! Now they're gonna find the vehicle and you could have KILLED us!"

Kade stood there, unsure of how to respond.

Rio persisted with clenched fists. "Am I making sense or what!?"

"Guys, we need to keep our voices down." John remarked.

Everyone looked at John, then realised he was right.

Kade continued, "Hey, don't worry about it. The vehicle is coated in eltrasium. They won't find our fingerprints or anything."

"And what about the rest of our DNA?" replied Rio. "You think there won't be any stray hairs lying around in the vehicle after a crash like that?"

"I, ugh. Rio, I'm sorry."

The four of them stood in silence for a moment.

"Anyone have idea?" Lev asked.

"John, how long do you suppose it would take law enforcement to secure our DNA from that vehicle?" Rio asked.

John thought about it for a moment, careful to give an accurate reply.

"They probably just arrived at the crash. The first step would be to secure the scene, then call forensics. They could be there in about an hour or less. Might take a few hours to do the sweep of the vehicle's interior, plus taking the evidence back to the station. Then, they would have to test it and determine the DNA match to their database of everyone's deposits."

"How long do we have?" Rio asked.

"I'd say half a day at most. Probably less."

"Okay, but Wesley wiped our DNA from Eva's database." said Kade. "We don't even have a social security number anymore. We should be good, right?"

Desperate for re-assurance, everyone looked at Rio, who stood tense and ran her fingers through her hair.

Kade sought after her reassurance. "Right?"

"Wesley couldn't clear John just yet." explained Rio. "The most recent security changes to her program locked him out and he hasn't yet found his way back in."

"You're telling me that in half a day, Eva is going to match my DNA to the crash scene!?" John asked with a tremble in his voice.

"It's worse than that." she replied. "From the tinkering Wesley has done to the vehicle, they are going to know that the car belongs to the Patriots. John, they are going to know about your involvement with us."

"Fuuuck." Kade exclaimed.

John went over to the wall, sat down against it, and rested his head between his palms. His legs grew weak at the recent unfortunate news.

"I have to report this to Farell." said Rio. "Wait here for instructions."

Rio walked further down from the group. When she found a distance suitable for a private conversation, she took out her cellphone and called Farell, giving him the full explanation of what happened, then eagerly waited for his instruction.

"This couldn't have gone worse. How could this be any worse!?" Farell asked rhetorically.

"Sir, is there anything we can do?"

Farell took a long deep breath, as if he felt shame, or regret, in what he was about to say.

"I'm afraid there is only one thing to do. We're unable to meddle with that data. The rest of us are safe, but John, I'm afraid he has become a liability. We cannot take the risk of his capture. They could learn too much from him. I trust you will do what you must."

"I understand Sir. See you soon."

Rio hung up the phone and made her way back to the group. John, Kade, and Lev stood around in a circle, desperate to come up with a plan. Rio approached John from behind and locked a solid grasp on the handgun she had tucked in her waist.

CHAPTER 7

Rio tugged on her handgun, then paused. She overheard John say something to Lev and Kade regarding a plan to infiltrate the police department's data. She thought to herself, "This sounds crazy, but it just might work!" The thought immobilised her and caused her to reconsider what she was about to do. She at least knew it would be best to have Farell provide his insight on the matter. After all, it's not like they could bring John back from the dead should they later change their mind. Rio released her grasp on the pistol tucked in her waist and rested her arms by her side, just in time for John to turn around and notice that she was standing directly behind him. Rio felt a sense of relief, both in knowing that John hadn't noticed what she was about to do and confiding in the possibility she may not have to kill him after all.

"Well? Sounds like it could work." said Kade. "What does everyone else think?"

Lev nodded.

"It's at least worth getting Farell's opinion on it." said Rio. "We should retreat to the base and fill him in, then go from there."

"Can we at least call Farell again and request to get picked up?" Kade asked..

"That's a bad idea." replied Rio. "Cops are going to be swarming all over the streets. It's *2:30* in the morning with no traffic out. Any vehicles on the road would be too conspicuous. We are going to have to make it back on foot, along a concealed route."

Kade expressed his disapproval. "Ahhh, that's so far! And we're soaked!"

"I don't think there is another way." John remarked.

"Stop complaining!" demanded Rio. "Everyone, get a move on. I know how to get back."

The four of them followed Rio back to the hide-out. Each step John took through the flooded streets and alleys only further soaked his pants and shoes. A grim breeze overtook the night, biting into John's drenched body, provoking desperation to return to the warm, dry environment of The Patriot's lair. It seemed as if his body temperature plummeted more with each minute, constructing doubt whether he would even make it back. John repeated the same thought to himself, "Just one step at a time! Left. Right. Just one more step. Keep going!" knowing that enough repetitions would eventually carry him to the goal.

* * *

It was a long, tedious journey, but they were eventually met at the entrance with dry clothes and towels, which Rio had called ahead and requested. John changed and left his previous outfit a sodden heap in the wash, then met with Farell, Wesley, and the other members of his team back in the lounge room. He sat, huddled a blanket and shivered violently as his body attempted to return to its base temperature. Rio then placed a large mug of hot coffee on the table in front of him.

"Wait until you stop shivering before you drink that, otherwise you're gonna spill it all over yourself."

"Thank you."

"Alright, John. Let's hear this plan of yours." said Farell.

John reiterated the plan he came up with to Farell. The shivers caused his voice to vibrate.

“There’s only a single evidence locker which is held at the head office. From my time in the police, I know my way around the districts. Farell, you mentioned you have a contact with the police? Is it possible to have Wesley copy the access code from his chip and upload it to mine?”

Farell looked at Wesley.

“Yeah, that’s easy!” he replied.

John continued his explanation, “Okay, so we need to set up an immediate meeting with him to get that data. Wesley can copy it and give it to me, so I should be able to have access to that building. The primary issue here is all the cops that would swarm the district. We would have to create an outside diversion to draw most of them out.”

“Alright, what are you thinking?” asked Farell.

“When I began my investigation to find Stephanie, there was a protest on the block. The place was swarming with police trying to get the mob under control. Drones were everywhere and the public street cameras were all panned over to focus on the riffraff. I know a guy named Jasper. I can tell you where to find him and if you bring a large amount of supplies for his people, I’m confident he could muster up a large and willing group of protestors for an effective distraction.”

“Jasper? Who exactly is this guy?” asked Farell.

“Uh, kind of like a leader among the homeless. It’s a story for another time, but look, he told me that some of his people don’t really mind going to prison for minor offenses. They get treated decently in there. If the incentive is generous enough, I’m sure he could muster up a large enough crowd. Just bring them as much food, toiletries, cigarettes and alcohol as you can, plus whatever else you think the homeless would enjoy. Make it plentiful. And tell them to do the protest just around the street corner from the department.”

"And then what?" asked Farell.

"Most of the officers will attend to the commotion. Some will have to stay behind, but the building would be more vacant. Fewer people around to notice me. Then from there, I steal our physical evidence from the locker, and I'm hoping that Wesley can provide some way for me to gain access into one of the police terminals so that I can change or delete the database data; therefore, clearing my guilt. Then I'm going to walk out. Hopefully."

Wesley jumped up from his seat. "I have the solution! It's called the Data Bandit 5000!"

Kade raised an eyebrow at him. "Data Bandit 5000?"

Wesley clarified, "A while back, I created an app that allows a wristlet to bypass a computer's security network and it just downloads all its internal and cloud files that the accounts on it have access to. I can put the app on John's wristlet, then all he has to do is sync it to one of the police computers and all the data on it would just transfer over! Awww man, I've been waiting for an opportunity to use this thing!"

"You are certain that this thing works?" asked Farell.

"Yeah! I mean, it can't bypass highly sophisticated security protocols, but should slip right through anything that would be used in a police department computer. I wouldn't be able to hack my way remotely into the police database before they determine a DNA match, but if John is there physically, then I'll get everything I need off the Data Bandit 5000!"

"John, this is a high-risk operation." said Farell. "We can't take the chance of your capture. How are you going to find your way to a computer without being spotted?"

John looked over at Wesley. "Hey, yesterday you were mentioning something about being able to control Eva's security cameras?"

"No, I can't control them. Just view them." he replied. "I've gained access as a spectator, but to gain physical control I would have to navigate past additional security measures, which I haven't been able to solve just yet."

"Okay, but you can at least view the ones at the police station, right? Like, you could observe me while I'm in there?" asked John.

"Yes."

"Alright Wesley, I'll have to be on the phone with you and get some wireless headphones. You'll be my eye in the sky. Watch over the precinct and tell me where to go and how to avoid danger. I'll follow your directions and slip through without being noticed."

"Hell yes!" shouted Wesley.

"This is a terrible idea!" Farell objected. "John, when they notice that the evidence is missing, they are going to review the camera information and Eva's face recognition software will identify you."

"Well sir, I figured I would probably just wear a mask or something." replied John.

"I got a better idea!" said Wesley. The rest of the room turned to look at him.

"Come on, guys!" he expressed. "You should know better than to count me out! I got a solution for just about anything. I'm a genius baby!"

Everyone continued to look at Wesley in long anticipation that he would specify his last comments.

"Well?" John asked him.

Wesley continued, "Yeah, right. So, you guys know about deep fake technology, right?"

Everyone else in the room nodded.

"Well, I can do something better! It's kind of like that, except you don't have to edit the footage. I have these, ugh, let's call them stickers. The stickers have these thin microchips in them that would create a disguise for your face over any type of digital technology. People would see your actual face in real life, but anything digital would pick up an edit that's sort of layered over your face in real time. It's highly accurate and would take a real video sleuth to discern, but even if they noticed the edit, there's no way for them to identify your actual face because the camera footage would have picked up the layering instead! By then, you would be long gone!"

"Ayy! My man!" said Kade in celebration.

Wesley continued, "One thing though, try to manipulate your normal body language, like the way you stand or walk. Eva has had some recent updates introducing breakthroughs in body-language identification. I don't know exactly how accurate it is just yet, but you also have to consider that over time, she is only going to become more complex. As her technology advances, I imagine that a future version of Eva could review and analyze past data with her modern capabilities."

John sought to clarify Wesley's statement. "You're saying that even though my face will be hidden, one day she might eventually match my body language to the scene?"

"Correct-a-mundo!" he replied.

"Good point. What if I put a sharp rock in my shoe or something?" John asked Wesley.

"I think you're on the right track. That should throw your normal movements off. And by the way, my workstation here will be synchronized to the app on your wristlet. As soon as you transfer that data, I'll have access and can review and alter the police files right away! You don't have to worry about returning to base for me to work on it!"

John turned to look at Farell. "Well? It seems like we've officially got a plan."

Farell took a moment to ponder everything he just heard. Then looked up at Wesley.

"How confident are you we can make this work?"

"Pretty confident boss. It's a good plan, and I know that my tech works."

"Rio, come speak with me in private." requested Farell.

Farell and Rio both left the lounge and entered an adjacent room. They closed the door and made sure they were alone before he addressed her.

"I don't like this idea at all. We should just take care of John instead of gambling on something as risky as this. It is unwise."

"I think John is useful to us. I hear what you are saying and to be honest I feel uneasy about it as well, but instead of asking ourselves how much we trust John, a better question may be to ask how much we trust Wesley. He seems confident in the plan and the guy usually comes through for us. Besides, with having that access data for police stations and Wesley's face distortion technology, PLUS an inside man in the Vancouver police department, we can't rule out the possibility of being able to send in a hitman should John be captured. You know, before they turn him over to federal powers."

Farell turned away and paced the length of the room. When he arrived at the opposing wall, he reached out and braced himself, leaning against it. He took several deep breaths, then turned around and walked back to his original position to continue the conversation with Rio.

"I can't believe I'm actually agreeing to this." he stated.

"Then let's tell the team. We don't have any time to waste!"

Farell took a couple minutes to make a quick phone call, then he and Rio entered the lounge and repositioned themselves in their previous seating arrangements. Farell then addressed the group in a regretful tone, void of enthusiasm.

"We are going ahead with the plan."

Wesley jumped up into the air. "Aw yeah!"

"Ayyy!" exclaimed Kade.

Farell then informed John, Rio, and Wesley that they would meet the contact and gave them the coordinates for the location. John gave Farell the details of where

Jasper could be found, a duty which Farell dispatched onto some of the other patriot members. Farell expressed to them the dire urgency involved in the matter before both teams departed to attend their fresh assignments.

John, Wesley, and Rio went to the garage and entered one of the Patriot vehicles. Rio as the driver, John as the front passenger, and Wesley lying down, sprawled out in the back seat.

* * *

They arrived at the meeting point to find an unfinished multi-level above ground parking lot, vacant of any signs of public life. Rio parked in the west corner far from any stairwells and the three of them exited and waited for their contact to arrive.

John squinted with attempt to adjust his sight to the change of environment. The light that normally illuminated their area of the parking lot was burnt out, leaving the space covert and somber. Due to the unfinished nature of the construction lot, John noticed that there were no surveillance cameras installed. John also couldn't help but identify many potential escape routes. Both by vehicle and by foot. It suddenly became crystal clear to him why the contact chose this location.

Nausea consumed John. Enough to make him vomit had he even eaten anything. He figured that if anything in his life was going to do him in, this would likely be it. His last adventure. He had done nothing as daring as the upcoming mission. He stood in near panic until he noticed the premature glimmer of an early sunrise breaking through the dark horizon. It was a marvelous craft among nature. Thin streaks of yellow, orange, and pink narrowly pronounced themselves across the dark blue canvas of the night sky, publishing the dawn of a new day. It captured John's attention more with each passing second until he was no longer there. The present moment was taken from him, replaced by a vivid, treasured memory from his youth.

"John, hey John."

John awoke to the gentle tremors of his father shaking his shoulder. Dazed and confused, he wondered why he was being woken up in the middle of the night.

"Hey John, it's Saturday morning. We were going to get up early and watch the sunrise, remember?"

John had forgotten the plans he and his father had made earlier that week. He had told his parents he recently learned about colorful sunrises in school but expressed that he had never seen one before. His father told him that on the upcoming weekend they were going to get up early so John could experience his very first one. John was excited, but not as excited as his father, a proud parent looking forward to sharing his son's first exposure with one of mother nature's most beautiful and adoring features. How old was he then? Seven? Nine? John couldn't remember. He took a moment to pull himself together before he could drag himself out of bed and get dressed. He and his father said goodbye to their mother, who promised waffles upon their return. They got into their family vehicle and made way for Sunrise Spot.

It was a bit of a drive, but they attended their destination before the break of dawn. John and his father made their way up to the summit of the park hill and fixed themselves onto one of the park benches that oversaw the beautiful landscape of Queen Elizabeth Park. A satisfied smile exposed itself across his father's face as he realized that they had found the perfect vantage point, almost as if it was an identical match to how he had previously envisioned. John's father took the radio he brought with them and perched it by his left side for a later use while John rested to his father's right. John's legs were too short to reach the ground from a seated position, leaving his legs to dangle and swing along with each playful kick. A typical expression of a child's innocence and naivety.

"Dad…"

"Yes?"

"This hill is really high! I bet I can run the whole way down!"

"Hah! Well, I bet you could! In fact, when we leave to go home, why don't I race you back to the car? Do you think I could still keep up with a rascal like you?"

John's father tickled him, leaving him to laugh and squirm along multiple dishevelled postures while he tried to defend. They soon reset their actions, sitting on the bench until John spoke up again.

"Guess what I learned in school!?" said John.

"What did you learn?"

"A sunrise can make all kinds of colors! It's because it's lower and there is less atmosphere to spread the molecules."

"Wow, hey that's pretty neat! If you keep going to school, I bet that soon you're gonna be smarter than your old man!"

The yellow tinge broke through the night sky and revealed the display they eagerly expected.

"Oh wow! Pretty!" exclaimed John.

John's father then turned over to his left so that he could reach the radio he placed beside him. He took out a cassette tape out of his pocket titled *Abbey Road* that had already been pre-wound to a specific track. John placed the cassette tape into the front of the radio and pressed play. The two of them sat in an elevated ambiance as *Here Comes the Sun, by The Beatles*, gently serenaded through the park, complimenting the alluring appeal of the budding sunrise adorned before them.

"Dad, who's that?"

"It's The Beatles! You ever hear of The Beatles?"

"No."

"Well! The Beatles were an amazing band! Probably the best band ever! They broke up a long, long time ago. You know your grandpa got to see them play many times!"

"He did?"

"Yup! Listen to this part carefully."

The song broke into its first chorus.

“Do you know what he means when he says that?” his father asked.

“No.”

“Well, it means that sometimes we go through bad times in life. Sometimes they can go on for a long time, but just remember that eventually there will always be another sunrise and the bad times are going to go away. It’s a song about hope. Just remember that! The tough times in our life don’t last forever, so never give up on hope, alright?”

“Okay.”

“Promise?”

“I promise dad!”

The rest of the song played through its course as the two of them observed the colorful display of the sunrise. As the song finished, John abruptly came to the realisation of where he was. He stood in the parking garage, now calm and fearless. Hopeful that he would pull through the difficult and dangerous challenges before him. Just as he promised his father.

CHAPTER 8

The three of them turned their heads down the sight of the parking ramp as the sound of a vehicle approached from below. It arrived slowly, parked, and a tall man exited alone. Wesley and Rio walked towards him in a friendly manner that instilled John with trust, to which he followed suit.

"You guys are really flexing your stupidity with this one, aren't you?" the detective asked them rhetorically.

"Nice to see you again too," Rio replied, "but I'm afraid we don't have time for pleasantries."

Detective Almas held his arm out for Wesley, who then approached him and engaged the Data Bandit 5000, which near instantaneously extrapolated the data from Almas' chip.

"Don't make me regret doing this!" The detective warned.

The detective then departed in his vehicle with quick edgy resolve that implied dissatisfaction or regret regarding his involvement in the matter. Having known that time was of the essence, John and Rio took their first few steps in return to their vehicle when John noticed Wesley had not followed. He looked back and observed him standing with a hunched over posture, peering down into his wristlet as if to take great concern to monitor it carefully.

"Hey! You coming along?" he asked Wesley.

"Yup! I should have what we need."

"Okay, well let's get going then!"

Eager to catch up, Wesley proceeded towards them with a slight hop and skip. As the distance between him and the vehicle became shallow, Wesley caught his foot on a loose piece of rebar, which caused him to stagger many steps forward. In a startled reaction, he reached out to brace himself from falling as he stumbled into the incomplete wall that made up the second level perimeter of the parking lot. As his weight made contact, one of the loose bricks fragmented from the structure. Wesley gasped and could only watch in a helpless tension as the brick fell from the second level striking a pedestrian on the sidewalk below who keeled over onto the pavement. Their body lay barren of any notable vital signs.

Wesley panicked, "Oh shit! Oh no! Oh no! Oh no!"

"Wesley!? What did you do!?" asked John.

The sound of an emergency siren precipitated throughout the city block. A face appeared on a large, mounted television screen on a large building across the street parallel to the incident. The face was a woman. Caucasian, in her mid-thirties and highly attractive, with long black hair and green eyes. John could recognize that face anywhere. It was Eva. Well, the regional version of her appearance. Eva had varying avatars allocated for different regions. After all, they designed her with the intention of being accepted by the varying cultures they would integrate her with. In some societies, Eva wasn't depicted as a woman at all, but a male counterpart using the name Evo, Yuvo, or Avo, depending on the dialect.

"Attention everyone, attention! There has been a critical incident in the area. I have dispatched emergency medical services and if anyone has any medical training, please lend your assistance. To everyone else, please clear the area. Help is on the way!"

The three of them froze completely gobsmacked, almost in disbelief until Rio's prompt to flee returned their senses.

"Everyone, get in now!" demanded Rio. "We have to get out of here!"

Rio fired up the engine and as the last door to the vehicle shut, she led them away from the area with a sense of great importunity, yet still within the confines of legal driving as to not draw attention.

Wesley ran his fingers through his hair while he rocked back and forth in the fetal position. "I can't believe I just killed somebody. I never killed somebody before. They're dead! They're fucking dead!"

"Wesley, shut the hell up!" Rio shouted. "Get control of yourself!"

Wesley continued to panic. "Ah! Oh man, I didn't mean to!"

"Wesley, we don't know that they're dead." John explained. "You heard Eva. She dispatched medical services. There's nothing we can do and I bet they will probably be fine!"

Wesley responded with heavy breaths and panicked whimpers.

"You're gonna be the death of me, kid!" Rio shouted.

"You guys can't tell anyone!" Wesley pleaded. "I'm already in the deep end with Farell. It was an accident, I just tripped. I could barely see anything!"

"You fucked up!" shouted Rio. "You think we should just pretend that didn't happen back there, huh?"

"Rio, pleeease. I'm begging you! You can't tell Farell. Please Rio, it's not gonna be good if he finds out about this." Wesley begged them. "You can't tell anyone! Either of you!"

Rio could only display a wide-eyed, jaw clenched expression of intense fury. Her knuckles became white from the vindictive death grip her hands contrived through the padding of the steering wheel.

"You know Rio, it WAS quite dark back there after all." John commented.

Rio said nothing. Wesley, too, was silent. He sought reclamation, but realistically did not expect someone to advocate for his defense. He existed momentarily in a state of suspended animation. All breaths and heart beats on pause in patience of what would be said next.

John continued, "I mean, it was the break of dawn, and the lighting was out. It was an accident that could have happened to anyone."

After a long pause, John prompted her for a response. "Rio?" he asked.

"Fine." she finally replied.

"So, you're not going to tell Farell about this? Or anyone at the base?" Wesley asked. Eager for her response.

"No."

The whoosh of a major sigh traveled from the back of the vehicle.

"Rio, um, thank you."

* * *

The journey back to the Patriot's base was silent. When they neared only several minutes away, a voice brought the reticence to interruption.

"Rio, pull over! I gotta piss like a racehorse!" claimed Wesley.

"What!?" she replied. "No, we're almost there. Just hold it."

"Yeah? Well, the thing is, I can't."

"What do you mean you can't!? You have to!" she said. "We don't have time for this!"

"Do you want me to pee in the car!? Rio I'm telling you I gotta go, as in right now!"

Rio could only respond with a vehement release of agitation. Her hands shaking on the steering wheel.

"UUURRRGGGHHH!!!"

The vehicle came to a halt. Wesley jumped out and crossed the road to seclude himself in a bunch of shrubs.

"I better get out to keep an eye on him." Rio said to John. "If he takes too long, I'm gonna drag him back myself! Finished or not!"

"I'll stretch my legs as well." John replied.

John exited the vehicle after Rio, then walked around the back end to meet her on the driver's side. They both stood and leaned back against the vehicle as their attention focused ahead on Wesley, who faced away from them as he unzipped his pants. Rio hadn't been working with John for long, but still respected him. Considering the potential for failure on the upcoming mission, she thought this might be her only opportunity for sentiment with him. What else were they going to do while Wesley held them up?

"So, why quit the police? Seems like a good career." she asked him.

"I didn't. They did."

"What happened?"

John felt reluctant to answer. There weren't too many other subjects she could have asked that would have felt more personal. He almost told Rio to never mind, but bit his tongue. He wasn't sure why he trusted her. It could have been the camaraderie between Patriots, or the need to confide in a team member during a tense moment. Perhaps it had nothing to do with the context of the current juncture, rather something within John himself. He hadn't recently allowed for many people to become close to him. Not since the divorce with Stephanie. Maybe he longed to relate to another person who would understand. Someone who had been through similar rough experiences. Like Rio? At least that was the impression she gave him.

"It was before the Conversion. Another officer was doing a traffic stop and called for a second unit to assist. I arrived to find my partner holding the man at gunpoint. He told him to exit his vehicle, but once he was out, he gave the man very mixed and conflicting instructions. The man did his best to follow along, but his hands fell by his sides for a single second and my partner claimed he was reaching for a weapon. He blew him away right there in front of me. Dead before he even hit the ground."

"Then what happened?"

"They conducted a major investigation. It turned out the guy had a prior assault charge, which was probably why my partner was so cautious. The poor guy did nothing wrong. He tried his best to understand what he was being told to do, but the officer wasn't clear. When his arms dropped, my partner interpreted it as a threat and opened fire. It was entirely unjustifiable. I became very spiteful that someone would do that to a father of a young child, who was left there crying in the back seat! A news outlet arrived and stuck a camera in my face. There's a strict procedure for constables not to engage with media. We are supposed to leave any comments or public engagement to the higher ups, but I lost control. I couldn't contain my rage. There I was, in uniform, ranting about my criticisms on the matter for all the world to hear. I should have known better, but there was no excuse for what I did. Cops are supposed to band together no matter what. It's how we survive. And as fate would have it, this happened just short of my upcoming promotion to Sergeant."

"What happened to your partner?"

John scoffed and turned away in disgust, but quickly recalibrated.

"Terminated, but dodged the murder charge. Funny how cops get special treatment sometimes."

Rio didn't reply. John could have stopped there. He had answered her question, but the same instinct that provoked him into his initial response now compelled him to share further. He took a deep breath before he continued. The flood gates had opened.

"It changed me forever. It overtook my thoughts and dreams. I tried some other jobs here and there. A little construction, retail, but I didn't have interest or skills in any other fields. It was hard. Then the Conversion happened, and that's when things truly became tough. Had I not been careless, I probably would have kept my job. After all, police were an essential service then. I know the Conversion was hard for everyone, but Stephanie and I struggled beyond repair. I was so angry. I couldn't provide for her. I lost who I was and eventually drove her away. So, that day at the traffic stop cost me more than just my career, but my marriage and sense of self-identity. It took me a long time to rediscover myself; although starting my business certainly helped with that."

"Damn. That's some heavy shit."

There was a brief pause. Rio adjusted her sleeveless shirt then brushed off a ladybug she noticed had landed on her arm before following up with another question.

"You still love her, don't you?"

John felt embarrassed. He couldn't help but feel he had over shared, but was too deep into it to back out now. He was a man who finished what he started.

"Yeah. Never stopped."

Several seconds went by before John felt the need to redirect the focus of the conversation away from himself.

"And what about you?" he asked her. "I've seen the look on your face whenever someone mentions Drax."

"Oh? Yeah, well……. good catch John."

As Rio completed her words, Wesley had just made his way back to the vehicle, slightly out of breath from the jog across the street.

"Jesus Christ! I couldn't stop that thing!" exclaimed Wesley. "It just kept going and going! I bet I could have watered the entire Sahara back there!"

"It's about time!" said Rio. "Let's get going already."

"Yeah, hey thanks for allowing the pit stop, Rio."

As he finished his statement, Wesley's hand contacted Rio's bare skin with a light, playful slap on the shoulder.

Rio gasped, "Did you just get your fucking dick germs on me!?"

"Ugh, I, ugh."

FWOP!

Rio punched Wesley directly in the solar plexus. The belching wheeze of the air escaping his lungs announced the panic and anguish that overwhelmed him as he slumped to the ground, desperate to breathe. Rio opened the rear passenger door to the vehicle and threw Wesley in, having not bothered to buckle him up or even place him in a comfortable position. The three of them drove the rest of the way back to the Patriot's base in silence, as Wesley no longer dared to speak.

* * *

When they arrived in The Patriot's underground garage, Rio stayed in the driver's seat and kept the engine running to prepare for John's speedy return. John and Wesley jumped out and sped walked through the cement lair. A sense of impending climax elevated the area's ambiance as the slap of their footsteps off the concrete floor bounced through the halls. They reached Wesley's workstation. He launched himself into the chair from a walking position. The momentum of his body caused it to glide across the floor before he propped his foot out and stopped himself from crashing into the adjacent wall.

"Grab that backpack on the couch over there and an energy drink from the fridge." said Wesley. "You'll need it."

John took the bag, then opened the fridge and inspected the various cans on the shelves. He read the flavours out loud. "Very berry, blue banana, mocha." The choice was obvious. John took the energy drink and returned to the corner of the room, where Wesley frantically typed away at his monitors. The rapid clicks of the keys on the keyboard dispersed like machine gun fire.

"Okay, give me your wristlet." requested Wesley.

John handed it over. Wesley plugged it into his computer and then transferred a bunch of files onto it.

"Alright, you have detective level access within the police station." said Wesley. "This will get you into almost all areas, including the evidence locker."

"Good to know."

"I'm just going to upload the Data Bandit onto your wristlet. In the meantime, there are some wireless headphones in the drawer just over there."

John went over to the filing cabinet Wesley had just pointed out to him and opened the top drawer.

"Wait! Not that -----"

It was too late. John had already opened the drawer and noticed the stack of vintage pornographic magazines along with a bottle of lubrication. Wesley stopped for a second in regret of the current moment.

"Hah, my bad! I meant THAT drawer instead."

Wesley pointed over at the cabinet adjacent to the one John had just opened. John went over and grabbed the headphones, then synchronized them to his cellphone.

"Those are fully charged." said Wesley. "Call me as soon as Rio drops you off."

"Will do."

"Oh, and you know those are some classic editions, by the way! Late 1950s! I only have them because of their market value. You know, being so old and such."

"And the lube?"

Wesley realised he couldn't talk himself out of the situation and let out a nervous laugh. He then handed John his wristlet, who then put it back on his arm.

"Oh, one other thing," continued Wesley, "your wristlet's digital ID is scrambled, so when they try to investigate whose chip it was that opened the doors in the station, it won't come back to you. It'll be a fake name. They will figure that out, of course, but it won't matter. Okay, now take a seat. I'll get you all dressed up."

John took a seat beside Wesley as he opened a drawer to his desk and took out a small white box. It popped as the lid came off, implying suction. He then took out thin transparent strips that appeared almost like tape and motioned for John to lean forward. Wesley then placed those strips along various areas of the outline of

John's face, above his eyebrows, a small circular one on the tip of his nose, and then another strip that was much thicker across his throat.

"That last one is to disguise your voice." explained Wesley. "I forgot to mention to you about Eva's voice recognition software. Her cameras have microphones as well."

John then got up and went to look at himself in the mirror.

"The one on my throat is ----- woah, I sound different!" exclaimed John.

"Yeah, that's kind of the whole point! Just make sure that you don't get it wet. I don't think it is supposed to rain today."

John finished the last sips of the energy drink, then crushed the bottle and threw it in the trash can.

"Are you ready?" Wesley asked him.

"Yup! Talk to you soon."

* * *

Rio drove John a block away from the police station, then informed him that she would wait in the same spot to pick him up. They waited for the action to begin.

"Are you gonna call Wesley?" she asked him.

"Oh, right."

John dialed the number.

Wesley answered, "Well, if it ain't my manny from another fanny!"

"We just arrived at the drop off point."

"I figured. How's the scenery there?"

"The protest hasn't started yet. There's quite a bunch of homeless people kicking around across the street. I think they are waiting for more of them to show up before they begin. Shouldn't be much longer."

"Hopefully, we don't have much time. I have the cameras up at the station. Look over a bit to your left, just past the bus stop on the other side of the street. Do you see the alley?"

"Yes."

"Once the riot starts, go through there. It's a side door that will lead you into the precinct."

"I'm familiar with it."

"Hopefully there's still time, eh?"

There was a long pause. Wesley could only hear deep breaths through John's end of the call.

Wesley laughed, then stated, "Man, you're so nervous!"

"Of course I am! I'm about to risk my life here!"

"Yeah, I know. I'm nervous too. Hey, don't worry, I'm gonna be looking out for you, alright?"

"I know. Thank you."

Over several more minutes, additional homeless people arrived at the protest location. When they became many, they shouted and began the protest. Some of them even fought with each other. John's hairs stood on end when the same emergency siren John heard earlier echoed through the city block followed by Eva's voice.

"Attention everyone, attention! There is a disorderly conduct of a larger magnitude happening in the area. I advise everyone within the block to leave the area. I have updated the safest and most efficient route to your personal wristlets."

It only took a couple of minutes before the police arrived with four drones. The police were scattered and perturbed as to specifically which actions of the involved individuals to prioritize. The police handcuffed some of them, while others were just told to stay back.

"John, it's time to go." instructed Wesley. "The station is nearly empty. There are only a couple of cops around now and everyone else in there looks like civilian employees."

"Copy!"

John took a big deep breath, then exited the vehicle. He took his first step onto the pavement and felt the shape of a jagged rock underneath his shoe, which slightly capsized the position of his foot. Just then, he remembered what Wesley had told him. He needed to find a pebble to throw off his movements. John took a moment to find the right one then, sat on the concrete steps to the nearest building to sit down and adjust the pebble into his shoe. He took a couple of steps and felt pain. He certainly couldn't put all his weight on that side anymore. John second guessed having the pebble for a moment. He wondered to himself, "What if I have to run?" then remembered the goal was to not become discovered at all. Wesley was going to make sure of that. When John put his shoe back on, he crossed the street and went through the alley until he came to the exit door of the building. He held his breath, then motioned to scan his wristlet on the door and thought to himself, "This had better work!"

Beep

The light went green, and John could hear the release of the door lock. The urgency of the situation sought not to waste any of the little time that remained. He was now trespassing.

"Alright, I just entered." John informed Wesley. "Where am I going from here?"

"I see you. First, we should meddle with the data, then get the physical evidence on the way out. Walk straight and enter the room on your first right."

John did as Wesley instructed but withdrew himself in a jerked reaction once he noticed two people with their backs to him in the room, pouring themselves coffee. John retreated into the hallway and confronted Wesley, careful to keep his voice in a whisper.

"What are you trying to do to me!? There are two people in that room!"

"Hah! Whoops. I meant MY right."

"What do you mean YOUR right!? Why would you give me directions based on YOUR right and left!? I'm the one who is in here!"

"Yeah? I'll take note of that. Go into the room on YOUR first left."

John found himself in a large workspace populated by various cubicles. A computer took up the center of each desk.

"Take your pick." said Wesley. "I imagine either of those should be good. Just engage the Data Bandit 5000 and scan the wristlet against the side port."

John engaged the app, then held the chip in his wristlet up to the computer port.

"Nice! I got it!"

"Already?"

"That's the big, beautiful speed of a 7G network, my guy! Oh, ugh, uh oh!"

"What happened!? What do you mean, uh oh!?"

"Someone's coming! Hide!"

John hid under the desk from the thumps of incoming foot traffic, followed by laughter and conversation by a man and woman.

"You did NOT!" said the woman.

"I did!" replied the man. "Taught him a lesson. He'll know better than to backtalk one of Vancouver's finest the next time we pick him up! What a freak!"

"Totally! So, how did you like, become so strong? You been working out with the other guys?"

"You know it! Been helping a few of them out. Inspector Nealy has asked me to develop a fitness outlook for the department. You know, help the other guys step up their game! Trying to get the rest of them in shape. You know how it is!"

John couldn't help but think to himself, "Wow, this guy is so full of shit!"

"John, lie low and be quiet." said Wesley. "They gotta leave eventually."

The man continued his conversation with the woman, “I’ve also been working on my aim. I’m finally outclassing the district’s top shooter! Making new records! I pulled a perfect game last time! Nothing but bullseyes!”

“You’re kidding me!”

“No! I promise! Ask Tyler. I’m sure he’ll back me up. Come on, let’s go ask him!”

John let out a sigh of relief as the man and woman left the room, then pulled himself out from under the desk.

“John, they’ve left. All clear.” said Wesley.

“Now I just gotta make it to the evidence locker downstairs.”

“Yup, but we’re taking the long way. Just exit this room and go to the end of the hall. Then follow it around the bend. On the second left, scan and go through the door.”

“MY left, right?”

“Yes John! YOUR left. Sheesh. Besides, don’t you know your way around here?”

“Of course I do! I’m just making sure you are calling things out the right way!”

John did as Wesley instructed and scanned through the door, which led into another hallway.

“Hey John, scan yourself in the last room on your left there.”

“But that’s the boardroom. Why would I -----”

“Just trust me, alright? Pop in there for a second.”

“Alright.”

John entered the boardroom. He had little experience being in here as a constable, but it brought back a memory. He remembered his first tour of the station as a recruit. His supervisor brought him there to meet some of the higher-ranked officers. He stood in the exact spot where he was now. Uniform cleanly pressed and eager to begin his career.

"What am I supposed to be doing in here?" John asked.

"Ok, see that television conference remote in the middle of the table there?"

"Yes."

"I'm gonna need you to bring that back for me."

"What? What the hell does this have to do with the mission?"

"It doesn't. I'm short of spare parts and this remote model has some pieces I could use. I could scrap it down and -----"

John threw his arms up in the air. "Are you kidding me!? We're not here for a shopping spree!"

"Yeah, whatever. Look, you're already right there. Just grab the damn thing for me, okay?"

John shook his head and clenched his fists, then quickly put the remote in his backpack and walked towards the exit of the room.

"Wait!" said Wesley.

John's heart skipped a beat. "What!?" he asked.

"Grab one of those mints in the bowl on the shelf for me too. I like those ones."

"Fuck you."

Wesley responded with a stream of laughter.

"Is the coast clear or what?" John asked him.

"Yeah. No one is around. Just make your way to the basement. You know how to get there."

John exited the room in faith of Wesley's insight. The place was nearly empty, with no one in sight. John made his way through the areas of the building until he reached the set of stairs that led to the basement. John made his way through the hallway and scanned his wristlet on the evidence room door. No one was inside.

"I'm not able to see where the evidence is on camera." said Wesley. "You'll have to search for it."

"Copy that."

John searched through the various shelves. There were drugs, weapons, bloodied clothes, but no sign of anything related to the Patriots just yet.

Wesley continued, "Also, you should know that I've just found my way through their files. Yeah, they recently got a match on you, but it doesn't seem like anyone has seen it yet. I think the riot distracted them. It seems like things have worked out just in the nick of time."

"Thanks. That is definitely good news."

"No luck, huh?"

"Hold on, still looking."

John went over to the other side of the locker and went through the various drawers. There were four transparent evidence bags with the same case file written on them. He saw strands of hair inside each of them. He knew one was his, while the other three pertained to Kade, Lev, and Rio.

"This has got to be them!" said John. "*Case file #2046-144000.* Does this match with the files you've observed?"

"Yes, it does. That's gotta be it, right?"

"Definitely. I'll bring them back, and there's nothing else here associated along with it."

John put the bags in his backpack, then closed the drawer. He stood for a second, frozen in disbelief that he had made it that far. There was only one thing to do now. He just had to make it out without being caught.

"I'm making my way out." said John. "Please tell me that the way is clear."

"Don't go back the way you came from. Take the other set of stairs. The ones that lead out more towards the main doors of the station. You'll have to go out from there."

“Copy that.”

John traveled through the underground level of the police station and up the other set of stairs. He visualized where it led to. It meant freedom. After everything, he would pull it off after all! John climbed the steps and opened the door to the main level. He turned the corner and walked through the main lobby towards the exit doors, but his movements were cancelled when he heard a voice from behind shout out to him, “Hey! Hey you there! Stop!”

CHAPTER 9

John couldn't believe it. He was so close. All he had to do was make it through that door and his mission would've been successful. He would have been free. John held his breath and waited for whatever would happen next. Frozen in place, he found himself unsure of what to do. The voice behind him continued.

"Hey buddy! Are you that attorney we've been waiting for?"

John released the tension in his gut through a lengthy exhale and considered that perhaps he could talk his way out of the situation. He would not give up on hope. Not with victory just a hop and skip away. John cleared his throat in preparation to reply while he kept his back towards whoever had confronted him.

"Ugh, yeah! That's me!"

"You're late! You've held us up for nearly two hours now! Your client is waiting for you in holding. What are you doing out here in the lobby?"

"Ugh...."

John looked to his left and noticed a sign that read: *Public Washrooms.*

"Yeah, I'm really sorry about all of that." said John. "I just got held up, that's all! I'm going to use the washroom quick, then I'll be right there!"

"Well, don't be long!"

John then entered the men's washroom and hid inside a stall. He found it difficult to believe that what he said had worked, but now wondered how he was going to get out unnoticed. He couldn't make sense of why Wesley had not warned him that the path was unclear. John needed the answers.

"Wesley! What the hell, man!? Someone saw me!"

"What happened!? Where are you now!?"

"I'm in the men's public washroom by the main entrance doors. Someone saw me trying to leave. They think I'm a lawyer here on a case. I told them I just had to use the washroom."

"Alright. We can work through this."

"What the hell happened man!? You were supposed to warn me!"

"I, ugh, became distracted from the monitor for a quick moment. I spilled hot coffee all over my lap. Sorry."

"You idiot!"

"Oh, I'm sorry John! You try to maintain perfect focus on something while your member is literally being SCALDED ALIVE!"

"Fuck sakes!"

"Heads up! Two people are coming into the washroom. Hide in a stall and wait for them to leave. I'll figure out a way to get you out of there."

John sat on the toilet and pulled his feet up, then held himself in a fetal position. The door to the restroom swung open in a squeak, and two unidentifiable people approached the urinals in conversation with each other.

"The boys sure are busy this morning, eh?"

"Yup! A whole friggin' riot is going on outside! Like, just out of nowhere! Seems like they are all homeless, too. I wonder what it could mean?"

"Who knows? It's pretty crazy though. I bet it'll make the news!"

"I think you're right about that. I'll be watching for it tonight. How badly do you think they are gonna screw up the details this time? It's a good thing we work for the police detachment. Asking people around here gets the facts straight from the horse's mouth!"

"I hear ya."

There was a moment of silence between them. The only sound in the room was the gentle trickle of urine hitting the bowl of the urinals.

"Yeah, there's really gonna be a lot of paperwork set out for them over the next while. Did you hear about what happened last night?"

"No?"

"Looks like a bad vehicle wreck. Flipped upside down and everything. Whoever was inside crawled out and got away before the police arrived. Turns out they were chasing an armored police van that was transporting a prisoner to a medical facility."

"What? Why would they be doing that?"

"Well, get this, they're thinking the vehicle belonged to The Patriots!"

"The Patriots!? Really?"

"Yup!"

"What would The Patriots want with a prisoner transport?"

"Don't know. They haven't figured that out yet, but they've definitely cracked down double time on investigating it. That is, until that riot outside happened."

"Huh, no shit. So how do they know it belonged to The Patriots?"

"That, I'm not sure about. I'm sure we'll get more information later. Anyway, see ya!"

The two of them finished their business and left a subtle squeak and thud behind them as the door opened and closed upon their departure. John found himself alone once again.

"Hey Wesley! I'm alone again." said John. "How are you going to get me out of here?"

"Hang on, I have an idea. When I say, make sure you exit the washroom and head for the front door. Got it?"

"Whatever you're planning had better work!"

About a minute had gone by before John heard Wesley's voice again.

"Alright, now! John go! It's clear!"

John retreated from the bathroom and observed the lobby's vacancy upon his re-entry. With the path now clear, he held a deep breath and thought to himself, "Only a quick dash to the finish line!" He sped walked and counted down the last remaining steps between him and the door. Five.... Four.... Three.... Two.... and One. John pushed his way out of the exit and walked onto the sidewalk, holding his hand up to shield his eyes from the sunlight that welcomed him. He couldn't stop now. John made his way back to where Rio had dropped him off, who waited with the engine running. John entered the passenger seat and buckled himself in as fast as he could while Rio drove them away from the scene.

"Did you get it!?" she asked.

"Yeah! I actually did!"

"You son of a bitch!"

"Hang on, I'm still on the call with Wesley. Let me patch him through."

John set up the call to be run through the vehicle's speakers so that he, Rio, and Wesley could all communicate with each other.

"Wesley, can you hear us? I made it back to the vehicle and Rio is driving us away!"

"Yeah, I hear you guys." he replied. "Man, that shit was some high stakes poker back there, huh?"

"No thanks to you!" expressed John.

"Oh whatever!" Wesley objected. "I got you out of there. It all worked out, didn't it? "

"What are you guys talking about?" inquired Rio.

"We'll tell you later." John answered.

Rio persisted, "But you guys did get everything, right? Like, we're totally good? One hundred percent?"

"Yes Rio." replied Wesley. "I wiped the files of the DNA test results clean before anyone saw it. They would have to run another one, except John stole the evidence. They've got nothing."

"I can't believe you guys actually pulled this off!" she expressed.

"Come on Rio! You should know me better than that by now!"

John thought to himself, "I guess I can take this rock out now." John took off his shoe and shook it until the pebble fell out, then put it back on his foot.

"Seriously though," said Rio, "tell me everything that happened in there."

"Almost got caught a few times, but slipped through." replied John. "I got the files for Wesley, then the evidence. That's it! Nothing more to it than that."

John then took out the four bags from his backpack to show Rio that he had them.

"John, what did that guy say to you in the lobby?" asked Wesley. "He thought you were a lawyer?"

"Yeah. They were expecting an attorney, and he thought it was me. I played along."

"They still got lawyers these days?" asked Wesley.

"Yeah, there's still some lingering around." explained John. "They exist for complicated cases that are highly contextual and need to be argued in depth within court. It's for stuff that Eva can't just immediately settle on her own."

"I mean, you are kind of dressed like a lawyer," Wesley pointed out. "except for the backpack. The backpack didn't give it away to him, eh? Ha-ha! Wow, what an idiot!"

"How did you get me out of there, anyway?" John asked Wesley.

"Well, that guy was a cop. I zoomed in on the lobby camera to see his nametag, then got the idea to call the dispatch asking to speak to him. I said I was a witness in a case of his and remembered more information to tell him. The receptionist then called him over, which granted the lobby clear for you to escape. You were boxed in otherwise! He was standing in the lobby waiting for you."

"Thanks Wesley. I'm sure you've got an answer for this, but just for my own peace of mind, what about the exterior street cameras?"

"Don't worry. They were all panned over to focus on the riot. Everything is golden, baby! I always cover my tracks!

"Let's never do something like this again!" declared John.

"Agreed!" replied Rio.

"What!? Oh come on, this was a blast!" Wesley objected. "Am I the only one not afraid to get my feet wet here?"

"Wesley, we'll see you back at the base." said Rio. "Great work."

"Hey how about some ice cream in celebration of my genius?" suggested Wesley. "Not to mention John's resolve. Think you could grab some on the way back, Rio?"

"I'm hanging up now." she answered.

Rio disconnected the call. The two of them drove back and parked in the garage. As John unbuckled himself, Rio turned to him and spoke her mind.

"Hey, great work back there today. I mean it."

"Thanks."

"Come see me sometime later today. Until then, get some sleep. We all need it."

John and Rio walked from the garage into their quarters. John stripped to his underwear and climbed into bed. The very moment his head hit the pillow revealed just how truly exhausted he was. His body became heavier with each subsequent breath, which provided a sinking feeling into the softness of the mattress. Desperate for rest, his mind soon became dormant until the world around him faded away.

* * *

When John awoke, he sensed it was much later in the day. His suspicion was validated as he checked his phone reading: *17:57*. He dressed, then remembered Rio wanted to see him. He found her quarters empty and searched throughout the Patriot base to find her. As he walked into the hallway, the echo of marching footsteps struck him. The sound ricocheted through the hall as Wesley and another Patriot that John hadn't been introduced to advanced towards him.

"So, I was trying to prove my point, right? Like I told him, a grizzly bear just doesn't have the same competition within its environment compared to a Silverback Gorilla. Those Silverbacks face larger and more dangerous threats. Grizzlies are even chased off by smaller creatures sometimes! Like, wolverines and stuff!" Wesley expressed passionately to the other Patriot.

"Actually, I hadn't thought of it like that."

"So yeah, I think a Grizzly might be a formidable opponent. But let's be honest, the Silverback is going to win this one at least most of the time."

They brought their conversation to a pause as they approached John, who stood in the doorway of the quarters.

"Oh hey, you're finally up." said Wesley. "Rio is off blasting rounds with Stoiya in the armory. You should go see her when you can."

"Thanks, I'll head over there." replied John.

The other Patriot spoke up. "I'm Simon. Good to meet you."

"I'm John. You too."

"What's that all over your face?" Simon asked.

John reached up and felt the smooth surface of the facial distortion technology. His previous desperation for rest made him forget he still wore it.

Wesley chuckled then said, "Ah, I was wondering how long it would take him to realise he still had it on! Ha-ha!"

"Can we get this stuff off me now?" John pleaded.

Follow me." replied Wesley.

Wesley and John parted from Simon and made their way over to Wesley's workstation. Wesley peeled the strips off John's face with a surgical precision and carefully placed them back into their previous storage conditions.

"That's one hell of a technology you've developed there." said John.

"Sure is! I wish I could officially put it on the market. I could make a lot of money, but then Eva would just develop around them once they've become mainstream. That's why my toys must remain as secrets."

"Are they reusable?"

"Yup! I just have to re-do the adhesive each time. That's all. Hey, wanna see the face you were wearing?"

John nodded. Wesley opened up a software program on his desktop and went through a variety of files before he opened a digital image of a person on his screen.

"That's it?" asked John.

"Yup! Meet the culprit who broke into the police station just earlier today! Well, that's what they are going to believe."

"He doesn't look anything like me! That's all digital? I could swear that is an actual photograph of somebody!"

"I'll accept that as a compliment. I made it myself. I'm happy to see the rock did the trick."

"Yeah. My foot is sore."

They both stared at the image John had been disguised with. Neither person knew what to say next, but eventually, the silence was broken by a curious inquiry.

"You're finding your comfort around here, aren't you?" Wesley asked him.

"I mean, we did just pull off one hell of a stunt together. I'm still trying to process it all. How are you doing?"

"Meh, I'm used to this by now. I've been involved with these guys for several years. It's become my way of life."

What Wesley said confirmed John's suspicions surrounding The Patriots' lifestyle. He knew that for the rest of his involvement with them; he was going to have to adapt to the stress and anxiety of impending danger. John said his greetings to Wesley and made his way over to the Armory to check in with Rio.

As he walked through the entry, he was first greeted by booming gunshots as they ripped through the air. As he turned the corner, he witnessed Rio's impressive marksmanship as she blasted away down range. Not one target was missed. Rio shot with confidence and a formidable posture that communicated her experience and familiarity. When the last target was hit, Rio handed the shotgun back to Stoiya as steam rose out of its barrel.

"You got a similar model, but with more kick?" she asked her.

"Do I have more kick!?" replied Stoiya, almost offended, "Girl, I'm the queen of the BAM BAM honey! Come on over!"

Stoiya led Rio back over to the wall and returned the shotgun to its placement on the shelf, then selected a similar model, which she gave to Rio. John could not tell the difference between the two, but the ladies seemed to know what they were doing.

"Looks like you've got an audience." Stoiya commented.

Rio glanced up at John, then continued to load several slugs into the shotgun. She retook her position at the shooting range and stood by for the next round to start. Stoiya took a moment to initiate the controls. The loud ding of the bell vibrated throughout the armory, signaling the beginning of the next round. A series of deep booms shook the room as the fired slugs nailed every target. The recoil of each blast penetrated through her supporting shoulder, ever so slightly knocking her off balance, causing her to reset her composition between shots. When the round finished, she reloaded the weapon, then passed it between several different positions in her hands to examine it thoroughly.

"Oooohh, I think she likes that one!" said Stoiya.

Rio replied with a smile. It was the first time John had seen her with one. He took it as a reminder that somewhere, even the hardest of people still had human aspects within them. John appreciated that.

Stoiya clapped her hands, then held them out to Rio. “My turn!”

Rio passed the shotgun to her and started the next round. Stoiya nailed all the targets. Each shot landed within the middle or inner circle of the targets, including the distant ones. She even got a few direct bullseyes. Stoiya’s prowess in marksmanship became clear. She was a true firearms master. John had never seen more accurate shooting. Not even from the Vancouver police tactical team. When the round ended, Stoiya winked at John, then went over to the wall to store the gun. Rio made her way out of the armory and signaled for John to follow her.

“I have something for you to look at.” she said to him.

John followed Rio over to Wesley, who beckoned John to take a seat next to him at his workstation.

“What’s going on?” John asked them.

“I’d like you to view the incident that took place when Drax was captured.” Rio explained. “Maybe you’ll pick up on something the rest of us missed.”

“I could do that. You have any video on it?”

“Yeah. Eva’s drone footage captured the whole thing.” said Wesley.

“Just a heads up, you’re about to witness a bloodbath.” Rio warned.

“Alright. Thanks for the caution.” he replied. “What do you guys know about it so far?”

“Nothing outside of what the video is about to show you,” said Rio, “and the fact that we were set up. Not sure how though, or who.”

John considered for a moment what he was about to witness, then mustered up the courage to proceed. Gore was never something that bothered him much.

“Play the video.” he said.”

Wesley clicked play on the video up on his monitor, which displayed a bird's-eye view roughly thirty feet in the air. It was in the middle of the night. Visibility was restricted, but John could still identify a group that comprised several people. The group scattered upon the entry of two Eva drones that illuminated the area with their bright headlines. Wesley then paused the video so Rio could better explain the context.

"That's our people. Drax is in the center with the blue coat. We were expecting to meet another group of Patriots from the Prince Rupert area to offer them supplies. They had some sort of upcoming job regarding shipment smuggling on the coast. I don't know all the details, but they requested borrowing some heavier duty weaponry, just in case. As you already know, we have plenty to spare around here."

"Right. So how did things go south?" John asked.

Rio took in a big breath. "Well, somehow the feds found out about it and ambushed our guys from Prince Rupert along their route traveling here, and then Drax and the others while we waited for our friends. The combat drones emerged first, followed by a tactical assault team. They had more numbers and better gear. We lost many people that day."

"Farell seemed confident the rat had been killed." said John.

"We don't know how they found out about it." said Rio. "Everyone on our side of things checked out. Mika confirmed the same."

"Mika?" asked John.

Rio elaborated, "She is the regional leader for all mid-province areas. Helmet test confirmed confidence in her end as well."

"And you trust Mika?" asked John.

"I don't know her personally, but Farell confides in her." she said.

"Very well. So, where did this take place?" asked John.

"Spanish Banks Viewpoint." she replied.

"Alright, let's see what happened." said John.

Wesley then played the rest of the video. With the area now in high visibility, the drones began shooting at the group of Patriots who quickly dispersed and took cover. The drones lobbed flashbang grenades among the battlefield which deafened and blinded the Patriot members before a large squad of armored soldiers entered the scene. The Patriots did their best to withstand the assault, but their weaponry was inferior and most of them were too staggered to hit a target. They dropped one by one as the bullets ripped through their bodies. One patriot popped his head out of cover to search for a better place to hide, but a bullet hit him between the eyes and exited out the back of his skull. An explosion of red mist painted the area behind him while his limp body collapsed onto the ground. Drax's body stiffened and timbered over as he was hit with the barb of a taser. The squad moved in and seized the remaining Patriot members, most of which were wounded and unable to continue fighting. Drax was hogtied and carried out of the area, then thrown into the back of a van. The video then concluded, implying that the drones had been powered down.

"Anyone have any idea what happened next?" John asked them.

"Based on the number of people on the assault team, there would have been at least two other vehicles in their convoy." said Rio. "They probably would have provided an escort away for the van that held Drax."

"Wesley, what about the street cameras?" John asked. "Surely there must be a trail we can follow away from the scene?"

"No. They figured out that we had viewer access to Eva's system." he explained. "They had all the street cameras out of service, so we wouldn't be able to see where they went."

John followed up with another question. "Okay, but there should be a trail of out of service cameras that would infer the direction they traveled?"

"No." he replied. "That entire area of the city was out."

John scratched his head, then asked, "Damn. How do you feel knowing that they are aware you can view Eva's cameras?"

"Obviously, it's not good." replied Wesley. "They changed their security, which locked me out for a while. I regained access, but I imagine they will be incredibly cautious from now on. Anything sensitive might not be captured on camera in anticipation that we might be spectating."

"That seems like a big loss for us." said John.

"It is."

Rio chipped in, "Our biggest loss that night was Drax."

Wesley nodded, then said, "As much as I enjoy using their own technology against them, I have to agree with Rio."

"What happened to the vehicles our members used to get to the meeting point?" John asked them.

"The agents seized them." answered Rio.

"More bad news, I'm assuming? I mean, couldn't they reverse engineer the modifications Wesley did to them to learn about how we've been evading Eva's technology?" asked John.

Wesley let out a heavy sigh before he replied, "Yup!"

"So, they will figure out how to improve her defenses?" John asked.

"Yes, which makes Eva stronger all around the world." Rio explained. "This is the consequence of failure. If one of us screws up, all Patriots must pay for it. We cannot tolerate mistakes."

As Rio finished her statement, she had a flashback of earlier that same day when she prepared to execute John under the bridge.

"It's not the worst thing in the world." said Wesley. "They'll figure out a new system and I'll figure out how to bypass it. It's going to create a gargantuan amount of homework for me, but I'll get through it. After all, I'm smarter than they are."

The dire reality of the impact of Drax's capture had sunk in for John, reminding him of the importance of not taking their enemies lightly. It was a necessary reminder of the brash confidence he freshly gained regarding his recent success at the Police Station.

"Why didn't they tamper with the video footage of the combat drones?" John asked.

"My best guess would be for facial recognition data." replied Wesley. "They might keep it for review to get Eva to identify our members. It would give them information on where they've been, what they've done, and who they've associated with. I've downloaded this footage, so even if it becomes erased, we've got it for good."

John issued a blank stare when an epiphany shot across his mind. "Uh, the facial recognition could lead them here, could it not?"

Wesley scrunched up his face and shrugged his shoulders while he gave his reply. "I've thought about this a lot, and I don't believe so. All our members are extremely careful about what we do in public, and our biometrics are all erased from Eva's database."

"I see." said John.

Wesley continued, "It could also be a taunt, but who knows? They probably figured there wasn't anything on there worth censoring and wanted the rest of us to view our own defeat. They have been petty to us before like that. Those dicks!"

"Can you show me the video from the second drone?" John asked.

As Wesley prepared to bring up the requested video footage, John remembered about Rio's connection to Drax.

"Rio, you sure you want to keep seeing this?" he asked her.

"Play the damn video!" she demanded.

Wesley looked at Rio, then back at John, before he shrugged his shoulders and pressed play. The video from the second combat drone showed the same sequence of events from the opposing angle. The three of them viewed it in careful silence to the end when the video feed was lost upon the drone being powered down.

Wesley looked at John, "Well?" he asked him.

"Any chance facial recognition would identify any of those agents?" John asked Wesley.

"No. That is highly sensitive information. That access would be restricted from normal system use, available only for higher-level government officials. Nothing that I would have access to."

"Play the last bit again." John requested.

Wesley set the video feedback at the remaining fifteen second mark and waited with prospect. He and Rio both hoped John may have caught on to something of relevance.

"There! You guys see that?"

"Yeah? It's just a coffee cup being thrown out the vehicle window." said Wesley.

"Authorities had immediately secured the scene." said Rio. "We couldn't get there that day and anything of importance would be long removed by now. What's so important about a coffee cup, anyway?"

"Do you guys recognize the cup design at all?" John asked them.

Wesley and Rio both replied, "Yes."

John continued, "So, we have a general idea of where that agent would have been prior to arriving at the scene. We may not have access to facial recognition technology, but we know what he looks like. We're going to do things the old school way. Wesley, I know it's going to take some work, but you could manually review the footage of every location of that restaurant branch until you see THAT man purchase THAT drink! Then we know where they were, and you could access the other cameras within the surrounding area to try to get a solid identification of the vehicle they were driving. And then from there -----"

Wesley couldn't let John finish. He knew where he was going with the explanation and couldn't contain his excitement. "And then I can view the entire database of image captures of that vehicle!"

Rio looked at them with squinted eyes. "You guys care to explain?"

Wesley took a deep inhale to prepare for a lengthy answer. "To make footage review easier, Eva can search for a specific set of conditions. Like for example, you could input to search for every time a pedestrian wearing a yellow shirt had been captured on image. Then you get a complete list of all cameras worldwide that captured a yellow shirt along with the location and timestamp. You could input to search for facial recognition technology if you wanted to know everywhere THAT specific person had been identified on camera by Eva. It's one reason she is so good at finding people. So, what I'm getting at is -----"

Rio interrupted him, "If you can get that vehicle information, you could input its details into Eva's search conditions, which would give you a list of every time that vehicle had been picked up in her system. And that would reveal the routes of where they came from and where they went."

"Yeah! Well, it's a starting point at least." Wesley replied. "It's a small lead with the potential to point us towards something bigger!"

A smile broke across Rio's face. "Good catch John. Wesley, it looks like you got your work cut out for you for the next while."

Wesley's wide eyes narrowed, and his elevated cheekbones descended into a frown once he realised the copious amount of footage review that lie before him. John jokingly patted him on the shoulder.

"Good luck, buddy! Let us know how it goes, eh?"

"Awww." he replied.

John then stood up and attempted to walk away before Rio stuck out her hand and stopped him.

"Not so fast John. Go find Simon. He's doing a supply run soon and could use some help."

"Simon? Oh right, I just met him. Any idea where he is?"

"He said he was going to take a shower." said Wesley.

"I'll check over there." replied John. "I'm glad I could help out. See you guys later."

When John arrived back at the quarters, he found Simon next to his bunk. Simon stood with damp hair as he buttoned his shirt. He noticed John entering the room and gave him an amicable head nod. An acknowledgement of a friend's presence.

"Rio said you could use my help with your supply run?" John asked.

"Yeah, I could! Thanks for that John. I'll be ready in a second here."

Simon's living area was orderly in contrast to how the other Patriots lived. Its presentable nature stood out, alien to the surrounding counterparts.

"Groceries? Toiletries?" John asked.

Simon sat on his bed, hunched over as he put on a clean pair of socks.

"Both, among other things."

"I hope errand boy duties aren't normally passed onto newbies or those of lower ranking, are they?"

"Kind of. I mean, it depends on what everyone's doing. Rio must have asked you to come with me because she has nothing else for you to do. We always try to keep ourselves useful down here somehow."

Simon stood up and checked his pockets. John could hear the metal jingle of a set of keys.

"Good to go?" he asked John.

"Sure am!"

Simon opened the vehicle app on his wristlet and remote started the vehicle, then beckoned John to follow him. Upon arriving in the garage, the sensor of the vehicle detected the approaching presence of Simon's wristlet, and both doors of the sports car automatically opened for them. John entered the passenger side but misjudged the low depth of the vehicle seat, which gave him a brief sensation of falling before his weight reassured into the soft, absorbent leather of the vehicle's posh design. Simon climbed in behind the wheel and the doors automatically closed.

"I bet you've been itchin' to get a ride in this hot mama ever since you laid eyes on her, haven't cha?" Simon asked.

"I've been pretty distracted as of late, but now that you mention it, I bet this thing knows how to take the edge off a guy's mind!"

A roar bellowed through the underground parking garage as Simon revved the powerful engine. "Does that answer your question?"

John replied with a smile. Simon backed out and directed them out of the parking lot. The acceleration of the vehicle was nearly instantaneous and took John by surprise.

"Not exactly an inconspicuous vehicle, is it?" said John.

"No need to worry. They don't even know to look for us. We're good! Sit back and enjoy the ride!"

* * *

They arrived at the grocery store, parked, and walked towards the entrance when a civilian calling out to them turned their heads. "Woah! Nice car dude!" Simon responded with a wave, but didn't lose any steps over it. Once they got inside, Simon handed John a piece of paper with several ingredients listed on it.

"You get those. I'll grab the food. Make sure you get everything on that list! Proceed to your own checkout and meet me back at the vehicle."

"Copy, I'll take care of it." replied John.

"See you soon."

They went their separate ways in search of the desired items. John collected typical things for household and hygiene purposes. When he entered a far aisle, he noticed a familiar blonde woman browsing items at the other end. It was Stephanie! John thought to himself, "How!? What is she doing here!?" He quickly proceeded down to the other end of the aisle. Each step filled him with more fervor. He was so glad to see that she was safe, but how did she get here? As John neared Stephanie, she turned her head down aisle and looked directly at him, revealing the full contents of her face. It wasn't her. Perhaps it was because she had been constantly on his mind that led him to be mistaken. That, or the desperation for her rescue, caused him to lose his mind. Within seconds, John's state of emotions transitioned between elation, to melancholy, and finally embarrassment as he realised the woman had noticed him stare at her, like he was some sort of moron or pervert. John quickly returned to his senses.

"Um, sorry!" he muttered.

He pushed his shopping cart past her and turned the corner to hide himself in the neighbouring aisle. An attempt to escape his sense of humiliation. Even though he was now alone, he felt like the entire world was watching him. John remembered his duty and got the rest of the items, then had them bagged at the checkout and returned to the vehicle to find Simon waiting for him. The trunk opened, revealing the drawn-out depth of rear storage space with reference to the fact that the rear seats had been taken out. They loaded up the goods and re-entered the vehicle for departure. After they pulled out of the store parking lot, Simon mustered up the courage to ease his mind, asking John about matters among the personal sorts.

"So, I gotta ask. I know you haven't been with us for very long, but if push comes to shove, we Patriots need to know each one of us will watch the other's back."

"Was there a question in there?"

"What I mean is, I'd be a lot more comfortable understanding my fellow man's ideas, goals, and philosophies. Those sorts of things."

"My absolute priority is getting Stephanie back."

Yeah. I know that, but are you willing to fight to protect your fellow patriot?"

"Everyone else trusts me. I passed the helmet and everything. You got a problem with Farell's judgement?"

"No! I know you passed. I was the one analyzing your thought patterns during the test, but Farell never offered you the question that I just asked."

John tried to come up with a way to respond, but was unsure of what to say.

Simon continued, "Look, neutrality is never valuable to any cause. We live in one hell of a time in history, and our purpose can't coincide with anyone who doesn't directly believe in our mission. If you aim to succeed with us, I advise you to figure out exactly who you are, and what you believe in."

"What I believe is that I am going to help you guys find Drax."

"I hope you do, John! I hope you do, but that may not be enough. Consider your stance regarding Eva's oppression of humanity. Silence and stillness are the greatest enablers of all."

"And what about you? What do you fight for?"

"I fight for those who cannot, or will not, against the corrupt elite and their infinite thirst for power and control. It's not rocket science. It's classic good vs evil. I fight, well, basically I fight for freedom."

"And what does freedom mean to you? Private conversations? No curfews? Democracy?"

"Those are superficial examples. Freedom runs deeper than that. It's about expression, attitude, and perspective. They may seek to control our possessions, our lifestyles, or our bodies, but it isn't until they control our minds that they truly own us. Freedom of thought, belief, and speech is partially what separates us from the animals. It defines who we are as a species! Freedom is the open window which pours the sunlight of the human spirit and human dignity."

John chuckled, then replied, "You writing a poem or something?"

"That was Herbert Hoover who said that."

"So, you fight for your own sense of individuality. I get that, but many people find Eva convenient and depend on her for their everyday lives."

"Dependency equals vulnerability for exploitation. The more that people need help, the less capable they become on their own. If you have the power to feed, you have the power to starve. If you can influence, you can control. That's all they want."

"They? Meaning the world elites? Those in position of global influence, right?"

"Exactly!"

"If you are so in favor of freedom, why can't you leave others to their own opinion about the world? Freedom is the ability to make up your own mind, isn't it?"

"You're missing the point! They're NOT free to make up their own mind! The government restricts and censors anything and everything directly outside of the narrative! With media, or digital algorithms, they are all designed to create echo-chambers. They give the population a customized experience of reality that was pre-selected to normalise us into patterns and habits of their choosing so that they can control us. The most effective forms of control aren't blatant, like physical force, but instead manipulate how people think or behave over time towards the benefit of their agenda. This way people will believe their actions are of their own free will, when realistically they are just mirroring. People are incredibly habitual by nature. Monkey see, monkey do."

"I suppose the illusion of freedom would negate the risk of revolt."

"Ah! Perhaps there's hope for you yet!"

"I think I understand. To fight for the freedom of humanity means to oppose the social programming from those in power, so that people become subjected to a wider world of varying perspective, and can therefore truly be free to think, speak, and behave of their own true, free will."

"Couldn't have said it better myself, Sir."

After a couple of minutes of silence, Simon turned on the radio to break the awkwardness. Placid electronic music quietly traveled through the length of the vehicle but didn't distance John from his train of thought. He sat mind absent from body. A bewildered daze between the clutter of recent intense experience and unanswered critical questions. He could hardly believe he pulled off the heist back at the police station, but what was the deeper meaning behind the kidnappings? And what was *Serum 3V-12*? If there was one thing John recently had identified, it was that The Patriots' philosophies became more understood to him with each conversation and John struggled to find any line of reasoning to persuade himself to disagree.

CHAPTER 10

Some of the other Patriots greeted Simon and John as they arrived, dismissing the need for a second haul. Lev carried the largest load. His gigantic hands supported at least double the number of bags compared to his companions. The groceries were unloaded first, then the other miscellaneous supplies as Kade withdrew large pots and pans from the cupboards and set them down on the stove tops. Their bulky girths overlapped the burners, revealing Kade's intention to cook for the entirety of their group. John took a seat in the lounge, which engulfed his body and provided him an allaying nirvana as he surrendered his weight into the pliable material. Living as a Patriot, rest was something not to be taken for granted, but cherished. John embraced the opportunity and felt his heavy eyelids sink into his face. His breath and heart rate dropped before he was abruptly returned from a state of drifting consciousness into the waking world.

FWOP

John opened his eyes to discover someone had thrown a pillow at his chest. He scanned his environment, trying to find the meaning of his disruption, and noticed Milton point over to Wesley, who waved over at John.

"Tired, huh?" he asked.

John sat in the seat beside Wesley and could only respond with a yawn.

"Well, no rest for the wicked, as they say. I'm going to need your attention. I found what we were looking for."

"Already!? How?"

"Well, I figured that there had to be a faster way than manually reviewing ALL the footage for ALL the restaurant locations. I was thinking about Eva's search conditions for her cameras and realised that since we know some basic information about this agent, what if I could search up those details for the specific cameras associated with this restaurant chain?"

"Okaaay......?"

"Well, this guy we're looking for was at the assault, but not involved in the squad. I think he's some sort of commander, like the brains behind the operation or whatever. As the drone landed at the end of the video, we got a clear shot of the agent's face revealing he's a middle-aged Caucasian male with brown hair, brown eyes, about six feet tall. So, I inputted those details into the search conditions within the restaurant chain. There were a ton of entries, but having a clean image to compare had helped a lot. Just a few minutes ago, I finished narrowing it down. Look!"

Wesley brought up the drone image of the agent and compared it to a zoomed in camera shot taken at the front counter of the restaurant.

"Wow! Yeah, I'd say that's him alright!" John said. "Any news of an associated vehicle?"

"I just finished that while you were trying to pass out over there. The exterior camera captured the vehicle, but I couldn't get the plate from that angle, so I viewed the street camera from when the vehicle was pulling out of the parking lot. Check this out!"

Wesley brought up another image of the vehicle leaving the lot with the license plate clearly exposed.

"Hey! I knew you could do it! Input those details already, and let's see what we can get!"

A cryptic sense of others behind him spooked John. He turned around to notice that everyone else but Kade in the room had taken interest and now lingered around Wesley's workstation. They all knew something of dire importance was about to become revealed.

"Yo! What's goin' down?" asked Kade from the other side of the room.

"It's the moment of truth!" replied John.

"Word? Hold up!"

The group waited impatiently as Kade urgently flipped the chicken breasts in the pan and set a timer on the oven. Confident that he had a moment to step away from the food, he leapt over from the kitchen to meet with the others. Wesley inputted the vehicle data into Eva's search conditions for Vancouver and the surrounding areas, which revealed everywhere it had been.

"Damn!" exclaimed Kade. "It's gonna take a while to sort through all of that!"

"Yeah, give me a few moments here, guys." said Wesley.

The air thickened as the room stood in suspense. Wesley searched through the video time stamps, tracing the agent's route in pursuit of any investigative lead. A few minutes had passed when John voiced a concern itching at his mind.

"Hey guys, so I was just thinking, couldn't they have used this same method of video tracing to track us back to the base? I mean, they seized the vehicles from the meeting point. I know the cameras were out, but Eva would have the digital history of everywhere those vehicles have driven, right?"

John sensed the atmosphere change from suspense into an uncomfortable energy he couldn't quite identify. Perhaps regret or sorrow? He looked around, seeking confirmation, but found no response.

"Guys?"

Just then, an answer arose from the other side of the room. Everyone turned around to face the interruption.

"That's right. And they did."

Farell approached the rest of the members standing around Wesley. John waited for him to clarify his previous statement. Farell took a lengthy inhale, then paused for a moment before he continued.

"There was a second Patriot base. Most of the members involved in our loss were from there. The vehicles they seized were from there as well and had never traveled to this location. We organized it that way, to prevent this exact type of thing from ever occurring. Otherwise, we would have become overrun too."

"What happened, exactly?" asked John.

"That's pretty much it. Our guys got hit, and they traced everything back to the other base." replied Farell. "The few people remaining there, along with weapons, supplies, and everything else, were lost."

"They didn't know?" asked John. "Someone couldn't have warned them?"

"They got hit almost right away." Farell replied. "Just about the time we were suspicious that something had gone wrong."

"Killed or captured?" John asked.

"We don't know." Farell answered. "If the Feds captured any remaining members, I'm certain they would have known little to nothing about the location of this base. We are still here, after all. We take precautions. Things are on a need-to-know basis only."

John scratched his scalp. "What about the rest of the team in Prince Rupert?"

Farell shook his head while he replied, "Gone. All assets involved with that region are lost. It was a smaller district, so all our members in that region were involved in the ambush. The Feds would have overtaken the base too."

John felt heavy in his seat under the reality of what he just heard. It seemed like every time he thought he understood the severity of Drax's capture, additional details would surface to prove it more significant.

Beep

The timer to the oven went off, and Kade returned to check on the food's progress. Farell crossed the room to join the others while Wesley searched through the remaining video logs and soon found something of interest.

"Hey, I got something here!" Wesley claimed.

Everyone around Wesley's workstation leaned in closer, honing their attention to the computer monitor.

"Earlier the same day, the vehicle made its way to this warehouse and met with someone." explained Wesley. "I can't see much from this angle. Hold on."

Wesley pulled up the exterior cameras of that property address and began cycling through them until he identified the view. The vehicle stopped at a side entrance to a warehouse. The agent left the vehicle and met with a younger man by the door. They appeared to be speaking for a few minutes, then they both extended one of their arms out to each other, but the camera angle could not capture the specific details of what happened.

"Anyone have any idea who that is?" asked Milton.

Everyone shook their heads.

"What are they doing? Is he giving him something or shaking hands?" asked John.

"Can't tell from this shot." replied Wesley.

"Cycle through one more time." requested John. "Maybe there's another one in that area that views from a separate angle."

Wesley cycled through all the cameras associated with that property, then replied, "No, that's the only one."

"I don't suppose there's any way you have access to the camera's audio captures?" John asked him.

"No, I haven't worked my way into that yet." he replied.

"It would certainly be great to know what they were saying." Milton added.

"Agreed, and we're gonna find out!" said Farell. "Wesley, track that person away from that location. I want to know as much about them as we can!"

"On it."

"You guys are having all the fun without me!" Kade exclaimed. Lev, take over for a minute. I've seen you cook a mean chicken before."

As Kade was swapped by Lev, he sprung over to join the others but failed to identify the suspect. Wesley took care to track the person from their location, identifying that they were a warehouse worker who locked up the facility and departed alone on foot. He took a bus route for most of the distance, then continued the rest of his course on foot; eventually arriving at his residence within a towering apartment complex.

"Ha! Got the bastard!" exclaimed Milton.

"That's a clean face shot we got of him in the lobby too!" Simon added.

Milton looked around at everyone in the room. "So, none of us know this guy? You think they could have been meeting about us?"

"It's a lead, at least." replied Wesley.

Milton threw his arms up in the air as he gave his next statement. "How could this guy possibly have known about our upcoming meeting later that same evening? And the weapons drop? Or that Drax would be there? Who the hell is this guy?"

"We don't even know for sure he had anything to do with it." said Kade.

Milton challenged him. "Think about it! The agent involved in Drax's capture met with that person earlier the same day! None of our remaining members are the rat! None of the people we lost that night would have put themselves in a deadly situation like that if they were a rat! It's gotta be this guy, whoever he is!"

Farell, Wesley, Rio, and Simon nodded in agreement.

"Wesley, where else has the agent been that day?" asked John. "Are you sure we aren't missing anything important? I just want to make sure we don't focus on the wrong details. You didn't see them come and go from anywhere that might indicate where Drax is held?"

"This is the only thing of significance that happened within the city." he replied. "The vehicle came in from Highway 99. Camera view is limited outside of populated areas, so for those regions, Eva relies upon wristlet or vehicle GPS tracking."

"There are no highway cameras outside of the city?" John asked.

Wesley elaborated, "Yeah, there's some, but it's very limited. Their plan is to put up more both inside and outside the city, but there's only so much labour that can get done over the last handful of years. They've prioritized their surveillance development for the metropolitan areas, for obvious reasons."

"Yeah, I understand." replied John. "Wait, doesn't that mean Drax is being held somewhere outside of the city limits?"

Farell chipped in, "Yes, and within reasonable driving distance. I figured it wouldn't be within the city. Probably some sort of secret facility in the mountains, not far off Highway 99."

"That's a good start." said Simon.

"Wesley, Eva is uploaded into the International Space Station, isn't she?" asked John. "What about satellite imaging?"

"I like how you're thinking, but no." he replied. "I don't have access to that, and anything worthy of a secret base probably could not be seen through a bird's-eye view, anyway. Especially in the mountains."

"Tomorrow will be Tuesday." John remarked. "Review his actions from Tuesday of the previous week."

Wesley took several minutes to fulfill John's request and identified their suspect working the same shift hours. He left the same time as the following week and took the same route home.

"What are you thinking, John?" asked Rio.

"I just wanted to see if Tuesdays are typically the same routine for this guy."

"Food is ready." said Lev.

Kade returned to the kitchen and took out the dishes and cutlery. Lev returned to Wesley's monitor.

"So tomorrow, we get this guy." said Lev.

"Yes, and our answers." Farell added.

"So, he's alone when he leaves work, right?" asked Simon. "Why don't we just drive up as he walks away and grab him right then and there?"

"That could be a fatal mistake." replied Wesley. "Remember guys, Eva is passively monitoring until something causes suspicion to provoke an investigation. When he ends up missing, Eva is going to wonder where he is. What do you think will happen when she backtracks her data and sees us pulling up to his workplace, forcing him inside our vehicle?"

Simon realised his error. "Oh, shit. Right."

"It's probably best to see if there's any cold spots along the way." said Farell. "There aren't too many of them, but they certainly exist. Those alleys look secluded before the merging point onto the main street. Take a look Wesley."

Wesley took a moment to bring up the camera angles for that surrounding area.

"Yeah, just as I thought, it's cold. Best to take as many precautions as possible. We'll park in the alley, intercept him there and lead him to the van at the other end, cutting off his escape routes ----- hold on, no, that wouldn't work. The camera from the main street would see our vehicle pulling in and out of the alley. Wesley, do you think Eva would associate that with our suspect's disappearance and track us back to base?"

"I believe that to be likely." said Wesley. "We need a different plan."

Kade rubbed his forehead. "This is making my head hurt. How about we figure this out while we eat?"

Simon felt his stomach groan before he replied, "Good idea!"

As everyone lined up to grab their portion of food, Stoiya entered the room.

"Geez, is it dinner time yet?" she complained.

"Yup! Come grab some." said Kade.

"You finally left your dungeon!" teased Wesley.

Stoiya flipped Wesley the middle finger, then grabbed herself a plate of food and sat down with the others. "So, what are ya'll doing in here?" she asked them. "Did I miss something?"

"Hah! I'd say so." Kade remarked.

Milton relayed the details about the investigation's progress to Stoiya until she was brought up to speed. With her mouth full of food, her reply came out muffled.

"Goddamn!" she replied. "I've been missing a party up in here! Well, if it were up to me, I would just show up there all like, POW POW!"

"And that's why you're just the brawn behind the operations." teased Kade.

Stoiya shot back at him. "You have a solution, then?"

"Ugh, no." he replied.

Simon sat up straight upon the epiphany of a new idea. "Alright, how about this? We break into his house wearing the disguise of Wesley's face chip things and wait for him to come home, then take him by force. The cameras won't identify us that way."

Rio challenged him, "And our vehicle?"

"Oh, never mind." he replied.

"Alright, how about another homeless distraction? asked Kade. "Jasper was his name, right? We could get them to do another protest or something to distract the street cameras, then just follow through with Farell's plan."

Farell shook his head and voiced his concern. "No. They would likely learn from their mistakes. We can't fool them with the same trick twice, especially back-to-back. We are risking too much with this operation, so the plan must be reliable."

"Plus, many of the homeless who were arrested from this morning wouldn't even have been released into the public yet." John added.

Kade dropped his posture and stabbed at his food with his fork. "Well, there goes my idea."

Simon voiced another idea. "What if we did something like how we grabbed John? We know there's a cold spot there. Wesley can disable the person's wristlet when we grab him, then he can set them up on that program Wesley has where it inputs fake daily logs into Eva's data, tricking her that our suspect is still around?"

Once again, Rio challenged him, "And what do you think is going to happen when his family, friends, and co-workers realize that he's physically un-accounted for?"

Simon realized she was right, but did not reply.

"Not to mention that would reveal my capabilities to do that." Wesley added. "Currently, the Feds are unaware of some of the things I can do to their system, and that is to our advantage."

"Wesley, why don't you just hack your way into gaining control over Eva's cameras?" suggested Kade. "Then on the day you obtain access, we can sabotage our suspect?"

Wesley placed his fork onto his plate to free up his hands for a double facepalm. "Oh gee, why didn't I think of that!? Yeah, I'll just hack her! Cause it's that easy, you know? It's not like there's numerous cyber security barriers. All of which are complex to the highest possibility to prevent that exact type of thing!"

Kade clenched his jaw and narrowed his eyes at Wesley. "Ok, fine. Don't be a dick about it."

Several minutes went by. The sound of metal scraping against their plates being the only noise in the room. Eventually, Farell spoke. “I have an idea. Everyone be quiet.”

Farell dialed a number on his phone and placed it face up on his armchair as it rang until the call was answered with a deep sigh.

“What?” the voice said.

“You’re on speaker. I gotta pick your brain about something.”

“Fuck you! Do you have any idea what kind of shit storm you guys have caused for me over here!? I’ve been assigned as the lead investigator on your case. YOUR case, from this morning! Or at least I was until the Feds came crawling all over it.”

At this point John realised the person on the other end of the phone call was the police detective he, Wesley, and Rio met up with earlier that day.

“I can imagine,” Farell empathised, “but it had to be done. Just checking though, we’re good, right? No loose ends?”

“We have nothing. We’re looking for a ghost in Eva’s database. Someone I know doesn’t actually exist, and I gotta somehow fake my way through everything. Not that we’re involved in the case anymore, aside from the grunt work. The Feds have taken over and anything we may uncover gets turned over to them.”

“There is a real possibility we found the person responsible for Drax’s capture. We gotta set up a way to grab them for interrogation.”

“That’s great news, but I won’t subject myself to that sort of risk. I’ve already gone too far with what happened this morning. There is a possibility they could already be investigating internally for a mole.”

“These are desperate times, Ricardo. I mean, for crying out loud, you even went to college with Drax! Are you going to abandon him during his time of need?”

“What do you even need?”

"We need some way to divert Eva's attention from the entrance and exit points to a cold spot long enough for us to make the pickup."

"Absolutely not! I must consider my own well-being. For my daughter. I won't help you."

John felt a wave of confidence wash over him. "Farell, let me talk to him." he said.

John took the phone from Farell, then cleared his throat as he returned to his seat.

"This is John. I'm a former member of your police department."

"I know who you are."

"I joined the police a long time ago. I wanted to be a cop pretty much my whole life because I knew the fear that existed in my city. People didn't trust their neighbour, couldn't walk down the street alone at night or leave any of their doors unlocked. Thefts and assaults were everywhere. I always believed the world should be better, so I wanted to help in any way that I could. I figured the best way I could make a difference would be to fight back, so my ambitions became centered on crime prevention. At the time, I wouldn't have known to define it this way, but recent experiences have made me reconsider the value of freedom. Now I can identify that's what it was ultimately about for me all along. I watched people's fears and concerns influence their actions and it stifled how they lived. I wanted to deliver people from their worries and create an environment where they could just be themselves and do the things they want or go where they need without having to look over their shoulder. That is freedom. To me it is anyway. How long have you been involved now?"

"Going on fifteen years."

"That's quite some time. I bet you've seen it change a lot. You stuck through it during the Conversion too. The job's not the same anymore, is it?"

"No, not at all."

"Tell me about it."

"Crime is quite low, which is good for the people, but most of what we do these days is largely customer service centered. It's boring."

"And Eva auto-processes most things for you guys, doesn't she? There's probably not a lot of making your own decisions. I bet the day to day entails a lot of strict protocols, bland routines, and helping people with frivolous or mundane tasks. Am I right?"

"Yes."

"Eva didn't make people safer, Ricardo. In fact, the threat among civilians is even more real. Crime in the traditional sense may have dropped, but what took its place? Instead of having to worry about the consequence of leaving your door unlocked or traveling through a rough area, people just face different consequences instead. The threat of consequence for disobedience. What happens if you say the wrong thing or don't make it home in time for your curfew? What happens if you miss your deposit appointment or waste too much energy? I'll tell you what really happened in the world. What really happened is that society traded one form of oppression for another. All Eva did was shuffle the deck."

"What's your point?"

"My point is that the younger and ambitious John Mason I just told you about would have grown to resent working in the modern police force. It wouldn't align with my values. Tell me if that sounds familiar?"

John received only silence on the other end of the phone. He continued, having known that he caught the detective's interest.

"What I'm saying is, I'm just asking that you reconsider your position. I bet your current professional duty does not resemble your deeper ambitions. Remember who you are and stick up for what you believe in. Your daughter would want that of you."

Again, John's statement was met with silence. John tried to prompt the detective into a response.

"Well?"

"Put Farell back on." said the detective.

John handed the phone back over to Farell and returned to his seat in the room.

"Hey." answered Farell.

"I'm not saying I'll help. I have some questions."

"Sure."

"Specifically, which cameras are the issue, and what day and time?"

"Tomorrow, around quarter past six in the evening. I'll send you the location details in a second here."

Farell sent the detective screenshots of the street view as well as a map GPS drop point showing the exact location he was referring to.

"I'll call you back."

The call ended. John stared off into the corner and tried to process what he had just said. He wondered if he really believed all of that, or if it was just a ploy of charisma to persuade the detective into helping them one last time.

Impressed, Simon looked over at John with admiration. "Good speech buddy."

"Yo, get my man a podium next time!" exclaimed Kade.

Stoiya mumbled, "Mghhhmmhgmmmhgmhmhhmgg!"

Kade chuckled, then asked her, "What?"

Stoiya held her index finger up at the group as she struggled to force down an entire mouthful of food in a single gulp.

"I said, who would've thought hot stuff over there would have a way with words as smooth as a baby's ass!?"

Most people in the room burst out laughing. Several minutes passed. The phone rang again as Kade went around to collect the dishes of those who had finished eating. Farell took a nervous breath, then answered.

"Hello?"

"At exactly *6:10* tomorrow evening, there will be a vehicle collision at the southern footing of that intersection."

"How did you manage that?"

"I know someone who owes me a big favor."

"How long will the cameras be distracted?"

"However long it takes to settle a vehicle collision. Bye -----"

"Wait!"

The call was silent while the detective waited for whatever Farell would say next.

"Thank you, Ricardo."

The call dropped. Farell stood up and faced everyone in the room.

"Ok team, we officially have a plan. A traffic collision at the base of the intersection would cause the alley cold spot entrance to become temporarily out of view. We will wait around the corner for the accident, then park in the alley. Simon, Kade, you guys will wait for our suspect in the alley out of sight. As he passes you guys, approach from behind and make him enter the van ahead, then one of you jumps in the back and the other take one of the rear seats. Milton, you are the designated driver. Rio, Lev, and Wesley, you guys ride the back. Tie him up and watch over him once he's in there. Wesley, you know what to do with his wristlet. John, Stoiya, you two take the other end of the alley in case he runs. When we get him in the back of the van, take the rear seats and consider yourselves a miscellaneous duty. I'll be the front passenger. We have to time things accordingly to enter the alley. Take him and depart before the collision can be sorted. Our suspect leaves at the same moment each day. It should be enough time to pull it off."

Some people in the room clapped while others threw their arms up in celebration. They finally figured out a plan to capture their suspect and get their long sought-after answers.

"Everyone, take a load off tonight." said Farell. "We finally have something to be optimistic about. Eat, drink, sleep, whatever."

Kade went over to the bar and held up a bottle of alcohol. "Did someone say shots!?"

"Not you Kade!" said Farell. "You're still in hot water."

Kade's jaw dropped and he stood up straight. "What! Seriously?"

Wesley broke out into laughter.

"You too Wesley!" said Farell. "Besides, you have work to complete."

"Work!? What work!?" he cried.

"You forgot? Finish your how-to tutorial videos and send them to the other Patriot groups. Do you want your skills and technology to die with you?"

Wesley didn't reply. His body drooped back into his seat as he covered his face with his hands.

"So get to work already! Kade, clean this place up a bit and see if you can get our treadmill working again."

Farell left the room, and Kade followed soon after. Wesley went over to his workstation and typed away at his projects. Simon went behind the bar counter and inspected their alcohol supply.

"Alright everyone, what are we drinking?" he asked them. "Lev, I know your type."

Simon took out a bunch of glasses and grabbed the Vodka bottle, then set everything down on the bar counter. Everyone else gathered around while Wesley peered at them from his corner with a look of jealousy.

* * *

A couple hours passed with the number of drinks forgotten. Rio and John were the closest to sober among the crew. Milton staggered over to Simon and patted him on the shoulder.

"Hey bud, come stand over here. Watch this!"

"Oh, you're performing another trick?" he asked.

"Ugh, yeah! You're short enough for this." Milton replied. "Check it out. Stand still and put that empty bottle on top of your head."

His drunken swagger caused several failed attempts, but Simon eventually balanced himself and the bottle.

"Should have asked for an apple and an arrow." he said

"I'm gonna kick it!" claimed Milton. "Check it out!"

Milton performed a spinning wheel kick aimed at the empty bottle, but caught Simon just above the ear with the end of his calf and knocked him to the ground.

"What the hell!?" cried Simon.

Stoiya scoffed at them.

"Hah! Pathetic!" teased Wesley.

"Wesley! Get back to work!" shouted Rio.

Milton tried to reassure the others of his abilities. "No, I can do it! I'm just a little rusty, that's all! Let me try again. I'll do it this time. I promise."

Rio scolded them, "You guys are gonna leave broken glass everywhere!"

"Nah, we won't." replied Milton. "I've had to rely on one of these bottles in a bar brawl a long time ago. Trust me, this thing is stronger than a human skull!"

Simon slowly made his back up to his feet and balanced the bottle again. Milton took a few steps back and performed a few practice kicks. His heel cleaved through the air in a perfect arch, clearly displaying an elegant technique only obtainable through a mastery of martial arts.

Stoiya's eyes widened as she puckered her lips. "Ooooo, maybe he's still got it after all!"

"Top Lightweight contender of the world! Hoo-hah! Hoo-hah!" Milton chanted.

Milton took a deep inhale through his nose, then held his breath and executed a perfect wheel kick that just barely grazed Simon's hair as his heel contacted the empty bottle. The impact sent it flying a few feet through the air and bouncing off the carpet until it found its resting place at the base of the couch.

"That was dope!" shouted Simon.

"Hah! See, I told you guys I could do it!" Milton bragged. "I still got it and the bottle didn't break either!"

"I ain't no fisticuffs expert, but that move was gust! Like SHERYUUUM, POW!" expressed Stoiya.

Rio rolled her eyes at them. "You guys had your fun. Now settle down before you break something or someone."

"Milton, what sport did you compete in again?" asked John.

"Karate when I was younger, then Mixed Martial Arts. You're talking to the Lightweight division top contender!"

"Top contender? Is that like a champion or something?" John asked.

"Close! It's the runner-up." said Milton. "I fought for the world title. Twice actually!"

"That's really impressive!" expressed John.

Wesley scoffed at him. "Yeah, but he lost BOTH times!"

"Fuck off!" said Milton. "A nerd like you couldn't fight your way out of a paper bag."

Wesley assured him. "I'd do better than you think."

"Hah! No, I don't think you would." challenged Milton.

"Actually Milton, this past Saturday I saw Wesley pull off an impressive move or two." said John.

Milton looked over at Wesley for confirmation, but his curiosity was only met with the flip of a middle finger.

"Milton, you think you could take on Lev?" Simon asked.

Lev scoffed. Everyone looked at Milton, eager for his response.

"Hah! I'm the Lightweight contender of the world!" he bragged. "Don't forget that! It's not the size of the dog in the fight but the size of the fight in the dog, as they say!"

Wesley challenged him. "Hey, aren't there weight classes in combat sports for a reason?"

"Wesley, if you don't get back to work, I'm gonna show YOU the meaning of combat sports!" warned Rio.

Wesley returned to his workstation muttering something inaudible under his breath. Simon and Milton went to grab another plate of food.

"So, how did you all end up with The Patriots?" John asked the group. "This life, it's quite the risk."

"What a downer." said Milton. "Always the serious one, eh?"

John apologized, "Sorry."

"Nah, it's fine. I just believe in the mission." said Simon. "Nothing special."

"Same." replied Rio.

"I like guns!" expressed Stoiya.

Simon chuckled before he replied, "Yup, she likes guns all right."

"Lev?" John asked.

"Yeah, I don't know your story either, Lev." said Simon.

Lev cleared his throat, then leaned forward in his seat to address the group. He spoke in partially broken English, clouded in a thick accent.

“After revolution, you know, like when different groups comes together and make Patriots, yeah? They send best soldiers around the world to fight and help with train other fighters. Sooner or later, I end up Vancouver.”

Simon’s eyes grew wide. “You fought in the 2040 Russian revolution!?”

“Yes.”

During 2039, a year amid the Conversion, the world governments announced they were going to come together to form a unified government as the recovery solution to their collapsed societies. It created little resistance at first as most people were unsure what that would mean, but over time, they released more details to prepare people for the changes. This included informing the people that an artificial intelligence would operate the world government, society would become a police state of strict surveillance, private property would be abolished, and many other attributes currently in place for the modern 2040s. This led to protests and riots all around the world. Those who were the most zealous banded together and fought, sparking all out revolutions in various areas of the world. People rose and fought against their governments with the revolutions in the United States, Russia, Eastern Europe, and some parts of Africa being the most considered for their violence and death tolls. Most people who partook in the protests and riots did not bear arms when the wars began, but some members of police and military defied their countries’ orders to fight against their own people, even leaving their duties to join the resistance. It didn’t take long for the various resistance groups to realise they shared the same aim and banded together, distributing information, resources, food, soldiers, and weapons amongst themselves. The Russian Chief of General Staff spread a conspiracy theory that it was the world authorities that caused the Conversion so they could implement a unified government. This led to a great widespread of disinformation campaigns aimed to discredit the theory, but those who believed it were just as ardent to spread it. This member of Russian office became one of the primary leaders for the early resistance and officially named their cause, which translated to English as *The Patriots*. He was captured and executed in 2041.

"Tell us what fighting in the Russian revolution was like." requested Simon.

"Bloody. Many people die." replied Lev.

There was a pause. Everyone looked at Lev and waited whether he would continue. Lev realised they expected more to the story and cleared his throat again.

"So, Russian chief of general staff, he lead the revolution, you know? We make fighting with the government but have more winnings than some other revolution groups because many people respected him as leader. So, we get many people in Russian military to leave and help with us instead. Then, we go to eastern European countries and help make with their fightings too. So, those governments try to stop our winnings by, ugh, you know, um……"

Lev opened a translator application on his phone and spoke a Russian word into it. The phone returned the translation into English in a robotic mono-tone voice. "Famine."

Lev sounded it out. "Fam, Fam-ine. So, they do like famine to make us weak and then fight with us."

"How did you survive?" asked Simon.

"We cook them like chicken."

"UGHH! Gross!" exclaimed Stoiya.

Simon looked down at his plate. His jaw unhinged, and he set the rest of his food on the coffee table away from him.

"I'm sorry I asked." he said.

Kade entered the room. "What's going on?" he asked them.

Rio replied with a question of her own. "Did you clean up?"

"Yeah."

She followed up again. "Is the treadmill working?"

Kade shook his head. "Nah, it's busted."

Kade sat down, then asked them, “What are you guys talking about?”

“Not much.” replied Milton.

“Looks like Lev and Stoiya are both checking out.” Kade pointed out.

Everyone looked over and noticed their dishevelled positions. Lev’s side slumped over the armrest of the couch. His arms nearly touched the ground. Stoiya lie perpendicular to the chair with her head and feet dangled off the edges.

“He was literally just talking!” exclaimed Simon. “What the hell?”

“Yeah, he’s a strange drinker.” Kade commented. “One moment it’s like he’s completely sober. Next thing you know, he’s drifting through outer space.”

“How many drinks did he have?” asked John.

“I don’t know.” replied Milton. “I lost count. Maybe thirty?”

Simon’s eyes grew wide. “THIRTY!?”

Kade chuckled, then remarked. “My man’s a tank!”

They spent the rest of the evening together in good company. Rio left for her quarters shortly after Kade’s entrance, which granted Wesley the opportunity to join in. Milton tried out a few karate moves. Some made their mark, while others only displayed his inebriation. Wesley would pipe up to poke fun at people as the opportunities arose. Kade finally got some drinks in him, and Simon became curious about policing in the old world and picked John’s brain with questions. John appreciated the comradery. It was a generous intermission for the stress that came along with being in The Patriots that rejuvenated their spirits and prepared their will for the challenge they knew lied before them the following day.

Chapter 11

Kade arrived the next morning with warm fast food and ibuprofen for those who suffered a hangover. The day carried on in a typical fashion. Lev in the gym, Stoiya in the Armory, and Rio yelling at Wesley to get him to finish his tutorial videos. When the time finally came, the team geared up and entered the van. When he buckled up, John reached at his side and brushed the holster of his sidearm with his fingers while thinking to himself, "I really hope I don't have to use this thing!"

"Everyone is connected to the group call, right?" Farell asked them.

The van filled with the short confirmations of each member as they responded to him.

He asked the group, "Anyone need clarity on their role?" but received no answer. The only sound was the rumble of the engine.

"All right then," he continued, "take us away, Milton."

* * *

Milton pulled the Van up to their waiting point just around the block from the intersection collision, then brought it to a halt. John took in a big breath as his heart rate spiked. The silence within the vehicle suggested to him that the others felt the same way. Farell checked the time.

"It's *6:02*. It should happen soon. About eight minutes. You got your eyes up, Wesley?"

"Sure do!" he replied.

"It's pretty cool you can view Eva's cameras from your phone!" John said to Wesley. "You don't even have to be at your workstation."

"It's nowhere near as efficient as being at my monitors." he replied. "I'm much more limited this way, but it's still better than nothing."

John followed up with another question for him. "You checked the warehouse interior cameras to confirm he's there today, right?"

"Do I look like an amateur to you!?"

"Remember Milton, we don't enter on the crash." stated Farell. "We enter when Wesley confirms that it's clear!"

"Right." he answered.

Farell addressed the others. "When you guys near him, keep your voices down. Just in case your words end up coming through to his wristlet."

"Whispering does the trick," said Wesley, "even if it does get picked up, it's not distinct enough."

"Good to know." replied John.

Several minutes went by, then John checked the time: *6:09*. He knew it would happen at any moment. A handful of deep breaths passed, then all ears within the vehicle perked up.

SREEEEEECH, BANG

Wesley held up his finger to signal to the rest of the team for the timing. "Hold on, Hold on. Alright NOW!"

Milton drove the team around the corner and partially up the street before reversing the van into the alley. John and Stoiya jumped out and hid behind a dumpster while Simon and Kade found some areas to hide further down the alley, closer to the warehouse.

"Where's our guy Wesley?" asked John.

"He's still inside finishing the lock-ups."

"Man, we don't have all day." said Kade.

"Relax. Everything is on schedule." assured Farell.

A few minutes had gone by, and the suspect exited the warehouse alone on foot. Wesley alerted the others. "He's coming! He just exited the building. Kade, Simon, you're gonna hear him soon!"

"Copy!" they replied.

Simon and Kade waited in their ambush positions. Their accelerated heart beats forced oxygen through their muscles and readied their bodies for combat, like predators in the wild waiting for prey. A gentle breeze blew. No one dared say anything. The area was silent aside from the faint muffled noises of city traffic that echoed in from the major streets. The calm before the storm. Every passing second only added to the rising suspense. The array of approaching footsteps became louder with each individual step. Their target passed them, now roughly ten feet ahead. Simon and Kade approached silently from behind. The scrape of one of their shoes along the pavement alerted him, causing him to turn around and notice their advance. "Can I help you guys?" He asked while increasing his pace. Simon and Kade matched his tempo; then Simon reached for his sidearm, which spooked their target to turn forward and engage a full sprint. Farell sought to alert the team from inside the van. "He's running! John, Stoiya, he's coming right towards you!"

John and Stoiya jumped out to intercept their speeding target. John assumed a grounded, sturdy position, like a football player ready to accept the incoming impact. As he braced himself, Kade caught up to the target from behind. Each step was a graceful, robust stride that exhibited an admirable display of athleticism. He wrapped the target in a rear bear hug and threw his momentum against him, sending them both to the pavement. A wrestling match between the two broke out while Simon distantly tried to catch up.

"John, let's go!" said Stoiya.

John and Stoiya made their way over to the scuffle just in time to prevent their suspect from returning to his feet. His palms had planted onto the ground in a supported position like a push-up and lifted his body weight in a desperate measure of escape. John arrived just before Stoiya. His experience with arresting criminals took over, and he instinctually grabbed one of the suspect's hands and pulled it out from its supportive position, which sent their suspect crashing back down into the pavement and lying prone once again. Aware he could not speak in a normal tone, John whispered to the rest of the group, "Get his legs. His legs" only to be drowned out by the screams of their suspect.

"Help! Someone please help me!"

Rio felt her heart race. "You guys better shut him up! Unless you plan on spending the rest of your short lives under federal interrogation!"

The struggle continued. To their surprise, the young man was strong and nimble for his appearance and freed both hands. He opened an application on his wristlet designed to dispatch emergency services. On the screen displayed four options: Police, Medical, Fire, or facilities. John recognized the man's attempt to dispatch police over to his location and tried to inform the others; however, the man's despair again suppressed his whispers.

"Is there anyone around? I need help! Please!"

The pleas ended abruptly when the man felt the shape of a metal cylinder pressed into the back of his skull. Upon recognition that his drawn firearm had intimidated their suspect into silence, Simon took advantage of the opportunity and whispered into his ear.

"Scream again, motherfucker. Come on, I dare you."

The young man dared not move or make a sound. John turned off the app on the wristlet so they wouldn't have to be concerned with any authorities arriving. Kade and Simon zip tied the man's hands behind his back, then the four of them picked him up. Kade and Simon escorted the man forward while John and Stoiya went ahead of them to open the rear van doors. They threw him in, and Wesley immediately tampered with the wristlet to dismiss the possibility of being tracked. Simon jumped in the back while Kade, John, and Stoiya took the rear seats. Everyone was now positioned in Farell's prior arrangements.

"Wesley, status!?" asked Farell.

"The collision is just wrapping up! The drivers are entering their vehicles again. We gotta go now!"

"On it!" said Milton.

The van pulled out of the alley onto the street and turned at the next intersection a mere two seconds before Eva's camera returned to its default position. A close call, but successful.

Wesley informed them, "You guys have no idea how fucking close that was!"

"Milton, slow down! There's no need for that." explained Farell. "We're in the clear."

"Sorry boss."

"How you guys doing back there?" Farell asked them.

"All under control sir." answered Rio.

Simon shouted at their captive. "Hey! What's your name!?"

"My name's Jeremy!" he replied in a panic." Who the hell are you!?"

"Don't worry about us!" replied Simon. "Why were you meeting with a federal agent outside of your workplace last week?"

"I don't know what you're talking about!"

Simon's rage grew out of control. He wound up and kicked him in the stomach.

THUD

"OOOOFF! Ugh!"

"SIMON! Save it for the chair!" demanded Rio. "Control yourself!"

"But, this is our guy! It's him!" he replied, then returned his focus to their captive. "Hey, tell me right now how you knew about the meeting that evening!"

"I don't know anything about that!"

"SIMON! Sit the fuck down!" demanded Farell. "NOW!"

Simon took a seat and restrained his impulses from future outbursts. Milton drove them back to the base. Their suspect refused to get up and walk out of the van, forcing the Patriots to carry him to the interrogation room.

"Simon, Rio, you guys stay." instructed Farell. "I'll come out and inform the rest of the team when ready."

The rest of the group did as they were instructed and waited in the lounge, anticipating answers. Shortly after finding their seats, John got up and went over to the kitchen.

"Hungry?" Kade asked him.

"Making coffee."

"That was pretty crazy back there." Milton said.

"He almost dialed the police." John remarked. "Next time we gotta do a better job with restraints."

John poured the grinds into a filter, then continued his line of thought. "Typically, there's a person beside them for each arm and one or two people for the legs. I was trying to tell you guys to get his legs!"

Kade challenged him. "Who made you the expert?"

John changed his voice to a strict tone. "I've arrested many people. I kind of know what I'm talking about."

"Oh, I suppose." Kade admitted. "We couldn't hear you over the yelling and screaming."

"Kade, I didn't know you could run that fast!" exclaimed Milton.

A grin widened across his face. "I did Track and Field throughout my entire youth."

Milton followed up with another question, "Hundred-metre dash?"

"Yeah. And long jump."

Milton gave him a nod of approval. “Nice.”

“Hey guys, I know the helmet can detect lies, but there’s no guarantee that he’ll even say anything to us, right?” John asked them.

Milton rolled his eyes. “Don’t be naïve John.”

“He will talk.” said Lev. “We always make them talk.”

“Rio is one smooooth lady with sharp edges!” Stoiya remarked.

“Yeah, and Simon is trained to operate the helmet well.” Milton added. “One way or another, we are going to find out. It’s just a matter of time.”

John’s concerns were coming true. He resented the fact that the interrogation would come down to torture. At least he wasn’t the one who had to do it, or even be in the room while it occurred. How far were the Patriots willing to go to get their answers? The guy they had just kidnapped was young, about early twenties. They wouldn’t murder a kid, would they? Nearly an hour had passed before Farell entered the room. The others perked up in interest, eagerly awaiting whatever he would say next.

“His name really is Jeremy.” Farell said. “He was a prospect of the other group that had a change of heart and decided to sell us out.”

“Prospect?” asked John.

Farell clarified. “A prospect is an aspiring member. People rarely join the Patriots by jumping straight into the deep end. There is a process. We need to know that each upcoming member is loyal and reliable. If they pass the helmet, they start out with simple tasks and are given very little information. Most of which is intentionally inaccurate and unique to that individual. That way, if they talk, we know who those details came from without the liability of having any vulnerable details exposed. It’s to ensure that they can pull through on less significant tasks before handling larger duties. You were an exception, John. Considering your skill set, motive, and the current state of our organization. We took a chance on you.”

“But none of you recognized him.” John remarked.

Farell elaborated. "He was a prospect for the other base. His sponsor was a friend of his and also his recruiter. He was a member killed in the incident when Drax was captured. Prospects are not supposed to know sensitive information about the group, but in this case, his sponsor had a loose tongue and shared more with him than he was supposed to. Seeing as how he believed they were friends. Apparently, the feeling wasn't mutual. He never should have been assigned as his sponsor. It was an obvious conflict of interest. A mistake which never should have occurred."

"Whaaaat!?" exclaimed Stoiya.

Kade threw his arms up n the air. "You've got to be kidding!"

"I'm afraid so." Farell admitted.

"Why sell us out?" asked Milton.

Farell answered, "He realised the Patriots didn't live up to his expectations. In his view, we are losing the war, so he reconsidered and contacted the police, who assigned a federal agent to the case. The one from the video. He's some kind of high-ranking officer. He sold us out for a large sum of money. That was what the meeting at the warehouse was about."

"Sheeiit!" exclaimed Kade.

"Motherfucker!" shouted Milton.

"What happens now?" asked John.

"All terrible things considered, there's an angle of advantage here." explained Farell. "I'm thinking we use him to set up another meeting. This time we're taking the agent himself."

Kade's eyes shot wide open. "For real!?"

Stoiya responded with finger guns firing into the air. "BAM! That's what I'm talking about!"

"You sure about that Farell?" asked John. "What's the plan?"

"We are going to have him call the agent and bait him into another follow up meeting." explained Farell. "Then we will form another plan like we did today and go for the son of a bitch himself!"

"That sounds incredibly risky." expressed Milton.

"Of course it's risky!" replied Farell. "Everything we do is risky!"

"How are we going to pull this off?" asked Kade.

Farell answered, "It's going to depend on the specifics, but first we must set it up. Wesley, you can capture Jeremy's facial identity into your system, right? Then create a digital filter of his face into your chips to create a disguise with his appearance?"

"Yeah. That's easy."

"Grab your gear and come with me." Instructed Farell. "The rest of you stay here and wait for more details."

Wesley grabbed his 3D imaging equipment, then followed Farell into the interrogation room. Jeremy sat restrained in the interrogation chair with the helmet on his head, visibly shaken but suffered no evident wounds, indicating that he had been an easy talker.

"Jeremy, you're gonna call this agent back and set up another meeting." said Farell.

"But I don't have anything more to offer them!" he objected.

"Make something up! Think of a story and make it believable. Your life depends on it!"

Jeremy took a moment to consider his story. His eyes swayed back and forth, indicating a process of deep thought.

"Alright. I think I'm ready." he stated.

"You think?" asked Rio.

"I am! I'm ready."

Farell called the agent from Jeremy's cell phone and held it up to him on speaker.

The agent answered, "Yeah?"

"Hey, I have something you would be interested in."

"What?"

"Let's meet again and I'll tell you."

"You can tell me now."

"Well, it's going to cost you again. I'll need you to give me my share."

"I have your banking information from last time. I'll send it wirelessly. Now spit it out."

"Thing is, it's an object. I'll have to turn it over to you."

"Tell me what this is about."

Jeremy took a second to consider his next words, then cleared his throat.

"The last time I was at the Patriot base, I took one of their spare wristlets. Its software is probably modified and could contain some interesting confidential data. I'm sure you guys would be interested in something like that, wouldn't you?"

"Why are you just telling me this now!?"

"You guys offered me a flat rate for everything I could give. Well, I wanted more, so I kept this as a poker chip for future bargains. Now here we are."

"Don't ever do that again! What else do you have?"

"Nothing. This is all. I promise."

"We will give you twenty thousand credits for it."

"What!? That's nowhere near as much as last time!"

"Last time, you had significantly more to offer."

"I want fifty thousand."

"Nineteen thousand."

"Wait, but that's less!"

"Eighteen thousand."

"Okay! Eighteen thousand it is."

"I will send you the details. Come alone and don't be late."

The call ended. Jeremy released the tension in his diaphragm in a major sigh of relief, only for it to return upon immediately realizing that he was still being held captive by The Patriots. His concerns were far from over.

"Simon, power it down. Wesley, get your gear set up." Farell ordered them.

"What are you guys doing now?" Jeremy asked.

Jeremy didn't receive an answer. When the helmet was taken off him, he observed that Wesley had set up various high-tech posts, cameras, and sensors centered on him and the chair he sat imprisoned within. Jeremy began looking around in all directions, desperate to make sense of whatever was about to happen to him, until Rio approached with a sharp, glimmering blade.

"Hold still!" she demanded. "Stop moving your head around if you want to keep it!"

Jeremy obeyed, understanding Rio's seriousness. Wesley's 360-degree display lit up, only to power down just a few seconds after. Wesley checked the quality of the images with great circumspect. Rio, Simon, and Farell observed Wesley, awaiting his analysis until he returned his attention to them. A crescent smile smeared across his face.

"These images will do excellently." he stated.

"In that case, I expect you to get on it at once!" said Farell.

"Is someone finally ready to tell me what the hell is going on!?" Jeremy asked.

BING

Farell opened Jeremy's phone and inspected the received message. It was sent from the agent and contained the details for the future meeting point. Farell shared them with Rio, Wesley, and Simon, then the four of them came up with a plan of action. When they had the plan established, Farell rendezvoused with the rest of the team, who eagerly awaited his return. All actions came to a halt upon awareness of his entry. He recognized their pause as an invitation to continue and took a deep inhale to prepare his explanation.

"I just got the coordinates. Listen closely everyone, the details are complicated. Wesley just took an accurate imaging read of Jeremy's face and can upload it into the chip. The same technology that John used to disguise himself in the police station. Simon has a nearly identical body type to Jeremy. He will be the bait and wear Jeremy's face. We're meeting the agent tomorrow in a public park at *11:30* in the morning. It's highly likely the agent will survey the area prior to establishing the connection. He'll use Eva's cameras to observe Simon, A.K.A Jeremy, waiting at the meeting point. The rest of us will be close, but out of sight. We'll move in behind him as he approaches Simon. Concealable weapons only."

"What about the rest of our faces?" asked Milton.

"Wesley recently created enough strips for a small team." answered Farell. "Face and voice. All fake. You guys will be good."

Milton followed up. "What's the full extent of the plan? How are we going to pull this off without getting caught?"

Farell answered, "Let me know if any of you spot a flaw. Kade is going to rent a moving cubicle van from the Horseshoe Bay area and drive it back down highway 99 towards Vancouver. I will make the relevance of this detail clear in a moment. It's important to note that when the agent met with Jeremy at the warehouse, he exited his vehicle and approached the side door of the building just as Jeremy was leaving. This means he has the habit of using Eva's cameras as surveillance before he approaches his subjects. He doesn't go into areas blind or stand around waiting. He's cautious. He's a federal agent, after all. Simon will wait for the agent at the meeting point, disguised as Jeremy. Myself, Rio, and Wesley will be nearby and also have our faces and voices disguised under Wesley's identity filters. Stoiya will be positioned at a vantage point on a rooftop just a couple of blocks away, providing sniper support. Her scope will allow her to oversee the area. She will inform us when the agent is advancing on Simon, then Rio and I will approach him from behind and lead him to his vehicle. We will strip him of his gear, handcuff him, and Wesley will work magic on his wristlet. We will enter the agent's vehicle. Rio will drive, Wesley as the front passenger, and I will be with the agent in the rear seats holding him at gunpoint. I know of a secluded trail just off Highway 99. That will be the first transfer point and we will get there by driving the agent's vehicle. When we arrive, Wesley will use his Data Bandit 5000 to extrapolate the data from the vehicle computer and cloud network. Considering all the data that's on there as well as the data Wesley would get from the agent's wristlet, he will get Eva's surveillance user log in credentials. This will give him remote access to Eva's camera controls and many other functions. Kade will then meet us with the cubicle van to transfer the agent undetected. We will then detonate an explosive destroying the agent's vehicle, and Kade will drive us back into the city. Do you guys remember the unfinished parking garage where Wesley, John, and Rio met with detective Almas? That project is suspended, so it should be vacant. Kade will drive us there in the cubicle van where we will meet the others in the Patriot van. From there, we transfer the agent one last time, just as an extra precaution, and return him here in our van for interrogation. Kade will then take the cubicle van elsewhere to be returned on the following day."

They could have heard a pin drop, should there have been any motion in the room. Silent, meticulous thought conquered their focus as their minds scrambled through the puzzle of given details. Eventually, some questions arose.

"How am I getting back?" asked Stoiya.

"After Kade parks the cubicle, he will claim the vehicle that we used to get near the park and pick you and Simon up." answered Farell.

“Hold on, how is Simon going to leave the park after we get the agent?” asked Milton. “When the Feds eventually review the video of their agent’s kidnapping, couldn’t they trace Simon’s trail?”

Farell took another big breath, then replied, “Wesley identified a cold spot between camera angles just a few blocks away from the park. We’re all going to wear a spare change of clothes underneath and then change our attire, as well as implement the identity filters at that location. When the next crosswalk light goes, a large group of foot traffic will come our way, granting the opportunity to blend in. New faces. New attire. Completely new identities. Simon and Stoiya will do the same among their departure, changing clothes and taking the filters off, blending their natural faces in as they slip away. If they end up tracking Simon, and likely will, at that point, they’ll be looking for the wrong person.”

Another concern itched at Milton’s mind. “What about Stoiya? She isn’t even at the park. Why do we care about covering her identity?”

“Think about it Milton.” replied Farell. “If the situation forces her to take a shot, don’t you think they could trace the ballistics’ angle back to her?”

“Oh, right.”

“You all should bring a change of shoes as well.” John added. “People often overlook that. They will return to the scene in different clothes but neglect to change their footwear. I’ve identified many criminals that way when I was an officer.”

“Thank you for the insight.” said Farell. “Anyone else?”

The room became silent again as the group returned to their studious problem solving. John ran the details in his mind on a routine, hoping to find a potential flaw that could compromise the mission. After a moment, a concern arose within him, breaking all reticence.

“Sir, I wasn’t a crime scene investigator, but if I’m not mistaken, I believe certain experts can discern accurate time stamps of when explosions or fires had occurred. I know there aren’t many cameras outside of the city and certainly not at the transfer location where we are destroying the agent's vehicle, but I'm worried about the timestamp of the explosion being linked to an expected arrival time at the point of first video capture Eva would have of the rented cubicle van entering the city limits."

"That is an excellent point!" exclaimed Farell. "In that case, we will use a timed explosive to provide a false indication of when the vehicle was destroyed. As an additional consideration, the trail is only about three minutes off from the highway. So, if we time things just right, the first video log of the cubicle van entering the city limits would not be outside of the expected twenty minutes or so it should take someone to drive a cubicle van from Horseshoe Bay to Vancouver. Suggesting it wouldn't have deviated from the expected route."

"Perhaps. It is still a slight delay." said Milton.

"Not if Kade adjusts his speed accordingly when leaving Horseshoe Bay." explained Farell. "A slight increase can shave off a handful of minutes without speeding."

"And even if an investigation was conducted on the cubicle van, Kade would have rented it with fake identification and one of our untraceable bank accounts." Stoiya added.

"That is correct." replied Farell.

"What about like, GPS tracking?" asked Lev.

"Right, thanks for the reminder." said Farell. "I have consulted Wesley and he will disable the vehicle's GPS once we get in. That way, it can't be tracked to the transfer point. The vehicle will have to be found organically, delaying its discovery. Wesley stated that he will teach Kade how to do the same thing to the cubicle van. Then re-enable it afterwards."

"You think Kade could handle that?" asked Milton.

Kade shouted, "Hey!"

“Apparently, it is a simple task.” said Farell. “To quote Wesley’s exact words, even a monkey with Down Syndrome could do it.”

“And then we’re meeting you guys at the parking garage?” asked Milton.

“Correct, but wait somewhere nearby.” answered Farell. “We don’t want any of Eva’s street cameras getting image captures of our van being associated with the second transfer. We know the agent has access to Eva’s surveillance system. So, after we pick up his wristlet, Wesley will get user access and be able to deviate any of her camera angles relevant to potentially establishing any sort of link from the rented cubicle vehicle to our van, or any association of our van with the second transfer point. So, when Wesley provides confirmation that he’s in her system, it should be easy enough to conceal you. Then you guys can drive up and manually remove the entry barricade. We have the tools for that handy. With the transfer taking place in a cold spot in another vehicle with disabled GPS and scheduled to arrive in the city within an ideally expected travel time, there should be no established correlation between the rented cubicle van and the first transfer point. Just to be certain, we are doing an additional transfer at the parking garage. Which is another cold spot. That way, the cubicle van never arrives here at the base. Then all that is left to do is bring the bastard in!”

They all looked at each other with a glimmer of skepticism in their eyes. They waited for someone to speak up. To point out an error in their strategy, but the absence of objection affirmed their enthusiasms. The room broke out in a roared celebration upon the simultaneous realisation that they had established a workable plan.

“I can’t believe it!” said Kade. “Farell, you’re a genius!”

“Thanks, but it wasn’t all me.”

“Woooot! Guess who’s about to kick some serious ass!” shouted Stoiya.

John’s throat was gripped by a choking sensation as he fought back tears. They had a practical plan to capture the agent. It may not be Drax himself, but certainly the next step towards the completion of his objective. A giant leap towards the finish line. John felt Stephanie's freedom get that much closer.

"Don't celebrate just yet, we still have to pull it off." said Farell. "Kade, go prepare the disposal tub. When it's ready, go meet Simon in the interrogation room. You guys know what to do."

"Disposal tub?" asked John.

Milton clarified, "Yeah, acid."

John's posture shot up. "Acid!?"

Kade groaned, "Awww man, me again? Why me?"

"Because it is your assigned duty!" replied Farell. "Now get to it!"

Kade let out an unenthusiastic groan, then stood and left the room. Farell dismissed the group to tend to whatever duties as needed in order to prepare themselves for the following day's mission. John's nerves denied him of tranquility and he went for a walk. He completed a lap around the base before he found Simon and Kade struggling to haul a long blue bag enclosed, full of concealed content out of the interrogation room. From his time as a police officer, John had enough experience with crime scenes that he recognized it as a body-bag. His mind drew the connection between it and the recent instructions Farell assigned to Kade in the lounge room. He leaned against the cement wall of the hallway, facing the opposing direction of his companions as to distract himself from the vivid impressions his imagination burdened upon him.

* * *

John laid in bed and stared at the ceiling. Although some might consider such context as purposeless or troublesome, it was moments like these where John found an opportunity for his conscience to process recent events. His mind had been hijacked onto a rollercoaster of thoughts and emotions, almost providing a slight sense of vertigo. How long had he been lying there? Two hours? Three? He couldn't tell. John sighed as he sat up at the edge of the bed and rubbed his face. After a few minutes, he went for a walk and was greeted by the pelting clicks of speedy keyboard work as he entered the lounge.

"Can't sleep, huh?" Wesley asked him.

"No. It's kind of difficult when we got one hell of a day in store for us tomorrow."

"Hell yeah we do!"

"Having trouble as well, I see?"

"No, I sleep like a baby! Farell gave me too much homework."

"Trying to break into various Eva databases?"

"No, I'm sure the agent's wristlet or vehicle info will grant me plenty of access! If there's anything to keep me up excited or wondering about, it's that! I could have a wet dream over it! Man, forget a pot of treasure at the end of the rainbow. This will probably end up like a whole damn GOLD MINE!"

"Yeah, ha-ha! I can see why you're excited. What are you working on, then?"

"Those damn tutorials. Other Patriot groups gotta learn my tricks in case something happens to me. Farell has had me working on these for weeks now, firing them off one by one as I finish them."

"So, you're the computer mastermind for all Patriots? Like, across the entire world?"

"Sort of. There are others with promise. I can't take all the credit. It's important that we share information and that keeps me busy."

John nodded in understanding but failed to think of anything additional to say. He turned on the television and took several minutes to flip through the channels, but fell short to find anything of interest. He knew Wesley was busy, but John needed something to occupy his mind.

"How did you get caught up with these guys, anyway?"

"They needed me."

"It can't be that simple"

"Well, it is."

"Come on. I'm betting there's more to it than just that."

Wesley's keyboard went silent as he stopped his actions and spun in his seat to face John.

"Oh really? You think you got me figured out? Huh Gumshoe?"

"Heh, I have a pretty good idea. People who are a master of their craft need environments where their work can flourish. What I'm curious about is why specifically a criminal organization? I mean, there's so much you could accomplish as a software engineer. From what I've seen, I'd bet you could even revolutionize the industry!"

"There's too much politics, ethical guidelines, and other bullshit involved with that stuff. Working with these guys, I am pretty much free to create and experiment at will. No holds barred."

"Perhaps, but I don't think that's the full story. You're telling me there's no deeper meaning to any of it?"

"Well, I hate the New World Order."

"I think it's about belonging. Isn't it?"

"PFFFFFFTTT! What!?"

"Come on, a guy like you? Too smart to be relatable for most people, absent father, and a rough relationship with your mother?"

Wesley gave John a surprised stare, like a deer caught in headlights, confirming John's suspicions that he was on the right track.

John continued, "You're just looking for somewhere you belong. A purpose and place of welcoming. I get that. There's nothing wrong with it, you know? This place is suitable for you. People accept you here. Hell, even depend on you. It's a position where your skills really get to flourish and help to complement your feelings of grandeur."

Wesley's face changed from its usual pigment into a scarlet blemish, although John could not identify whether it had been because of anger or embarrassment. Wesley scrambled to find something to say, either in defense, denial, or deflection, but sat mute as his thoughts tripped over themselves.

"Don't worry buddy, it's nothing to be ashamed of. Does your mother at least know you're doing alright?"

Wesley's throat flexed as he swallowed heavily. He turned away, refusing to face John's confrontation, but then soon found his composure.

"Yeah. I send her emails now and then. Not telling her anything specific about where I am, or what I'm doing, of course. During the times I have the access, I sometimes view the cameras to check up on her too."

Wesley resumed his frantic typing. John recognized that he struck a nerve and withdrew himself from his follow-up questions. He returned to the futile attempts at channel surfing and eventually surrendered hope of discovering any captivating programs. John returned to bed more exhausted than the previous attempt, and shortly after his eyes had shut, he finally found what he yearned for.

* * *

The minutes of the following morning dragged along with minimal conversation. John lost track of the number of times he checked the clock. Farell eventually called for a group meeting where they reviewed the plan along with the addition of a few last-minute details. The members then connected themselves to a group call and departed for their assigned roles.

Wesley, Stoiya, Rio, Simon, and Farell took one of the spare vehicles and parked it several blocks away from the meeting point out of caution it would not be linked to the upcoming incident. Wesley pointed out that around one of the nearing building corners was the cold spot they previously arranged. They changed their clothes, then Wesley applied the facial and voice identity filters to the five of them and left a bag of sneakers idle for Simon and Stoiya to claim later. Wesley eased their curiosity and showed them their new identities on his cellphone, then Stoiya departed from the group, making her own way to the vantage point while the others walked to the meeting point. Simon took his seating on the bench centered in the middle of the park, while Rio and Farell hid themselves separately in thick shrubs, awaiting the cue to strike. Wesley stood on the public street just outside of the park grounds. The park was extensive, occupied by a couple of families and dog walkers, but much of its landscape was unpopulated. Simon couldn't get his restless leg to stop shaking. This was the most significant role Farell had ever assigned him. He took off his backpack and placed it on his lap, but the compulsion persisted. He pulled out his phone. The time read: *11:24*.

"Stoiya, you see anything?" asked Simon.

"Possibly." she answered. "There was a vehicle that drove by I thought might be him. Stand by honey."

"Just breathe Simon." instructed Farell. "You can do this. We got your back."

Simon replied, "Yeah, ok." then took a moment to focus his breathing into a steady rhythm.

There's a vehicle circling around for its second time." Wesley pointed out. "It might be him. Stoiya you should see it in a second."

"I got it." she replied. "Yeah, that's the vehicle I had my eye on previously. Let me zoom in on the driver."

Stoiya adjusted the lens to her rifle, then waited for the focus to adjust.

"That's him. The black tinted Jeep. Stand by everyone!"

The agent parked the Jeep, then sat in the driver's seat while the engine ran for several minutes.

"He must be scoping the grounds." said Rio."

"He is." confirmed Wesley. "Eva's cameras are panning and zooming. You and Farell are out of sight and I'm far enough away. We're good. Just chill."

A few more minutes passed, then the engine shut off. The driver's door opened, and the agent stepped out. He brushed dirt off his black suit, then stood for a moment overseeing the area before embarking towards Simon on the park bench.

"He's heading towards Simon!" exclaimed Stoiya. "Wait until he closes the distance more. I'll tell you guys the exact moment to act!"

"Copy!" said Farell and Rio.

The agent slowly closed the distance to the meeting point. His calm walk suggested the upcoming scenario met his expectations. Stoiya held her tongue and eagerly awaited the right timing. The moment became clear when the agent had covered half the distance from his vehicle to the park bench.

"Alright now!" she yelled.

Farell and Rio disembarked from the foliage that concealed them as quickly as they could without the agent's detection. Farell approached directly from behind as Rio made a circular route that would eventually lead to a pincer approach. Farell closed the distance silently, but was slightly too slow to catch up before the agent reached the park bench. The agent walked around the side to the front and sat down. He spoke to Simon under the impression he was Jeremy, but didn't turn to look at him until halfway through his sentence.

"Let's make this quick. And next time ----- wait, WHAT!?"

As the agent was struck with the realisation he had been fooled, his right hand shot down to his holster reaching for his weapon only to feel the firm grasp of a stranger behind him on his arm holding it in place while the metal barrel of a handgun pressed against his upper back through the jacket pocket of his unknown offender.

"Let's not do anything brash." said Farell. "We wouldn't want to make a scene in front of all these lovely people, would we?"

Rio approached them from the front, standing cross armed and grinning. The agent recognized it was The Patriots who sabotaged him, but he knew he was cut off.

He couldn't run even if he dared to challenge whether they were bold enough to shoot him in public. Simon reached across the agent's waist and unbuckled his weapon holster, then zipped it up into his backpack.

Farell commanded the agent, "Stand and walk."

Stoiya pulled her finger away from the trigger, as Simon, Rio, and Farell calmly led the agent back to his vehicle. Farell tightly gripped the gun in his pocket, ready to act should the agent attempt to flee or challenge them.

"Wesley, they've got the agent!" said Stoiya. "Meet them at the Jeep!"

"YOOO! That's what I'm talking about!" shouted Wesley. "Kicking some Federal ass!"

"Just get the hell over here, now!" Rio demanded.

"I know, I know! I'm coming!"

Rio handcuffed the agent and patted him down as Farell watched over them with his concealed weapon. When Wesley caught up with them, he began tinkering with the agent's wristlet, then opened the hatch for the vehicle computer access and scanned the Data Bandit 5000 to the port. Farell and the agent were now in the back seat, and Wesley sat as the front passenger. Rio adjusted the vehicle's mirror angles, then used the agent's keys to start up the engine and drive them away.

"I knew you guys were desperate, but I didn't expect you to be dumb." said the agent.

"Your cooperation will benefit your well being. We're going to find out where you are keeping Drax. It's up to you how inconvenient the process is going to become." said Farell.

"We'll see about that." said the agent.

"Yes, you will." Farell assured him.

"Kade, they just rolled out from the meeting point." said Stoiya. "Are you on track to arrive on time?"

"Hell yeah I am! I'm still in Horseshoe Bay. I got the timer set and I'll leave with the van accordingly."

When the timer went off, Kade departed with the cubicle van. Rio drove the team out of the city limits, over to the transfer point on the secluded trail just off Highway 99. They parked and forced the agent out of the vehicle. Rio then placed the explosives on the seat to be armed upon their departure.

"When the van is prepped, we need to leave immediately." Farell reminded them. "It should be here in a few minutes."

"You can't imagine what we're going to do to you." said the agent. "You signed your own death warrant."

Everyone stood in silence. The only noise came from the simple wildlife that surrounded them until the rumble of an accelerating engine approached from the distance. Kade pulled up in the cubicle van. Its large and clunky structure bounced and shook in an unstable pattern as it struggled to trek through the natural terrain. The vehicle parked and Kade exited. His boots proclaimed a loud thud as his weight was introduced to the ground.

"Man, this thing is totally not built for off-roading, like at all!" he said.

"Open the back!" ordered Farell.

Kade opened the back, revealing the barren storage unit. He and Wesley then took out hammers and nails and began creating hooks into the inside walls. Kade then took out some portable lights and hung them on the nails so the team would not be in darkness during their travel. Farell and Wesley led the agent into the back, then Rio set the timed charge on the explosives. Kade shut the heavy sliding door behind them, leaving the four of them in a dimly lit ambiance before he jumped back into the driver's seat and drove them away.

"Yo team, we just transferred the agent." he said. "We are coming back into the city."

"Excellent news!" Milton exclaimed. "We're ready whenever Wesley is."

"Right on. What about you Simon?" asked Kade.

"Well, after nearly shitting myself with fear, I left the park and found the shoes you left for us behind that building. We just finished taking the strips off and changing attire. We slipped out the other direction Wesley showed us and merged right into the city foot traffic."

"Excellent work Simon!" said Farell. "Is Stoiya with you?"

"I'm nearby." she answered.

"After the next swap, Kade is going to park the cubicle van, then claim the vehicle we used to get near the park and pick you guys up." explained Farell.

"Did the Data Bandit get anything good?" John asked Wesley.

"Hah! I'd say so! And then some! Man, I can't wait to brag to you guys about it!"

"Everyone focus." instructed Farell. "Let's not get carried away just yet."

"Wesley, we're ready." said Milton. "How does the parking garage look?"

"It's empty. There are no cameras in there, but give me a second to divert the street cameras so there's no video of you guys entering the parkade."

Wesley fiddled with his phone for a moment, then replied to the others. "Ok guys. You're clear to enter."

Milton drove the van into the parkade and waited until Kade caught up with them. Rio gave Kade the keys to the other patriot vehicle, then Lev assisted Kade with the back door and escorted the bound agent over to the Patriot van. They pulled a cloth bag over his head and threw him in the back component. Rio, and Lev climbed in and supervised him while Wesley and Farell allocated themselves into one of the other seats. Both vehicles departed. Kade drove off to park the cubicle and claim the other patriot vehicle, picking up Simon and Stoiya on the return while the others brought the agent to the base. They escorted the agent through the hallway towards the interrogation room. He remained stoic, albeit full of awareness of his impending doom. They positioned him in the interrogation chair with his bound hands resting coyly on his lap. Milton put his gun against the base of the agent's skull.

"Rio, cut him loose so we can put his hands in the arm restraints. If the fucker moves, I'll blast him!"

"You moron!" said Farell. "Don't you think he's gonna struggle on purpose just to receive a quick death!?"

Milton removed his weapon's barrel from behind the agent's head, then retreated a couple steps backward. Rio then walked up to the agent and pressed her right heel against the inside of the agent's left thigh, spreading it open, then placed the sharp tip of her knife along the surface of the crotch of his pants, pinning his penis in place.

"You're going to die in that chair." Rio said to him. "It is up to you how many extremities you lose along the way."

The agent made no facial expression. His only visible sign of fear was a heavy swallow. Lev approached the agent from behind and pressed the bone of his thick forearm across the agent's forehead, barring him in place while Rio cut the ties that detained his hands. Upon their release, John and Milton each guided an arm through the loops of the armrests and engaged the restraints. Upon completion, John conducted a follow-up inspection, taking confidence in his efforts while Lev engaged the horizontal restraints that bound his torso. The agent looked to his left and observed a surgical tray that contained various syringes and torture instruments, then looked down and noticed the rusty brown tinge of aged blood along the floor tiles. He clenched his jaw and fists as he exhibited a deep inhale that inflated his chest to the widest degree the restraints would permit. His eyes shut briefly, only to be startled open again when the attention of the room was diverted to the familiar buzz of an electric pair of hair clippers.

CHAPTER 12

They shaved the agent's head to prepare for Simon's return. Each Patriot considered an appropriate line of questioning suitable for the peculiar opportunity before them. A few of them became impatient, prompting Farell to remind them to refrain from their passionate and curious outbursts, and to save their rabid energy for the official interrogation. With the moment of reckoning nigh, each revealed their anxiety in a signature expression. John paced back and forth along the length of the room, stroking his goatee. He didn't doubt the transparency for the upcoming interrogation, considering the helmet's accuracy and Rio's methods of persuasion. Instead, he focused on considering which relevant inquiries would most benefit The Patriots, prioritizing Drax's rescue and well-being. After all, that was the key to finding Stephanie.

* * *

Their patience was killed upon the growing echo of approaching footsteps, preceding the homecoming of their fellow members. Fully reunited, they prepared themselves for the significance of the next phase of the mission. Simon seated himself at the computer behind the agent and launched the program while Milton coated the agent's scalp in the chemical gel. The air thickened with a familiar and offensive stench that launched a sharp sting deep into John's nostrils, encouraging him and many others to pinch their nose closed and breathe through their mouths until they found themselves adjusted. Déjà vu struck John. The vivid images eloquently coursed through his mind, reminding him that recently, he underwent a similar experience. John granted a temporary extension of empathy towards the agent; although, his feelings were soon estranged considering the antagonism of their captive and how his approaching doom struck no resemblance to John's previously favorable outcome. With the agent fully equipped in the helmet, Simon took a couple minutes to affirm the status of the program, then glanced over to Farell to provide his assurance who then began a line of questioning.

"Let's begin with matters of discretion. How long do you figure before they realize you are missing?"

The agent stared at the ground, reluctant to answer, until a glint beamed off Rio's blade and provided him the incentive to answer as it twirled and spun playfully within her possession.

"Likely tomorrow." he replied. "I don't have much on today's itinerary other than case reviews."

"Where is your partner? Federal agents don't usually work alone."

"Parental leave. They will re-assign me someone for anything necessary, but for minor tasks we can do them solo when short on personnel."

"Is Drax still alive?"

The agent didn't respond. As Farell finished the question, the agent retreated his eyes, returning them to focus on the ground below.

"That syringe beside you, it's meant to inject adrenaline. It's quite useful in the prevention of fainting. Either from pain or fright. That blowtorch is another handy tool. We use that to cauterize wounds. That way, our guests don't end up bleeding out and we can savour our valuable time with them."

The agent returned his focus to the tools on the surgical tray and took a deep inhale before reconsidering his matters of participation.

"I think so." he answered. "They haven't updated me in a while."

"Where is he being kept?"

"In one of our facilities."

"No shit! Where?"

"Underground. Outside of the city limits."

"In the mountains, close to highway 99, right?"

"Yes."

"How do we find it?"

"That's hard to explain. There's a subtle unmarked turn off about fifteen minutes north of Horseshoe Bay, which leads to a hidden trail. After a couple of turns, there is an underground entrance disguised as a dead-end."

"Don't worry too much about that." Wesley said to Farell. "I can pinpoint it based on info I've received off the data-bandit."

Farell continued with the line of questioning, "How many guards?"

"I don't know. I've always seen a few here and there while visiting, but as I'm present, I'm not scouring the full premises. I'm there for specific purposes. In and out."

"What information have you extracted from him?"

"Heh, not much. I have to give him credit. He's tough."

Farell took a moment to consider the next questions, rubbing his chin in thought and diverting his eyes across all areas of the room.

"Why are you kidnapping civilians?"

"We don't. That's just a conspiracy theory."

Simon yelled, "Lie!"

Rio approached the agent in the chair and struck the blunt end of her blade's hilt down upon the bridge of the agent's nose, breaking it upon impact. Streams of blood flowed from his nostrils, pouring onto his chest.

"AAARRRYYGGHH!"

"We're going to ask you one more time." said Rio.

"FUCK YOU!"

"Milton, give him the adrenaline!" commanded Farell.

"NO!"

Milton filled the empty syringe with a clear liquid, then approached the bound agent and injected the needle into his vein. The agent's eyes widened, and his pupils dilated. His breath and heart rate spiked as his body tremored with intensity.

"Answer the question!" screamed Rio.

"URRRGHH! AAAAAARRGGGH!"

Rio took the agent's trembling hand and cut off his left thumb. He retreated the remaining fingers into a tight fist while yelling in anguish. Rio then pressed the tip of her knife into the back of the agent's hand, telling him to release his gasp. When his hand opened, Milton used the blowtorch and welded the wound closed.

"Answer the question!" Farrell demanded.

The agent lowered his head, then his eyes shot up to their horizons, looking upwards at Farell, all the while baring teeth in revolt. Like a rabid canine determined to strike.

"FUCK YOU!"

Rio sparked a similar reaction to the previous as she cut off another finger in the same hand. When Milton cauterized the wound, the agent's demeanor resigned from its previous hostility into a more defeated state, suggesting submission and the inclination to cooperate. A repugnant scent among the mixture of iron from blood and burnt flesh overtook the room. John braced himself against the wall, combating a wave of nausea. He shut his eyes as his mouth increased salivation and slowly counted to ten. Each passing number added towards his recovery. Farell continued a line of questioning with the agent.

"What is your interest in kidnapping innocent people?" asked Farell.

"They are genetically experimented on!"

"Surely it isn't random. What is the selection process?"

"No. We only take those determined to be of promising value!"

"How do you determine that?"

"From their deposits!"

John's suspicion had come true. He never really bought into the explanations the media and medical industry provided to the public. It became clear that the deposits were never about health, rather a survey meant to seek valid candidates.

"Tell us about these experiments!" Farell commanded.

"We are looking for specific genetic traits among the population. Those who have such uncommon traits have the potential for certain……. enhanced characteristics, you could say. The experiments are conducted with the intention to unlock these qualities and test for the possibility of replication onto others."

"What kind of enhanced characteristics?"

"Things you couldn't even believe! Physical and mental capabilities beyond the limitation of your imagination!"

"Are you talking about mutants? You're not being clear."

"They are still human, but their genetics have been modified through a series of artificial mutations. So, in that sense, you could refer to them in those terms."

"For what purpose!? Are you trying to build an army of some sort? A battalion of super people?"

"No. It's not like that."

The agent paused and took a moment to breathe and collect himself. He shut his eyes briefly, then looked over at his hand, a trembling, bloody, soldered mess.

"We're building a better world. An improved society. Humanity 2.0. This is not just the next step in evolution. It is a giant leap! It is the artificial selection of traits sought to advance all humans from Homo-Sapien to an enlightened species free of our current flaws. *Homo-Illuminatus*!"

"Homo-Illuminatus? Is that Latin?" asked Kade.

"Yes." the agent replied. "It means *Enlightened man*."

"Let me get this straight," said Milton. "you guys intentionally brought an apocalypse into the world to create a New World Order of total and complete control over all people just to subject them to a variety of genetic tests!? Is this really just one big science experiment for you!?"

"How insulting and shallow of you to assume so little of our ambitions! Of course not!" the agent replied. "We're.... uuurrggh. None of you would understand!"

Rio approached the agent again and flashed her blade at him. "Spit it out!"

The agent swallowed heavily, then continued. "Imagine a world where people lived without fear of their fellow man. War, tribalism, false ideology all a thing of the past. Imagine a world where people would seek truth rather than preference, thought without bias, and where logic and reason triumphed over impulse and emotion. No disease. No famine. No physical ineptitudes. Social equality and opportunity for everyone! Imagine a clean, healthy planet hospitable to all flora and fauna! Imagine if every person lived with intelligence that exceeded even our modern standards of genius! We're trying to make a better world for everyone and everything! And......... It's you! You are fighting against the future of humanity! Against prosperity! You people are standing in the damned way fucking everything up!"

"The Conversion killed hundreds of millions of people!" Milton objected. "You think you can just change the rules of life? Take people out of their homes away from their families so that you can play GOD!? How dare you!?"

"Don't make me out to be a monster. Every great accomplishment is not without great sacrifice. It isn't just about making humans better. We are doing what we MUST to prevent ourselves from our own inevitable demise!"

"What are you talking about?" asked Farell.

"We've known since the 1970s. Experts have been warning of the consequence of humanity's recklessness for generations! You idiots! Think about it. I'm talking about climate change, mass deforestation, plastic in the ocean. Do you know what the quality of much of the earth's soil was like a mere decade ago!? It was malnourished, resting on the brink of infertility! You talk about the Conversion as an apocalypse, but you don't get it. The Conversion PREVENTED the apocalypse!"

"He's full of shit!" exclaimed Stoiya.

Farell looked over at the computer monitor. "Simon?"

"It's the truth." Simon replied.

Milton shouted at the agent, "BULLSHIT!" You couldn't think of any better solution but to oppress the entire world!? What about our freedom? People are not meant to be living under a leash in servitude to a fucking computer! Even if I were to believe you about the state of the planet, or humanity, there is a better solution to the issues we face than to resort to such an extreme and unjust matter!"

"Oh really? Tell me then!" the agent challenged.

Milton's eyes darted across all directions as he scrambled for a reply. "Well, ugh."

The agent followed up with the rest of them. "Anyone?" he asked, then looked around at each of them and waited for an answer, but did not receive one. "That's what I thought! You think all of this was the immediate conclusion? The world's best minds have pondered these questions for longer than you know! They ruled out every other possibility. This was the only way to prevent our extinction, and it is the only way to ascend into the following step in evolution!"

Simon spoke up from behind the computer to address the agent in a contentious and mocking tone of voice.

"So, the New World Order, and Eva. It's just one big probationary period for mankind while you guys use your big brains and your big cocks to figure everything out, huh? Oh, how superior you all must be to us ordinary simpletons."

"Mock me all you like. I told you that you wouldn't get it."

"There is a better way. The world wouldn't have to be like this if you would just be transparent with everyone about what's going on!" Milton suggested. "Look at all the progress humanity has aspired towards all on our own prior to the Conversion! Hell, the very people who caused the Conversion, the Enlightened, were created by advancements of those who were not. The very existence of this fact refutes the very premise of your argument! It's inconsistent to believe people need to become Enlightened to advance or to find solution and drive innovation. You built your entire philosophy upon a fallacy!"

"Yeah, hah!" remarked Wesley.

"Checkmate BITCH!" teased Simon.

The agent shook his head. "You really think it's that simple, do you? I figured you to be stubborn and ignorant, but I didn't expect naivety. You suspect that if we told people how to behave and left it entirely up to their own matters of responsibility, that they would just follow suit irrespective of their personal desires, instincts, and conveniences? What planet are YOU from!? That's not how people are at all! You could lay it all out perfectly for each person and very few will even care. And even for those who do care, even less will partake in personal sacrifice for any sort of benefit to the greater good! If you told someone to renounce their religion because it was false or to change their consumer habits indefinitely from their preferred methods to lower their carbon footprint, do you truly believe enough of them would obey? How foolish of you! Humans, at their core, are selfish and impulsive. Concerned only with the variables that surround the shallow vicinity of their immediate existence! I am wearing the helmet. You know I am not lying to you. I have given you the harsh truth, yet you still reject it. Your state of denial and devotion to your detrimental worldview only serves as additional proof of my claims!"

Milton stood still as his gaping mouth drooped. Unsure of what to say, he looked around frantically at the others, hoping someone would have a comeback. Hoping anyone could remark in his defense.

The agent continued, "Drastic times call for drastic measures. The only way to limit the recklessness of humanity is to limit humanity itself until we've successfully ascended past our primitive instincts and archaic compulsions."

"You said the Conversion prevented an apocalypse. Fine, crisis averted." said Farell. "So, restore humanity as it once was and allow us to learn from our mistakes!"

"That is unrealistic. Our carnal nature would eventually promote future catastrophes."

Farell shook his head at the agent. "I think things could have been handled more appropriately over a longer period. Then there wouldn't be a sense of desperation for drastic measures. You said we've known about this since the 1970s? This is a failure on you and all of those who have been in power since then for not taking the measures at the appropriate times! World leaders consult experts and advisors who are supposed to be at the forefront of global policy, yet you blame us!? How is any ordinary person supposed to know better!?"

The agent looked away from them and shook his head. After a pause, he returned his focus to them.

"Have you ever heard of boiled frog syndrome? We evolved our fight-or-flight response to react to immediate and abundant threats of danger, such as lions or falling out of trees. Humans don't think in terms of far future consequence. Not even those in power!"

"No, that's not an excuse." objected Simon. "It is still their duty! They made an oath upon entering office and are responsible as leaders for steering their people in the right direction! It's not our fault! Blame the rich! They are the ones with all the money! The larger the empire, the more responsibility to do the right thing! I don't see the billionaires planting trees or picking up garbage! How is the average person supposed to do anything? We don't have the money, power, or influence to make significant change!"

"Yeah!" shouted Stoiya.

"Things among larger significance arrive in smaller steps." explained the agent. "You blame capitalism for your problems? There's truth in what you say, but how do you think the rich obtain their wealth? It is your responsibility as the consumer how you conduct your purchases and prioritize your investments. Who made them rich? Do you deny your involvement in the grand scheme of reality? As an example, how many people do you know that will invest in local farms and food production? You think olives are native to Canada and are always in season? Nearly all people disregard where and how their food arrives. All because they want to eat avocados or drink almond milk in the middle of December! You guys think of my philosophy as a contradiction? Well, let me point out a contradiction to YOU! Humanity has become a walking contradiction. The very instincts we've depended upon for millions of years of survival have now become the same factors responsible for our demise. Overpopulation, overconsumption, and overdevelopment of weapons and technology capable of mass destruction and mass influence greater than our abilities to responsibly utilize. Technology has grown beyond our ability to match socially. We are primitive beings flirting with complicated and dangerous toys. Through recent generations, we may have increased our worldly knowledge and technological advancement, but our maturity has stifled. This is the seed to humanity's peril, and all we're trying to do is clean up the mess!"

It was like the earth stopped spinning. No one could speak. The only perceivable noises came from the agents' burst of quick and shallow breathing, complimented by the faint, timid hum of the helmet sensors engulfed around their captive's head. They stood around him bewildered and pondered what to ask next. The suspense was broken when a curious voice, having remained bashful, finally roused from the far side of the room.

"What is Serum 3V-12?" asked John.

John's question perked the attention of everyone else in the room, especially the agent. The other Patriots turned and looked at their captive in interest, craving an answer.

"How do you guys even know about that!?"

"Answer the question!" demanded Rio.

The agent turned his head away in defiance, only to resume a neutral posture, knowing any resistance would be futile.

"After the experiments have been concluded, we hope to reintegrate the subject back into society. We aim to prevent unnecessary suffering. If it is possible."

"You guys release the people after you're finished with the genetic experiments?" asked Kade.

"Yes. We try to."

"So there's a bunch of superhumans walking around the planet!?" asked Milton.

"No. Well, yes. Those in power. Genes can be de-activated. The test subjects are returned to the world in their prior status."

John persisted for an answer, "But what does the serum actually do?"

"First, we put the subject in a deeply medicated state. The serum enhances their proclivity for suggestibility. Almost like a deep hypnosis. The subject is then exposed to a series of ideas, hopefully convincing them of an alternative experience to explain their absence."

"You brainwash them?" asked Simon.

"That is an oversimplification, but yes."

"We have learned that not everyone responds positively to 3V-12." explained Farell. "What happens to them?"

"Correct. Even with the serum, each subject has varying levels of agreeableness. Those who fail to assimilate cannot be released back into the public. Their awareness of their own experience would be a severe liability."

Kade pursued the agent, "So, what happens to them!?"

"Their……. **sigh**. Their files are discontinued."

Kade gasped before his reply, "Discontinued? Meaning you KILL THEM!?"

"We were right to peg you as a monster!" challenged Simon. "You're soul-less! These are people you are talking about, and you refer to them as test subjects!"

Stoiya piped up from across the room. "I've heard enough! We know where Drax is. Let's just kill this fucker already!"

Farell stretched his palm out at them, then said, "Not yet! Not until we're certain the interrogation is over."

The agent scoffed at them. "Ha! After learning all this, you guys still cling to your pathetic worldview." he remarked. "Your very existence highlights the stubbornness of humanity. What do you expect from us!? To do nothing while our own carelessness drives us to the root of extinction!? How else do you expect us to reach the integration!? Fine. I have lived for a greater good and my sacrifice will not be in vain. I atone for and concede nothing. Do as you must."

Rio gripped her blade tightly and advanced towards the bound agent. Her eyes narrowed with focus and intensity. "Stoiya's right, enough is enough."

"Rio, wait!" said John.

Rio stopped in her tracks and looked up at John. The others focused upon him as well, wondering what relevance he may believe the agent to still hold. John approached the agent's side and asked him, "What did you mean by reaching an integration? What integration?"

The room turned to look at the agent. His posture straightened and entire face uplifted in shock as if coming to the immediate realization that he had made a critical mistake.

"I misspoke. I meant enlightenment."

"Lie!" said Simon.

Rio punched the agent square in the face. Her knuckles drove into the indent of the caved-in bridge of his already broken nose, reopening a heavy flow of bright red blood marking his clothes without restraint. The agent screamed, cursed, and yelled for a minute until he regained a minor composure.

"I don't know! I really don't know anything about that!"

"He's lying guys." said Simon.

"No! I really can't tell you anything about that! I won't do it!"

"Let's continue our playtime." said Rio.

"NO!"

The torture resumed for several minutes. John and a few other Patriot members became queasy and turned away from the violence. With the agent's persecution still audible, their minds filled in the visual gaps with vivid interpretations of the abominations committed upon him. The iron scent in the room grew stronger as more blood oozed its way down the slope of floor tiles into the drain. They drilled holes through his hands and Lev broke his legs with the repeated impact of several sledgehammer swings. The agent screamed and begged for mercy, only to have his pleas returned with proposals of the previously asked question. The agent remained firm, refusing to answer until his will was broken. Rio undid the agent's belt and pulled his pants down to his mangled ankles, exposing his lower body in nothing but underwear. She then pressed the sharp edge of her blade against the agent's crotch.

"I've had enough foreplay." she expressed. "It's time for the main course! Answer the question or I'm going to filet it right here in front of you! Layer by layer!"

"Alright." the agent conceded. "If it'll grant me death."

Rio persisted, "Answer the fucking question! What did you mean by the integration!?"

The agent spat a thick gob of blood onto the floor, then looked back up at Rio with tame and weary eyes.

"We refer to them as *Amicus-Dissideo*. The *Amicans* for short. They originate from a distant star system on the other side of the Milky Way; although they have long since expanded their species among varying home worlds."

"Ummm, say what?" asked Wesley.

"They've taken an interest in us since 1947. Shortly after the second world war. It was the detonation of the atomic bomb that lured them to earth. They remained spectators for a while before making official contact. It's arguably the world's most significant event kept secret by the world's governments."

The agent looked around, anticipating follow-up questions. As he found none, he continued with his own accord. "They are truly magnificent beings, from what I've heard."

"You haven't met them?" asked Farell.

"No. That is not a privilege reserved for my rank."

"So, all this UFO stuff has been true all along?" asked Simon.

"That's right. Most of the details surrounding the myths are fabrications. Some are organic while others have been government disinformation strategies, but the core concept is true."

"What the hell is this integration? Tell us!" demanded Stoiya.

"The Amicans are a benevolent species. They are aware of the issues we face and want to help. They've advised us on various subjects throughout the recent generations, but much of the things they wish to teach us, our species is far from ready or even capable of learning. The enlightening of our species is about much more than survival. Once we have fully become an ascended society where all Homo-Sapiens have been left behind as a historical footprint in the human evolutionary chain, that is when we can truly learn from them! The social integration of Amicus-Dissideo and Homo-Illuminatus!"

Milton looked over at Simon, behind the computer monitor. "Tell me he's full of shit!"

"I'm afraid not." he admitted.

"That just means he's not lying, right? asked Kade. "He just believes what he's saying. It doesn't mean that it's actually true."

"I doubt someone in his position would be clinically insane considering all the psych evaluations part of the enrollment process." said John.

"I told you the truth." said the agent. "Do with it what you will."

"You mentioned most people can't become enlightened. So, what exactly do you plan on doing?" asked Rio. "Create enough of your Homo-Illumi-whatever, then throw us normal people aside when you can take over?"

"We are not bloodthirsty. We are going to make manipulations to the human genome over a large period that will populate through subsequent generations. Either through active or inactive DNA traits. This technology is in its infancy but is advancing faster than you could understand. We have enlightened members working on it, after all. This process is going to take time, but will be accomplished through the inferior traits dying out of the human gene pool. Not through genocide or whatever else you're imagining."

"If these aliens are so great, why don't they just do it for us rather than sit around and wait for us to catch up?" asked Wesley.

"What good would that do for our species' maturity? Haven't you been paying attention to what I've been telling you? We're already too immature and irresponsible for the things we know and control, and you expect them to just come down and give us more? Capability must always balance readiness and our species has had the scales tipped for a long time! They may hold our hands a little here and there along the way, pointing us in the right direction, but it is ultimately upon us to attain the goal ourselves."

“How can you be so confident these beings have our best interest in mind?” asked Farell. “Why do they even care about us?”

“A species does not advance to their level of sophistication without benevolence. Any species that cannot overcome its lewd nature does not progress much further than from where we currently reside. They usually end up destroying themselves or become destroyed by another. Living by the sword brings death by the sword. It is a simple concept. They care because they care. We all share the same universe and when a species struggles, like we are, they take interest. They’re like our big brother just trying to look out for us.”

“I think we’ve heard enough.” said Farell.

“Yes! Finish me off already!”

Rio awaited orders. Farell took a hesitant moment to examine the other Patriots in the room, assuring himself of the group’s collective acceptance to conclude the interrogation. He received no resistance. Each of them remained satisfied with the moment, albeit understanding they could never revisit the unique opportunity that lie before them. Farell gave Rio a nod, and the agent shut his eyes and held his breath before the full extent of a long blade was driven deep into his neck.

CHAPTER 13

Rio turned away and wiped her blade clean as thick spurts of blood shot out from the agent's neck. The first stream almost hit Farell and caused him to pull his feet back to dodge the impact. The agent squirmed in the chair until his frantic actions diminished. He knew he was dying. A short act of gurgles and shallow breaths defined his last moment until his mangled body slumped inert. Some stared at his corpse while others their feet or a random spot in the room to divert their attention from the obscenity before them. Having noticed the heavy dismay, Farell directed the focus on commencing the next scheme of details for the mission.

"The agent stated it'll be a while before they know he's missing. Once they do, they will either move Drax or reinforce their security. Probably both. Not to mention resetting Eva's cyber security barriers. We're going to take advantage of the opportunity before us and hit them hard tonight! I'm going to assemble a team among our best soldiers from the province, Alberta, and parts of the US. They will all arrive within several hours. This is the night we free Drax. I need to make the calls. Stand by everyone."

Farell left the room in a hurry, leaving the others to figure out what to do next.

"Kade, Milton, take care of our friend." instructed Rio.

Milton went over to the corner of the room and took a body bag out of a large container. He unrolled it at the base of the chair, then undid the restraints that bound the agent while Kade stared at the body and took no action.

"Kade?" asked Rio.

Milton turned back and looked at him. "Hey buddy, you helping or what?"

Kade stared at the ground for a moment, then offered his reply. "No."

"What do you mean no!?" asked Rio.

"I'm not doing this anymore." he stated.

"What the hell do you think you're talking about!?" shouted Rio.

Her eyes slowly changed from a narrow projection to a wide arrangement upon the realisation of what troubled him. "You're not seriously buying into all that bullshit, are you!?"

Kade stood silent.

"Where the hell are you gonna go!?" she persisted.

"I don't know. Just not here."

Kade left to pack his belongings. Rio's entire body filled with tension as she raised both fists above her head, almost as if to scream, but at the last moment refrained from outburst and turned away. She stood facing the wall and ran her fingers through her hair.

"I will help with body." said Lev.

Lev got up and assisted Milton with dragging the agent out of the chair and loading him up into the body bag. The remaining members went into the lounge, aiming to regain some lost composure. They all sat silent for several minutes. Overtaken by the heavy reality of the information they recently learned and the brutality they witnessed. Eventually, Wesley found himself unable to hold it in anymore.

"Fucking aliens? Can you guys believe that?"

He didn't receive a response. Farell entered the room in earnest. He addressed the others, slightly out of breath with resolute intensity.

"Okay everyone, they're on the way! Tonight, we are storming the base and bringing Drax home. Stoiya, you will receive a list of required gear shortly. Have it prepped. You and Lev will take part in the assault. Wesley, we'll have you on surveillance, of course. You're going to be directing us to the base and through it while we're in there. John, Simon, make us all something to eat and prepare for several guests. We're all going to need a full stomach. Kade......... where's Kade?"

"He left." replied Simon.

"He left?" Farell asked. "To do what?"

No one would answer. It took Farell a moment, but the realization eventually sunk in. He stood for several seconds trying to process his feelings on the matter, then left the room, seeking privacy. Had he associated Kade's departure to a failure of his leadership? Perhaps he too had his perspectives affected by the agent's words? It was too early for him to tell, and he had a duty to fulfill.

* * *

Nightfall hit and the convoy arrived. An intimidating rumble filled the hallway as the soldiers marched on through, making their way into the lounge and filling their stomachs as Farell and Darcy (the squad leader) relayed the plan details of the upcoming assault to the rest of the team.

"Let's go over the details one last time." said Farell. "Wesley surveyed the area. As expected, it is certainly guarded, but the fact we are taking them by surprise gives us the advantage. Our squad will also have superior equipment. It should be a success. Wesley will guide you to the base entrance. He has copied the access code to your wristlets, so you'll be able to enter. Then he'll provide a watchful insight while the team makes their way through. This is an extraction mission concerned with Drax only. Who knows who or what else you guys may encounter in there, so be on guard and keep your minds solely on the objective. Once you have found and released

Drax, there will be a series of vehicle transfers similar to how we captured the agent. That way, no investigation could lead the Feds back to the base. Keep your helmets on at all times. We can't have your faces exposed."

"We should have enough time for a direct in and out strike before any hope of reinforcements can arrive." Darcy added. "It is an isolated facility, after all. Move and act quickly. Eva will be alerted to the first guards killed, if not sooner. Any questions?"

The squad members remained silent. The only sound was that of the scrapes of cutlery against their plates as the last of them finished their meals.

"In that case, make your way over to the armory." said Farell. "Stoiya is expecting you guys and will help equip you with the remaining needed gear. She will join the team. Get to it!"

The soldiers leaped to their feet and departed for the armory in single file. Having recognized the opportunity, John approached Farell seeking to relieve a concern that itched his mind.

"You know, this could be the same facility Stephanie is being kept at."

"It could be," replied Farell, "but we're not there for her. Upon Drax's rescue, you would have fulfilled your duty to us, and we will uphold ours."

"But she's just right there! Since we're already in there anyway -----"

"She is not the priority! We will not divide our focus among multiple objectives. The longer we stay in there, the riskier it becomes. Wesley can sign for her release later. Now, if you'll excuse me, I have a matter to attend to."

Farell stomped out of the room, leaving John in a daze of unresolved solicitation. Farell arrived in the armory with the rest of the team. He observed Stoiya handing out high-tech weaponry to the squad members, explaining to them how it worked. He spotted Rio in the corner as she examined different firearms dressed in a fully armored uniform.

"What do you think you're doing?" he asked her.

"Taking my pick."

"You're not going in."

"What!?"

"This matter is far too personal for you! We can't have emotion clouding the judgement of any squad members! It could compromise the entire mission!"

"But sir -----"

"I said stand down!"

Rio slammed her helmet down on the ground and stormed out of the room. It bounced multiple times, then found its resting place in the corner. Farell didn't care for the theatrics, but he knew she would understand once the hysteria settled. She was a competent soldier, but her outburst was exactly the type of reckless behavior Farell sought to prevent. He turned to look at the others. A silent, cohesive intensity filled the armory as each soldier assembled their various load outs. One of them performed a series of calisthenics and minor acrobatic movements to test the nimbleness of his armored attire. The team finished their preparations, and upon their readiness, John and the others watched the squad disembark into the suspenseful night.

* * *

Wesley gave them the directions to the highway turn off. They drove along a quiet, dark, and recluse trail, which, after several turns, led to what appeared as a dead end. The trail ceased to continue as it met the towering dirt wall of an enormous cliff that stood before them.

"Okay nerd, this is it, right?" Darcy asked Wesley.

"Don't call me nerd." he replied. "Yes, you're there. Activate the code on your wristlet and it should remotely open the way for you."

Darcy pressed the button displayed on his wristlet application. The team waited for an action, but nothing occurred. Darcy threw his arms up in frustration. "What the -----"

SWOOSH

The dirt wall split from its vertical center line, revealing a set of mechanical doors disguised as a part of the cliff. Darcy and the others leaned forward and squinted, trying to see into the unknown passage before them, yet not even the dynamic high beams of their vehicle could penetrate the thick cloud of dust before them. "Yippie-o-caiya," said Darcy as he rolled the vehicle in. They drove down a steep and lengthy ramp that led to a colossal set of fortified steel doors supervised by two armed guards. One of them raised his hand towards them as a gesture to stop as they slowly advanced. Darcy rolled his driver and front passenger windows down to engage the guards, who approached with skepticism.

"Business?" the guard asked them.

"Got another one for you." replied Darcy. "Orders came in last minute. Some lady from Surrey. It seemed like an urgent detail."

"We aren't aware of this."

"Well, consider yourselves now aware. Like I said, it was last minute."

"I don't know you. Show me your identification."

"Yeah, no problem."

Darcy and the Patriot in the front passenger seat gave each other a nod of understanding as if they rehearsed this exact moment. They stuck out their wristlets for the agents to scan them and as their focus became distracted to their profiles; they pulled out their sidearms from inside the vehicle and shot them, leaving the piercing echo of gunshots and a loud heavy thud as their dead bodies collided with the smooth pavement. Darcy and the other Patriot exited the vehicle and claimed both guard wristlets for interior access purposes. They then scanned one of them along the control panel, opening the fortified gate ahead of them before returning to the vehicle and making their official entrance into the federal facility.

"The clock is officially ticking." said Darcy.

"When you guys go through, stay to your right." said Wesley. "Swipe the wristlet you picked up to get through that door and progress through the long hallway."

"Copy." replied Darcy.

They advanced into a hangar. Several workers were loading various materials off the back of trucks, but there were no guards. The Patriots parked their long van facing the exit readying an effective get away position. All doors shot open as the squad members disembarked and formed themselves in a tactical position. As they scanned through the door, they noticed the skeptical and curious glares of the workers in the far distance behind them, but the assault team knew they only needed to concern themselves with anyone armed. The door led them into a long hallway with several rooms aligned along its entire depth.

"Where to nerd?" Darcy asked Wesley.

"You're looking for laboratory *114-A*." he replied. "Just a little further down."

The main lights shut off, and the facility lit with emergency strobe lights as the sharp squeal of a siren pierced through the area. The team took a moment to turn on the flashlights associated with their assault weapons, then continued onward with improved visibility.

"Press onward everyone." said Darcy. "We have time."

A Patriot scanned the entrance to the door, granting access for the team. They entered in a tactical formation that covered all angles.

Darcy attempted to update Wesley on their advance. "Alright we just -----"

Wesley shouted out to them, "Look out! On the far side of the room!"

POW POW

A series of carefully directed gunfire performed by Darcy and another Patriot dropped two guards that entered the lab. He then re-established communication with Wesley.

"Thanks nerd."

"I told you! Don't -----"

"Where to now?"

Sigh "Go through where the guards came from. The door leads to the second part of the laboratory."

"Copy."

The team progressed to the other end of the lab. There were a few scientists who dropped everything they held and ran for their lives. The Patriots found themselves surrounded by several dozen large tanks filled with a strange green fluid. Each of them occupied by a nude person wearing an oxygen mask fed by a thick attachment that seemed to link to the ceiling in a secured connection. They were unconscious but seemed alive.

"Jesus Christ!" exclaimed one of the other Patriots. "What the hell are they doing to them?"

"Stay focused!" replied Darcy. "We're moving through!"

"Hey! Stop yelling in my ear!" said Wesley.

"It's fuckin' loud in here!" replied Darcy.

"Not for me!" said Wesley. "Keep your damn voice down! You have mics for a reason! Sheesh!"

They progressed to the other end of the room and scanned the wristlet to enter the following component. Upon the immediate breach of the doorway, the team was greeted by an array of speeding bullets.

"Nerd! What the hell!?"

"Sorry, I couldn't see them." said Wesley. "Hold on."

Wesley used Eva's surveillance system to survey the next room. A guard looked up and noticed the camera pan over at his location. He fired at the camera, terminating its view and leaving Wesley with nothing but a blank screen on his monitor.

"Shit!" he exclaimed.

"Having trouble?" Darcy asked him.

"They knew I was watching and shot the camera out!"

"Alright, don't sweat it! Kerry, throw an imaging grenade!"

One of the other Patriot members took a small electronic device with a large screen that consumed most of its surface area, along with a grenade from his pockets. He wound up and threw the grenade towards the center of the next room. It released a blinding flash of light and sent a 3D image of the room and its contents onto the screen of the device Kerry held in his other hand. He used his fingers in a pinching, spreading, and swiping motion to zoom, pan, and tilt the image as he examined the details of the room before them.

"There's two of them." Kerry described. "They are both on the catwalk above. Eleven and Three O'clock."

Darcy gave a series of hand gestures to Lev and Stoiya, who popped out of cover to engage their enemies. Aware of the guards' locations, they fired with advantage and slew them both. Two loud bangs commenced as the guard's assault rifles fell off the catwalk and crashed onto the floor of the main level. Stoiya looked behind her and saw the indents of bullet holes in the wall beside her. A close call.

Grunt

Stoiya looked over and noticed Lev collapse onto the ground.

"Man down!" she yelled. "We've got a man down!"

"Pull him to cover!" ordered Darcy. "Nerd, anyone else coming?"

"You're good!" replied Wesley.

The Patriots pulled Lev to a more secure location and inspected his body for wounds. Stoiya ripped through his first layer of clothing and observed a bullet lodged deep into his vest. She checked around the impact site and let out a sigh of relief upon confirmation that there was no bleeding.

"Hey big guy, it only hit your armor." she said to him. "You're going to be fine!"

Lev crutched his arm into his ribs to comfort the pain as he responded with a series of violent coughs. When he regained his composure, he looked up at Stoiya and gave her a thumbs up. She responded with a smile, and with the help of the others, Lev returned to his feet.

"Make your way down the staircase in that next room." Wesley explained to them.

The team advanced to the lower level. Wesley directed them to an additional hallway that led far into the facility's depths. They looked frantically for Drax's cell until finally arriving. Darcy held his breath for a second, then scanned the wristlet on the door. The room was a small dungeon of torturous and barbaric instruments. The dimness of the room complimented the horrific design of the atmosphere, courtesy of a single flickering lightbulb that dangled loosely from the ceiling. There he was. Drax. Tied up and hanging naked by his hands. Several blotches along his skin had been stained a reddish-brown tinge of his own dried blood. His unstained portions were pale, suggesting a major loss of fluids. He was missing an eye and some fingers. A Patriot approached him and held his index and middle finger against the side of his neck.

"Pulse is faint, but he's alive!" he exclaimed.

Stoiya grabbed Drax by the jaw and slapped him around, but he would not awaken from his comatose state. "Come on, you bastard! Wake up! We need you to get up and come home with us right now!"

"Try this!" said Darcy as he approached Drax, then engaged his taser and thrust it into his ribs. Drax jolted to revival and struggled for a desperate gasp of air. Lev withdrew a knife and cut him loose. He recognized what was happening and could partially walk with the support of an ally. They moved as quickly as they could get Drax along, having picked him back up each time he fell. Wesley directed them through a separate corridor from which they arrived, then brought them to a halt.

"Hold on! There's a guard there waiting for you to come out. The entrance through is far too narrow. It's a death trap!"

"Byron, send the hornet!" ordered Darcy.

One of the other Patriots took out a small box and opened it to reveal a robotic hornet. He inputted a series of commands to his wristlet, which caused it to animate and fly into the next room. The guard swatted at it in a panicked frenzy, but the drone penetrated its stinger into his neck, releasing a tranquilizer. The man screamed and missed with a few bullets as the hornet flew back through the doorway and returned to the team, nesting back into its originally stored condition. They waited several seconds, then heard the guard collapse onto the ground. Darcy took out a mirror and held it down sight at an oblique angle to confirm a safe advance for the team.

They returned to the vehicle and stored Drax in the back as they quickly scrambled for a get-away. As the engine started up, their vehicle was met with distant gunfire. The van's posture capsized as a bullet penetrated one of their rear tires. They exited the hangar and approached the ramp that led out. A Patriot opened the back door to the van and littered the ground with caltrops, diminishing their adversaries' hopes of a vehicular pursuit. Their vehicle swayed with instability along their departure, but successfully reached the transfer point. Drax was swapped, then led towards the Patriot base cloaked of Eva's detection as Wesley diverted the relevant camera angles.

* * *

When they returned to the Patriot lair, Farell fought to hold Rio back while two squad members carried Drax into an isolated room prepared in advance for his devoted recovery.

"Let me see him! Let me go!" she shouted.

"Hey, Rio, relax! He's fine! He's going to be fine!"

"No! I need to see him! Please!"

"He's being taken care of! You must let him recover first before I can let you in there! You're just going to get in the way!"

Farell felt her resistance dwindle as she slumped to the ground in a fetal position, clawing at her own hair. She let out a quick series of emotionally purgative screams until the gradual return of rationality settled her hysteria. Farell took his time checking on Drax's condition as the Patriot assault team unloaded from their highly dangerous and adrenaline-fueled assignment. The rest of them waited in the lounge room and celebrated victory. The cheerful rejoicing and rowdy consumption of alcohol overtook the environment. Except John, who sat shy in his seat and wondered about the potential upcoming success of his own mission. Was Stephanie still alive? The Patriots would hold up to their end of the deal, wouldn't they? John noticed Wesley peer over at him periodically but couldn't identify the motive. Perhaps he had something to share with him? Eventually, Rio and all other absent members joined them. Milton and Simon tried to get John to drink, refusing to accept his rejections, but their efforts were brought to a halt when Farell returned. His wide smile clearly represented a conscience full of jovial and optimistic tendencies desperate to break out of him.

"He's in rough shape, but stable. One of our doctors from the US is on their way up and will stay here with him to oversee his recovery."

Farell's statement was returned by the spirited elation of rejoicing Patriots. He held his hand up to signal for repose. A request for the opportunity to pursue his thoughts.

"Merely a few days ago, all hope had seemed lost. I want to take a moment to express to each one of you how proud and grateful I am for your incredible efforts and loyalty. You all played an important role in this prosperous victory. Thank you all so very much!"

"And here's to Farell and his outstanding display of leadership! Rising to the occasion in Drax's absence!" said Milton.

Farell assumed a blotchy redness as the room broke out into a lively act of applause, excluding John's participation. Instead, he sat stagnant and stared at the ground. An impression incongruous of the otherwise festive energy in the room. Farell read his thoughts.

"And let's not forget the relevance of our special guest." Farell continued. "John, could you please stand?"

John captivated the focus of the others as he stood and met Farell in the center of the room.

"John, we never would have come this far without your help. Your intuition played a critical role in the favorable outcome of our mission! A service for humanity and a service for freedom!"

"Let's hear it for John!" said Stoiya.

The room broke into another ovation. A smile broke across John's face, but did not linger among the murky nature of his deeper considerations.

"It pleases me to announce Wesley's success with the manipulation of data files pertaining to your subject of interest." Farrell revealed. "Congratulations Sir!"

"Wesley, you did it already!?" asked John.

"I had all the files already completed in advance." he explained. "The only thing left to do was to submit them upon Drax's immediate rescue."

"Thank you." said John.

"So, what's next for you?" Farell asked John. "A return to your normal ways of life?"

"Well, I guess so."

"You're welcome to stay with us and celebrate if you wish."

"Thanks Farell, but I think I'm gonna go."

The Patriots stood in honour of their friend's departure and patiently waited for their opportunity to bid him farewell. Farell shook his hand first and extended a contented and proud smile.

"Thank you again. Take care of yourself and good luck!"

"Thank you, sir. You as well."

"Looks like we both got what we wanted." Rio said to John.

"Looks like it! Take care of Drax for me, Rio."

Wesley was next. His chin visibly undertook the compression of unkempt wrinkles. A result of his quivering lower lip.

"Aww, you're not gonna miss me too much, are ya buddy?" John asked him.

"Shut up!"

His face assumed a scarlet blemish as the room broke out in laughter. Simon patted Wesley on the shoulder, straightening out his retreated posture.

"When can I resume my normal routines?" John asked him.

"I'll discontinue the program by uploading your false daily logs shortly after you leave."

"Thanks buddy."

John handed Stoiya the firearm and holster she lent him, then bid to shake hands. She rejected his offer and instead wrapped her arms fully around him in a warm, steady hug. She held him longer than he expected, and John exhibited a slight jump as she pinched his rear end along her retreat.

"Bye handsome!" she said.

"Take care, Stoiya."

John gave a gesture to Simon and Milton, who returned with a salute. Next in line was Lev. He hunched over from his injury, allowing John to address him at an equal height for once.

"You know," he began, "In Russia we have bold saying. If man keep honor, he can tame leopard, but if man forget honor, he can tame only pigeon."

Wesley burst out laughing from across the room. "Ha-ha-ha! What the hell does that even mean!?"

"Thanks Lev." said John. "Take care of yourself."

John received waves and head nods from the remaining Patriot members foreign to the Vancouver base. He turned to leave but stopped upon noticing Farell had one last thing to say.

"If you ever feel the need to do some real good in the world, you know where to find us. Consider this an open invitation."

"Thank you." replied John. "I'll keep that in mind."

"At least allow us to offer you a ride. We'll take you anywhere you want to go!"

"Thanks, but I plan on walking home."

"Are you sure? That would take hours!"

John looked away as if he reconsidered his thought, then returned Farell a sharp, confident smile.

"Yeah. I think I could use a victory lap or two."

John took one last look at them all, then began the long foot journey home. Upon immediate exposure to the night's cool wind, he felt the long-anticipated release of tension held in his chest. An awakening of bliss. Each step was a proud and gracious stride while his mind replayed the details of his successful experience working with The Patriots. The hours passed, and he became weary as he neared his home, almost regretting rejecting the offer to be dropped off. Once he arrived at his residence, he left the click of his apartment door behind him as he propped himself onto his couch and groaned as his weight surrendered to its flexibility. The vibration of his phone returned his senses, swaying him to view a text message from a concealed number that read:

Just got confirmation. She's on her way home. Congratulations, buddy.

- W

John didn't have the energy for a phone call. He sent Brian a text message informing him that Stephanie should be returning home shortly and requesting that he speak with her. John shut his eyes for a moment, hoping that Wesley was correct and that his risky efforts were about to pay off, then fell asleep.

* * *

He awoke later that afternoon and noticed he had slept through a call from Brian's phone. John played the voice message. Brian was frantic and curious about knowing the specifics of what had happened. Answers which John could not provide. John spent the rest of the day anxiously around his apartment, failing to amount to anything productive. He considered calling Brian several times, but didn't know how to start the conversation. He couldn't risk telling him about the details of his investigation, about The Patriots, or how the Government subjected Stephanie to experiments. Not over the phone. Eva would be listening. John knew he owed Brian an explanation, but he had to be cautious about the approach.

John contemplated what he would say to Stephanie. He felt the need to clear his conscience. To express how sorry he was about how he acted and how things ended between them. Otherwise, the guilt would eventually drive him mad. He respected her decision to leave him and move on, but he never let go. He couldn't.

The sky broke into nightfall. Ready or not, John promised himself he would contact Brian the following day and if Stephanie hadn't come home by then, well, John figured he would have to pay Wesley an unfriendly visit.

* * *

Ring* *Ring* *Ring

Disoriented, John rolled over and checked the time that read: *07:02 am* and thought to himself, "Who would call this early in the morning?" He took a second to pull himself together, then groggily answered the phone.

"Hello?"

"John? It's Stephanie!"

"Stephanie!? What? Hey, um, where are you?"

"I'm at home with Brian."

"How long have you been there?"

"A couple of hours now. I think."

"Are you alright?"

"Yeah. I just have this terrible headache that won't seem to go away."

"You have been gone for quite a while. What do you remember?"

"I don't know. Everything is so foggy. It's like trying to remember a vague dream from a long time ago."

"What do you remember?"

"I was leaving my shift at work. I thought I passed out because I woke up this morning sitting in my parked vehicle at the kitchen. I drove home thinking it was the same day, but Brian filled me in on everything. John, he said that you knew I was coming home soon. Is that right?"

"Yes."

"How?"

"There is an explanation for everything, but I'm afraid I can't tell you over the phone. I promise I'll explain everything. Just not like this."

There was a brief pause as they were unsure of what to say next.

"I really need to see you." John admitted. "Can we meet in person? Please? I think you should try to rest today, but how about breakfast tomorrow morning? I'll fill you in then."

"Yeah, uh, I suppose."

"Okay. Great. One more thing. This is going to sound strange, but I need you to promise me that you and Brian will not go to the authorities until we meet. Please. It's important."

"What? Why not?"

"I just need you to trust me. I'll explain everything, just not like this. Please. Don't go to the police. Not yet. Promise me."

"Alright, sure. I promise."

"Thank you."

"John? Is everything okay?"

John took a deep inhale and a smile spread wide across his face before he offered his sincere reply. "Yeah. Everything is going to be just fine."

They said their goodbyes and then John climbed out of bed and exited his bedroom. He set his phone down on the kitchen counter, then brewed a cup of coffee while he browsed through his music library. Upon his selection, he looked out his apartment window and bared witness to the bright tinge of dawn's pronunciation while he sipped his caffeinated beverage along to the luscious and nostalgic melody of a familiar Beatles song.

About The Series

Eva 2040 is an Action Sci-Fi anthology series written by Tyler J Sluys that is set in a near future dystopian world. The book entries contain no continuity with each other and can be read in any order. At this time (February 2023) only the first entry to the series has been published with others intended to follow. If you enjoyed this book, please consider leaving a generous review.

About The Author

Tyler J Sluys was born and raised in Surrey, BC, Canada, and moved to Calgary, Alberta in 2013 where he currently resides. He took up writing as a hobby in 2022 and published the first volume of the Eva 2040 series in February of 2023. He has worked many jobs among varying security details, including Private Investigation and holds formal education in Security management. Such credentials include certification as an Associated Protection Professional (APP) from ASIS International and certifications as a Certified Protection Officer (CPO) and Certified in Security Supervision and Management (CSSM) from the International Foundation for Protection Officers. Aside from writing, his interests include Martial arts, weightlifting, hiking, gaming, heavy metal music, and reading science fiction.

Tyler J Sluys can be contacted via the email address listed below:
tsluys@shaw.ca

Made in the USA
Las Vegas, NV
04 March 2023

68522767R00134